BIG HEAVEN

Charlotte Hebert

Savant Books and Publications
Honolulu, HI, USA
2016

Published in the USA by Savant Books and Publications
2630 Kapiolani Blvd #1601
Honolulu, HI 96826
http://www.savantbooksandpublications.com

Printed in the USA

Edited by Suzanne Langford
Cover by Daniel S. Janik
Cover images: (1) Fluffy Clouds by Karen Arnold, (2) Statues Of
Angels by George Hodan and (3) Car Keys by Marina Shemesh, all
from|publicdomainpictures.net through CC0 1.0 Universal (CC0 1.0)
Public Domain Dedication; and (4) Pills and Bottle by Daniel S. Janik
with permission.

ISBN: 9780996325509

Dedication

For Tom and Evan. And for Paramahansa Yogananda.

Acknowledgements

Thanks so much to Suzanne Langford, Savant's editor-in-chief, a true Godsend (how else to describe her?), who was enthusiastic about BIG HEAVEN from the start, and who was a constant champion of the book. I would also like to thank the rest of the Savant team, especially Daniel Janik, owner and publisher of Savant Books and Publications, for his time and kindness, and for having the vision to start Savant and the desire to give back to the writing community; Wendy Dunn for starting the editing process and suggesting many useful changes; and Sabrina Favors, for picking up the reins at the end and doing an excellent job. A big thanks also to my friend, Vicki Meager, who has read almost every piece of fiction I have ever written and provided invaluable feedback. Thanks to our son, Evan, for bringing true joy into our lives. And a huge thanks to my husband, Tom, for more than words can say.

BIG HEAVEN

Chapter 1

Shoot. He's there. I can see through the window. Not that I should be surprised, for he's *always* there. At least since my mom died, he is. It means that I'll have to sneak in, try and rush straight to my room in order to meditate.

Let me back up a bit. My name is Maureen. Mo for short. I'm sixteen, but I'm going to be a senior this fall 'cause my birthday's in September, so I'm really almost *seventeen*; and I've decided, only tonight, that I'm going to be a nun of the Swami Order, which has its origins in India. That's why I'm starting my story right here, by the way. You have to begin with a hook is what I figure, and this is mine. Becoming a nun is a pretty big deal, you have to admit!

Anyway, I decided this in part 'cause of a talk I attended tonight in Cambridge, Massachusetts, near where I live, put on by the group for whom I want to be a nun, which I'll tell you about later—I promise —though now I am on a mission. I have to go meditate now. I promised my guru. Plus, the meditation we did tonight as a unified group was *so* great you just want to do it again as soon as you can. Even *without* the special blessings granted a group.

Oh. And a few more things you should know before we launch in: My mother died, as I mentioned, three months ago now, very suddenly, which was really super hard. As a result, it's just my father and me in the house, which is *also* really hard. And there was a prophecy told about my life, right after a near-death experience I had when I was twelve, and I was wondering just what it all meant, and now I know.

It all gelled tonight.

I'm supposed to be a nun at sixteen—which is now. The timing is very important according to the prophecy. More on that later, as well; it will blow your mind.

Anyway, here I am, home from the talk, and my father is also at home, as I mentioned. It's nighttime right now, and dark, so one would *expect* one's father to be home, but even if it was broad daylight out, he still would be sitting at home since he's newly retired and has nothing whatsoever to do. His being retired makes sense as he's not all that young: not quite as young as you'd think to be the father of a sixteen-year-old. He's sixty-five. My parents had me when my mother was forty-four and my father forty-nine. They didn't believe they could have children then, but I was their "happy surprise" as my mother always told me. I was never "the mistake," 'cause they'd wanted a family, they just didn't believe they could have one by then. So I wasn't "planned," but neither was I in any way "mistaken."

In any case, my father, age sixty-five and newly retired, is watching TV in the family room. It's Frasier. I know 'cause it's ten PM. I know all of my dad's favorite shows because of when they air.

"Hi, Dad," I "casually" say as I try to get by.

"Mo!" he says. "Maureen!" And then I am gone. If I give him *more* time, he will lavish me with statements like: "To what do I owe the *pleasure*?" Or: "Well this *is* a surprise! Are you planning to join me? I'd relish the honor of your *company*!" Or: "I was beginning to think you were a ghost!" And then he would flash a sweet smile my way.

Not that I don't want to hear all of that (I don't want to hear all of that), but I am on a mission.

I can't get sucked in at this point.

My guru is waiting.

I slip into my room, feeling only minor convulsions of guilt, which I quickly push away. Once here, I realize I wouldn't mind some water, or a nice Diet Coke for that matter, or even a cold glass of lemonade—it's summer right now, and hot, and I walked from the bus —but if I *do* go back out in the hall, I know I'll be made to converse, so I stay in my room without the water. I don't want you to think I am mean, but some actions come first.

I bow before the picture of my guru, then I take my seat.

In the picture I have, he is smiling, his eyes looking into mine, his hands pressed together in prayer like he's giving me his blessing. All of him—his eyes, his smile, his face—are sweetly "all-knowing" you would say, though there's a hint of humor in them, too, as well as real empathy. It's as if he is saying: "I know." It's as if he is saying, "Don't give up. I am giving you my blessing. Look: my hands are folded in prayer." It's as if he is saying: "I'm smiling at you"—he's a nice guru—so I bow and then straighten my spine to get ready to begin.

In addition to the picture of him, there's also a candle on my table-turned-altar, an incense holder without incense, and a vase holding dead dried-up flowers—oh, well. One thing you should know about this path: Your guru loves you unconditionally—dead, dried-up flowers or not. This makes it easier to get away with some things that you might not get away with ordinarily, but don't tell my guru I said that.

That was a joke, 'cause he already knows—the guru knows all. He's a bit like Santa Claus in this way, 'cause of his omnipresence, which is really like God's omnipresence, more than Santa Claus's, for, I'm told, that's where that Santa-omnipresence stuff came from to start. In any case, I'm glad for the "unconditional love," 'cause it's hard to supply brand new flowers every week, trust me.

But getting on: I bow to my guru, say a prayer, and then I start to meditate. I know that other girls my age are posting on Facebook, or checking out Twitter, or sharing pics on Instagram, but this is what I do. People call me an "old soul."

I am a minute or maybe two in, unfortunately thinking about Cameron—his smile and eyes and neck—when I hear a "Knock-knock" outside my door. The words, this would be, not the rapping. It's good that he bothers to "knock" is what I think…

This is good. "Yes?" I tersely reply.

"It's your fa-ther," he pleasantly says, as he opens the door. This is his joke, 'cause he knows *I* know it's my father. Then, "Mo. Do you know where my hair tonic is?" *Why* he feels he needs hair tonic now, I don't know, but I guess that he does.

I get up, bow to my guru and say, "Excuse me a moment, Guruji," then I amble past my father and into his disheveled bathroom, which is off of his bedroom, and which used to be his and my mom's room, of course, before my mom died, which happened a goodly three months ago now, as I've said. I go to his medicine cabinet, open it up, and—*voila!* There is the hair tonic. Like magic. I take the bottle *out* of the medicine cabinet and place it on the counter for him.

"Thank you," he courteously says, having followed me in. "You're welcome," I courteously reply with a nod of my head before going back to my meditation room, which also stands in as my bedroom. Before I sit down, I bow to my guru again, then give him a look.

This time, I am four minutes in, or thereabouts, again partly thinking about Cameron, or okay, thinking about him *a lot*, when there's another "Knock-knock."

This, I guess, could have been predicted.

"Mo?"

"Yes?"

He comes in. "I was wondering if you've seen…the mustard?"

I get up after bowing to my guru, go to the kitchen, which is yards away from everything else—it's a very small house—open the refrigerator door, look on the lowest side shelf, and locate the mustard for him. I remove it and place it in his hands.

"*Well done*!" he says magnanimously.

"I have a knack," I answer in kind, before returning to my room. Perhaps you can see where this is going—I can.

There is a "Knock-knock" before long. That makes three. I inwardly cringe.

"Come in."

"And Mo. I can't seem to find the jar of mayo. I know we just had it," he says.

He is looking a little bit tired at this point, so I get up. "A million apologies," I say to my guru, while bugging my eyes. Then I go past my father back to the kitchen.

I could assemble the sandwich myself—and save everyone all the pain—but I'm trying to 'rouse independence in my father: a sense of "can-do" in the man. My mother never did this, and you can see where it's led. Her death's been a terrible blow, of course.

I look for the mayo in the fridge. It's not there—though it's really *supposed* to be there. I start opening cabinets, drawers. Eventually, I find it under the sink, next to the compost bucket and Drano and a bunch of other objectionable objects too grody to name. I don't even want to *consider* how the mayo ended up there. I take it out.

"Huh. I wonder what the mayo's doing *there*?" my father remarks.

I don't reply.

"Thank you," my father says next, with an affable smile. He is polite, my sweet, aging father. If there's one thing he is, it's that.

"Do you require anything else before I depart?"

"Only the pleasure of you," is what he says in return.

I know. We talk funny. Or rather *he* talks funny—for real—and in his presence I sometimes do, too, 'cause I find it contagious though I try not to do this in front of my friends 'cause I'd never hear the end of it.

"You've got it," I reply. "Only it'll have to be some other time, 'cause I'm trying to meditate now." I point towards my bedroom as proof.

"Of course," he graciously says, "of course." Then, "Thank you again, dearest Mo."

"You're welcome." The jar of mayo was supposed to be in the *refrigerator,* but I'm not even going to *consider* that right now.

I turn to go back to my room, but then I pause and get him bread, turkey, cheese, two different butter knives—one for the mayo, one for the mustard—I mean, why anyone would want to put *both* on a sandwich *I* don't know—a plate and a tall plastic glass which I fill with Barrel Head root beer for him. I let him make the sandwich on his own. "I'll be back," is what I say next as a kind of a joke, 'cause, after all, this is where I live.

"I'll be here," he answers, liking all jokes.

When I return to my room, I sigh and give my guru a look as if to say, "See what I'm up against?"

My guru only smiles at me.

BIG HEAVEN

Chapter 2

All right. So that didn't go "exactly" according to plan, but we're not going to dwell on that now, 'cause now I have a mission: I am going to be a nun, and that is the story that I *really* want to share. So for now, I'll give you just a *glimpse* into what that's about—what we on this path believe—and, that way, you get to see for yourself why I want to be a nun, and I get to focus on *being* a nun. So that works! Ha!

Basically, we believe in the "perennial teachings of the East" (the *Bhagavad Gita* and such), which state that God—we'll start with Him, ha—can best be described as "ever-conscious, ever-new bliss." However, when God created the world, He used not only *Himself* to create it, He also introduced *maya* into the mix, which is delusion. He did this 'cause you need duality in order to have a world. You can't have white-upon-white, to quote an example that is used. You couldn't see it. Plus, if you have dark, you'll appreciate light a lot more. So 'cause of all this, God, and also our souls—which are really little parts of God—are the only bits of creation that are actually "real," while the rest of the world is not. So we'll never be satisfied by the rest of the world. Not *truly* satisfied, anyway. Not way down deep in our souls, which is where we *need* to be satisfied. For how can something that's real be content with what's not? See what I mean? It all makes great sense if you think about it! And here is the *real* kicker: God actually created the world like this on *purpose*, 'cause He wants us to go back to Him. In the end, we are his little kids.

That, I think, is *really* cool.

Anyway, here's a story that illustrates this. In particular, it addresses the nature of desire. How worldly desires are endless, and how they're never *completely* fulfilled in the way we would like, and how, even when one desire *is* fulfilled, there soon arises *another* desire, and another, for that's just the nature of desire. But when we have God—who is ever-conscious, ever-new bliss—all desire ceases.

I think you can see why I'm excited by this!

Anyway, here goes. Here's the story:

There once was a devotee who lived in a hermitage. One day, he said to his teacher, "Master. Everything here is work—all day long. There's not enough spirituality. I'm going to leave the hermitage and go meditate in the woods," and his Master said, "You must not. You have to work for God, or else you will fall." But the devotee ignored him and went on his way. He took nothing with him except for a rag to serve as his loincloth, and a single wooden begging bowl. He went and sat under a tree, feeling terribly proud. The very next morning, however, he noticed a mouse had chewed holes in his loin cloth and he became really mad. He looked up at the sky and said, "Lord. I have given up *everything*, and now you want to munch at my *cloth*?!"

Soon, a man came by and asked him what was wrong. The devotee said, "I'm worried 'cause there's this mouse that is eating my loincloth," and the man said, "Sir, that is simple. You need a cat," and the devotee said, "What a great idea! But how do I get one?" and the man said, "I can bring you a cat." So, soon, the devotee had a cat—the mouse fled—but now he had to go to the village every day to get milk.

The next time he saw the man, he told him about his new problem, and the man said, "That's easy. Get a cow." The devotee replied, "Cow?! How do I get a cow?" and the man said, "I will give you one." So now the devotee had a cow *and* a cat.

The cow was known as "the saint's cow," which meant he was allowed to forage in everyone's fields, which caused a big fuss. Soon the villagers began complaining.

"Sir," they said. "Your cow is eating all our crops." The devotee said, "Well how am I going to *feed* my cow?" and the man from before stepped up and said, "Why don't you have your own land?"

The devotee said, "*Land*? How will I get *land*?" and the man said, "I will give you some."

"But how will I *tend* it?" the devotee asked.

"You need some children of your own to tend it," said the man."

"*Children*? Sure. But how?" and the man asked,

"I'll give you my daughter in marriage."

The devotee began seriously thinking about this—about marrying, and having children and so on—all to support his field, his cow and his cat.

Before long, his Master showed up and said, "I thought you had renounced the hermitage 'cause there was too much work. What's this, then? I hear that you're going to get *married!*"

The devotee said, "Master. This, believe it or not, is all for a *rag!*" Then he added, "You were right. I'll return with you," and away the two of them went, back to the hermitage.

Anyway, that is pretty much it. That's the story.

Desires, as you can see, are a big dead end.

Maybe you can understand the appeal of this nun thing now!

BIG HEAVEN

Chapter 3

As I said, my mother died three months ago. It was due to a stroke. There were complications, so it didn't take long. She never got to leave the hospital. She was only fifty-nine. And though I *really* don't want to have to talk about my mother, 'cause it's sad, and 'cause my story isn't about her, I will tell you this, which will tell you *something*—it would be weird not to mention her at all, after all; it would be like not paying her tribute: She was the glue that held my father and me together. She was the one who kept us engaged; who was always brimming with life; who made us a proper, whole, family.

I'll give you just a few examples, starting with me.

She would give me advice, tell me her thoughts on the world, open herself to me. We had loads of cherished "mother-daughter times." Regarding boys, for instance, she'd say: "You need to find a boy who *understands* you"—her very most pressing advice on the topic, and though I'm not sure I knew what it meant at the time, and I can't ask her *now*, and I'm indeed going to become a nun so I really don't *need* such advice—it sounded good. It sounded like she really knew her stuff.

By way of confiding in me, she'd say right before we'd leave the house: "I better put some lipstick on. I don't want to end up *scaring* anyone." It was her joke. She was implying she was scary-looking, without a thick dollop of lipstick on, though she wasn't. Yet by telling me her little joke, she was sharing herself—the hardships of aging, the vanities known to our sex—though doing it all in a fun way. It was a mother-daughter kind of thing: A being-initiated-into-womanhood thing.

You can't easily replace *that*. Or this:

We'd talk. I know that sounds awfully trite, but we would. Every single day after school she'd be sitting at the clean kitchen table, eagerly waiting for me, and we'd talk about our day. Mostly, she'd ask about mine and I'd tell her. It was girl-talk. We'd talk for *hours. S*he was my *mother*.

It's funny, but the conversations always seemed to take place in the winter—five o'clock in the afternoon is the way that I remember them—when it was already dark out-of-doors, and the kitchen was glowing and warm—thick, yellow light, barring the black from entering—a chicken was roasting slowly in the oven, filling the kitchen with its scent, though we must have talked in other seasons, too. But I always remember those chickens roasting.

Anyway, that is just a *glimpse* into what things were like.

We were close.

And as for my father, he completely adored my mother, and she him. It simply and clearly was that way. You could tell. An example: He used to make jokes just to hear my mother laugh, and she *would* laugh. She was his number-one fan. That's how you knew they were happy together.

I recall one time, for instance, they tried for weeks to get their toilet flusher fixed. I don't remember what was wrong with the flusher, and that won't help further my story at all, so suffice it to say *something* was wrong, and that my mother was constantly calling people up, and that either those people couldn't come, or said they would and then didn't, or even *did* come, but couldn't find or fix the problem. Finally, a plumber showed up and the toilet was fixed, hooray! As the plumber was leaving, and my parents were showing him the door, my father was raving about him, saying things like, "Gee. *That* didn't take very long. We're *extremely* impressed." And, "If there was a genius grant given to plumbers, I'd nominate you. You're quite a guy."

My mother was beaming, partly 'cause the toilet was fixed, but mainly 'cause of my father. She thought he was great. Corny. Fun.

The plumber also seemed to think he was great, and then my father said, "In fact, you did *such* a good job, we also have a typewriter that needs looking after, if you care to fix that."

Mom laughed. He made the joke mainly for her—he was happy owing to her is the way I saw it. The plumber guy had a laugh, too. Life was this big bowl of cherries all around. And though I remember thinking at the time: Corny! Embarrassment! Ick! Save me from them! *Please!* Even *I* could discern it was happy-vibe time: Happy vibes spread all around.

So that is what it was like in our house: Happy.

She was our family glue—my mother.

We both loved her.

And of course, that doesn't begin to paint the whole picture for you. That captures only a hundredth of it, a millionth, really, so I'll also say this: Right after my mother died, a lot of things started to change around our house, which of course is what you'd expect, though you can't really know till you know.

For one thing, nobody filled the napkin holder. The napkins in the holder ran out, as they're likely to do, and the next thing we knew

—that was it. The basket *stayed* empty. We had always kept the napkins in a basket on the table...it's a throwback from my mother's days. It's corny, but also kind of sweet.

Also, and I know this sounds lame, but for a couple of days there at least, nobody replaced the main toilet-paper roll. My father has his own bathroom, but sometimes he uses the main one just off our little hall, so he had to have seen. I, for my part, just used Kleenex from the box on the sink. It was survivalist time, you could say.

Even a couple of our pictures went crooked on the walls. The refrigerator collected old food, and no one disposed of it. We just let it fester. I won't even describe the kitchen floor for you. Suffice it to say, it took some time to see all my mother did—all of the things she attended to daily. It quickly became clear that my *father* wasn't about to shape up, so I did. I got the napkins out of the drawer, stuffed the things into the basket, wrote "napkins" on the long-neglected list. I went to the store and purchased new ones.

And, of course, that is just the lame, superficial stuff—the how-one-manages-a-household garbage—not the stuff that really truly matters, which I'd rather not think about, since it's too sad—way way way too sad—though it just goes to show how even the lame, superficial stuff adds up.

Chapter 4

Janie's over. She's my best friend. We're in the family room. My dad is next door in the kitchen—it's an "openish" floor plan, I'd say, so "next door" might not be the proper term, though he *is* beyond the small archway of where we both are. We could be hanging out elsewhere, of course, like at the river, or at Wendy's, or at the park, so no place *that* great, but I sort of thought it best to be around this afternoon—not 'cause he can't be alone (he certainly *can*), it's just that he seems to like it better when I'm here. So here we are. In any case, Janie and I have the alt-rock station on (channel 914 on Charter Cable —we refuse to listen to "pop"), and a box of Ring Dings right between us, and bottles of Maybelline nail polish out for our toes, since it now is high summer, which means sandal-wearing time. I have a nice, subtle mauve 'cause I look best in "earth tones" I'm told. Janie has a loud, garish red 'cause—well, she is Janie. You will soon see what I mean.

Anyway, I'm about to tell Janie what's going on—about my deciding to become a monastic and all—but Eddie Vedder fills the air waves singing *Black*. It's my favorite of all of his songs. I know Eddie's ancient and all, and that he's been rocking out and living it for years, and that Pearl Jam's considered "old-school" by my peers, still

—I love-love-love-love Eddie Vedder. And 'cause I love him so much, I wait a stretch of time before I speak—I have to hear Eddie Vedder *sing!* His voice could seduce you in a second. All right, Chris Cornell has an even far sexier voice, which means Chris could seduce you in, like, *half*-of-a-second—he's the sexiest singer alive if you ask me and you can trust me—though Janie says no. She says that Maynard James Keenan of Tool is somehow even sexier—though Janie is wrong. Anyway, I'm not really supposed to be thinking this way, seeing how I'm going to be a nun, though, I'm not a nun *yet.*

I say to Janie, "Eddie," and then I make goo-goo eyes at her—man-in-the-moon-pie-eyes—to say I'm in love.

I'm joking, of course, though not really.

Once Eddie Vedder is done—*aaagh,* it's *over!*—I tell my bud Janie my plans, a smile on my face.

"A nun," Janie replies.

"Yup."

"And next week will you be joining the circus?"

I smile even more. "I don't think the monastics will let me. Is there good work to be done in the circus?" is what I say back.

"Always," my best bud replies, so I smile again.

Then I tell her the desire story—about the devotee, the loincloth, and the mouse, so she'll understand—and then about my prophecy—which I *promise* I will tell you—and how it points to my being a nun. Right now. At sixteen.

It really does.

And *then* I tell her how, even though I *love* Eddie Vedder, *and* Chris Cornell, *and* Maynard James Keenan of Tool, how what God has to offer is better, and is what we are actually seeking when we seek, and is not of this transient world…it's pretty profound heady stuff, trust me.

Janie is doing "her look." Then she says, "How will Cameron feel?"

"What?" I ask.

"You know. Cameron."

"I don't know what you're talking about," I say and reach for a Ring Ding.

She continues to do "her look."

Right then, right at the *peak* of "her look," my dad yells the single word, "Mo?"

I go to the kitchen, which is, like, five feet away pretty much. Janie comes, too. To observe. She likes observing.

"I can't get this can opener to work," my father complains. He is standing by the counter, looking at the opener. It's not even held in his hands.

In my father's defense, it *is* one of those "new" kinds of openers that you have to place on top of the can—just so—so the blade can dig in. It's not the kind they used to have where the opener worked on the outside of the can. And it certainly isn't the hand-cranking kind from days of old. So, it's not what he's used to, I mean, though we've had it for three or four years. Still, it's not, you could say, what he "grew up with." I guess my mother used to open the cans. I open it for him. Tuna. Then I get the mayonnaise out, and a bowl, and a fork for the mixing. I'll let *him* scrounge his own plate. I say as gently as I can: "Now that Mom's not here, Dad, you should really learn to do things for yourself. It really would be good, I think."

"Oh," he utters, turning on the charm. "Why would I want to do *that* when my *daughter's* right here? Am I right on that, Janie?" he adds.

"Right back at you on that, Mr. P.," is what Janie says.

I give my bud Janie a look.

She gives me the look back.

We return to the family room, and the almost full carton of Ring-Dings and the red and mauve polish. Death Cab for Cutie is singing their song, *I Will Follow You into the Dark.*

I love them, too.

We listen to the song—at least the rest having missed the beginning doing the tuna-fish thing—and when Death Cab is finished, I sigh, then I tell Janie more. How it's said that *everyone* is searching, even those folks who don't *know* that they're searching. And how it's said you can either do it now—go back to God and give yourself over to Him—or after a hundred-thousand-million-zillion lives, but you'll still have to do it. And how all of the monastics seem happy, like, blissed to the max.

"Who isn't happy?" Janie says, shoving a double-stuffed Ring Ding in her mouth. She's funny, my very best friend.

Right then, my father calls. "Mo? Are we out of root beer?"

I know: You've heard all this before. I have, too.

I sigh and roll my eyes, and then we get up and go to the kitchen. I find the root beer in the fridge and take it out.

"I could have sworn on the bible I looked in there."

"Want me to *pour* the root beer for you, too?" I next ask.

"You're reading my mind."

I pour him a glass over ice. Then I start mixing the tuna, which hasn't been touched. I get the bread from the breadbox, go ahead and make the whole sandwich. As I am doing this he says, "I've got this kid under my thumb. You know that, Janie?" He winks.

"And a very nice thumb it is, Mr. P.," she replies.

I give ole Janie the look.

She sends it back.

As I'm cutting the sandwich, he says, "Please don't take all this the wrong way, but, Mo, you're a *very* good cook. You know that?"

He is vigorously cranking up the charm.

"No offense taken," I say, being swayed by the charm, just a bit, without really looking at Janie, though I sense her looking at me. Then I say, "There," handing him the sandwich, a trace of finality in my voice. We go back to the family room, where Snow Patrol's song *Chasing Cars* is on.

I probably don't have to say this, but I *love* Snow Patrol! I go on with the happiness theme, which is where we left off. How it's been said by my guru, who is dead but really "ever-living" as they say, "Be happy, for sorrow is an offense against the bliss of Spirit." And how Saint Augustine once said, "By being happy my child, thou dost please me." And how it is said that we should *always* think positively—*never* negatively—for our thoughts help create our lives and influence the whole *world*.

Janie—ever the funny one—quips, "I'm '*positive*' I've heard quite enough," which is really quite droll.

My father cuts in with a "Mo?"

"He's used to Mom doing all this," I say, as I move toward his voice.

We go to the kitchen together.

"When did you say my dad's coming by? He's taking me out to get ice cream," Dad says.

My dad is sitting at the table. His sandwich is almost all gone. Janie looks at me, puzzled. I have to explain how his father is dead—has been for some time. It's not the first time I've had to explain this, though it's the first time for Janie.

"Is that right?" is what my dad says as he looks into my eyes. "That's too bad…*gee*."

He looks crestfallen by the somber news. I quick-pat his arm. "It is," I say. "I know. I'm sorry, Dad."

We go back to the family room, where the Chili Peppers' song *Tell Me Baby* is on. The Chili Peppers top off my list. I go for some Ring Dings, then for the subtle mauve polish, then for the remote—not sure which task I should tackle straight off.

Janie looks at me. She keeps looking. She *keeps* looking.

I say, "Well the thing that you *don't* know is that he's on these new pills: to help…I only just found them…they were there in the drawer of his night-table next to his bed." Then I say, "I don't think that he has been taking them regularly." And *then* I say, "It's something I'm really going to work on—his taking his pills."

Janie looks askanse, then says, "I hope they take *fathers* at your monastery."

She goes for the garish red polish.

"That color's *gauche*," is what I say next—a lot like a hurt child.

Janie says, "Haven't you been reading your *Cosmo*? Red's *never* ever gone out of style. At least, never yet."

She blows on her toenails to clean them, just 'cause she once saw it done, I believe.

I think it's pretty idiotic.

Chapter 5

Anyway, okay. So the cat is out of the bag. My father "has something." I'm not quite sure what, or if it's ever been diagnosed for sure, like, one hundred percent, for neither of my parents ever mentioned it to me, yet it's becoming more clear that there's *something*.

What my father *could* have is either dementia (the plain, old, regular, old-age kind—though he's only sixty-five), or Alzheimer's. I'm guessing Alzheimer's: early stage, which has dementia as one of its symptoms, or maybe even vascular dementia, which is mini-strokes occurring in the brain, that slowly kill different parts. Any way you slice it, it isn't good, although dementia, I guess, would be the lesser of the evils, though I did find these pills in his nightstand which are used to treat Alzheimer's Disease—I know 'cause I Googled the pills.

Still, until someone tells me he's definitely got it, I can't quite be sure, 'cause I have also come to understand this: Alzheimer's is hard to diagnose. At least fully. I know 'cause I visited the website on this— really really quickly—I didn't want to hang out too long. But in order to be sure, like "one hundred percent," you need to perform a full autopsy of the brain. You need the person under suspicion to fully be dead. There are other odd tests you can do to try and make the diagnosis, like brain scans and psych tests and blood tests and whatnot. I don't know if my father's had any of those. My mother just suffered her stroke and then she was gone, without saying anything. So all I *really* can tell you for sure is that he's now on these pills…and the pills are for Alzheimer's Disease—hey, I'm only sixteen! I don't know for sure that he's got "it." I'll have to wait and see. And just 'cause my dad likely "has some condition," it doesn't mean I'm altering my own plans. I'm still going to become a nun. This summer. At sixteen. It's what my prophecy stated. I just have to stay one step ahead of things is all.

All of that said, my father asking questions about *his* father *is* pretty worrisome—I won't try and kid about that—but I am also serious about his pills: He needs to take them daily. I know that he's not, since the prescriptions were last filled in March and it now is mid-June, and there are still loads of pills in the bottles.

All these facts are swimming about in my mind before I leave for work in the morning—it's my very first job—I'm a "concession attendant" at Embassy Cinema and have to be wholly reliable, seeing as how it's my first job—I leave my dad's morning pills on the table for him with a note. The note states, "Please take your pills." Simple, considerate, clear. I use the largest-size notepaper we have, and write it in big capital letters. I reminded him last night that I'd be leaving this note with his pills, and that it was important he *take* his pills, and that the note would serve as a reminder for this. He said, "Fine," but when I get home from Embassy Cinema, the pills are still there—I counted them.

"Dad, you still haven't taken your *pills*. I went over all this last night with you," I say. It's become the first thing I say when I come home, which isn't that nice, but I guess I'm not really feeling that nice.

"Is that right?" is what he usually says back, which isn't that great.

It's a little like getting a job, I decide. You need experience to land a good job, but in order to *get* experience, you need a job. That is, you need to take the pills to remember to take the pills.

He wasn't like this when Mom was around—I think 'cause he was taking his pills—but I have a job, a future, a life. I can't be nursemaiding him all the time. I'm just a kid.

The difference, they say, between regular dementia and Alzheimer's, which has dementia as one of its symptoms, is that with dementia, you can't find your car keys at times, while, with Alzheimer's, you can't remember what your cars keys are actually *for.*

I know my father's not *that* bad.

Anyway, it's kismet, it's karma, it's fate—someone up there is smiling on me—for I'm outside, partially checking the weather (it's nice), partially checking the perennials that border our stairs that my mom planted eons ago (they're going to pot—or is that seed?) when Mrs. McClancey comes out of her house and asks how it's going. Note: She wasn't *already* outside of her house. She *came* out. That might be a clue to you. She knows about my mom dying, of course; she knows it's just my father and me in the house.

I tell her "Okay."

She's Irish, in case you couldn't tell from the name, though McClancey could be her married, not maiden name, which, owing to the "Mrs." in front, I'm sure it is), and her maiden name might *not* be Irish, which means *she* might not be Irish, but—married name or not —Mrs. McClancey *is* Irish. And seeing as how she is, she's interested in me, I believe, as a result of the potato famine. I mean—people *had* to show an interest in each other back then, otherwise they'd *starve.*

And, too, she's a mother of three, but her children are all grown, and I think *all* people who are mothers take an interest in other people's kids once their own leave the nest so to speak. It's, like, a requisite maternal trait. I know. I'm a kid, but I'm not a kid.

Anyway, after I answer "Okay," she asks about Dad. How he's doing.

"Okay," I repeat, which makes her stop and look at me. Everyone is always looking at me: Janie, Mrs. McClancey, everyone! So then I say—thinking maybe she's got some wisdom to share, and thinking I could use some wisdom right now—"I'm actually trying to get him to take his pills. He's always forgetting. It's important he take his pills." I don't mention what they're for, 'cause I'm not "fully sure," as I said. They could be for minor high-blood pressure for all Mrs. McClancey knows—and one of them is, by the way—which is to say that I say the words really casual-like, though not really.

We go on talking in that vein about how I have a job now at Embassy Cinema, and so am not always home for Dad's pills, though he needs to be taking them, and before long, Mrs. McClancey tells me about these pill boxes they have at CVS with the days of the week printed on them, and multiple compartments for each day, in case you need to take pills more than once a day—which Dad does—and not only that, they have this alarm that can be set for various times so that when the alarm makes its sound—*voila!*—the person takes his pills. I want to hug Mrs. McClancey. I want to hug the higher power that sent her to me.

She says she could always drop by with a stew or something if I'd like—the Irish are *always* at home cooking stews, I believe—and at first, I don't know what to say. Part of me wants to say, "Stew? Bring it on! In fact, come over anytime and just take over, why don't you?

We'd certainly welcome the help!" Then this other part doesn't want anyone knowing our business or trying to butt in. Who *knows* what could transpire then? People might see something's up with my father. They could put my dad into a home and send me off to odious foster care since I'm not an adult. These parts engage in a battle till the chicken part wins.

"I make a mean beef stew," is what she says.

"I'm vegetarian," I say—not totally true, but partly so, "though I do eat chicken," I blurt out. This last part *is* true, which means I'm *not* vegetarian *per se*, and which also means that I want to pull her in, and yet I don't. Mostly, I think that I don't, so then I have to cover my tracks quickly. "But really. We're fine. We are…though it's nice of you to think of us."

"Well let me know if you change your mind. You know where I live," she tells me, and winks as she utters these words since she lives right next door.

I smile, nod and wave as she goes into her house, wishing I could summon her back once she's gone. Her children are grown, as I've said. Her husband is dead. It's her all alone in that three-bedroom ranch right next to ours. We could become her new family, though she is much older than Mom—close to seventy-five I would venture; my mother was fifty-nine—and she already takes on a lot with Saint Anne's Catholic Church, which is just around the corner from us, so I'm not all that sure she *needs* a new family right now. For all I know, she might have orphans she remotely takes care of from a war-ravaged country in Africa—Catholics, I think, are well known for all that— though if she *does* come to want a new family, we're certainly here. Though, again, I think she's too old.

A little bit later, I call Janie and tell her I just bought a pill box with a built-in alarm to serve as an aid to my father. I explain the glorious concept to her: how you can set it for all different times so the person takes his pills.

"A pill box with a built-in alarm, huh? Well let's just hope your dad isn't too absorbed watching *Dr. Phil* when the pill box goes off, as we know he likes to do. And let's just hope that an *ambulance* doesn't go by at the very same time. And let's just hope that a *plane* isn't flying overhead. And let's just hope that he doesn't need pills on the half or the full or quarter-hour, so the bells of Saint Anne's aren't deafeningly pealing the minute he does."

"Huh," is what I think then.

Sometimes I'm not sure Janie really wants me becoming a nun.

In any case, I have a plan I set into motion at six that night. I wait until after we've eaten to start—I don't want my dad being so hungry he won't hear what I have to tell him. Also, I wait until after he's taken his three evening pills. I sat and I got him the water, watched as he took them and nodded as I saw them go down. It turns out—and I didn't tell Janie this exactly, and I didn't tell Mrs. McClancey, and I don't think I told *you*—but it turns out that Dad must take *two* kinds of pills: some for Alzheimer's, and some for high blood pressure. Two of these he has to take two times a day, and one of them once a day. One is yellow and round, one is pink and round, and the largest is oblong and white, so you won't mix them up—this I am especially glad about.

We're out on the deck. It's a beautiful night—late June—still early enough that mosquitoes haven't chased us inside, which means too early for fireflies too, which is too bad, but that's how the whole of life is at its core: a mix. It's never purely unalloyed. There's always duality. Like you get to watch fireflies fill the night sky, but the whole time your ankles are getting attacked by blood-sucking fiends...but then, I digress...

So here's the scene: We're sitting outside on a beautiful night with the pill box on the table. The table is mesh, by the way. We used to have a glass-top table, but somebody left the umbrella wide open one night when there was a storm, and the umbrella flew off and smashed the glass table. I believe it was my father who committed the *faux-pas*, though I'm not fully sure. And anyway—now we have a mesh table top.

So I'm explaining the facts of the pill box to my dad, who is here, and, I want to add "who is listening," though I can't be too sure of that.

"So, Dad, here's the deal. It says, 'Monday, Tuesday, Wednesday, blah-blah'."

"It says '*blah-blah*'?"

He loves this. Absolutely. It's a chance for him to tease his daughter.

I smile, though it's really a smirk, though really a grimace.

"No," I say. "It doesn't. It says the days of the week. Here." I tap on the pill box for emphasis. I would turn it to face his way, but it already is.

"And there is more than one compartment for each day—three actually—so you can take pills up to three times a day. And I'll set it. It has an alarm, like I said, so that on Monday, for instance, in the morning, the alarm will go off, and that will be your sign to take your Monday morning pills. The ones for the morning. Just those."

I'm hoping I am making it clear.

"Morning," he says with a nod.

"Yes."

"By the way," he says, "I've been meaning to ask how the piano is coming?"

This is way out in left field.

"I don't take piano, Dad."

"You *don't?*" he asks with big eyes. "I'm surprised. You have such nice long fingers." He leans forward, admiring my fingers.

"Thanks. But I never took piano."

"Well that is a definite *shame*," he replies.

I smile/grimace at him. "Okay," is what I say next. "So what I'm going to do—and you're going to watch as I do it to get the idea—is I'm going to fill the box for the week with all of your pills."

I open the Aricept pill bottle first, since that one he takes only one-time-a-day, which is easier, I figure. As I do, he touches my arm and says the word, "Ope!"

It's a game from my childhood. What happens is, when I'm not looking, or not really paying attention completely, he touches me, just with his finger, and says this to me. It's cute when you've newly turned two. Maybe three. But I'm not two or three anymore. I smile at him, though the grimace is coming out more. I hate to have to admit this, but he still plays the "Ope!" game with me. He's a sweet man, my father, deep down, though less sweet when you're trying to get something done.

I go ahead and fill the whole pill box—Aricept just in the evening slots, Namenda and Lopressor in morning and evening. All of the middle compartments are free, which I'm thinking is good, since they lend the box space.

"Okay," I say. "So say the alarm goes off while you're eating a sandwich."

I stop there, wishing I hadn't begun with a sandwich, 'cause I don't want him asking what kind, or if *I'll* be so kind as to make it for him, which is something he's likely to do to be "funny," and I don't want him being funny right now. Besides, I'm not sure whether you take any of the three pills with food, so I alter my course.

"Or," I make myself say, "say you're watching TV. Though you can't have it turned up too loud, 'cause it'll trump the alarm…" I wish I hadn't mentioned TV, but I carry on. "Maybe you have it right *next* to the TV," I persist. "And anyway, it's Monday, it's the morning, it's nine, and the pill box alarm goes off. *What do you do?*"

"What?" he says with big eyes, which is him being "fun" again.

"No, Dad. This isn't a guessing game. It's Monday; it's morning; here's the box. The alarm goes off. *What do you do?*" I look at my father with my own big eyes.

"Why, I look for *you*, of course."

This is his charm-working trick, but I don't let it work.

"I'm at work," I dryly respond, biting my lip.

"Oh. Well that would be a real *shame*. I'd certainly *miss* you."

This is the point where I snap.

"*Dad! What do you do?!*" I insist.

He says, "I *know* what to do, Maureen," using his "father voice" now, his eyes squeezing down to small slits.

"Good. Tell me. What?" This is important. My being a nun depends on this.

"I take my pills."

"Yes. Which ones?"

"The ones for Monday," he tells me.

"In both of the compartments, or one?"

"Both."

"You're *kidding* me by saying that. Right?" I know that it's mean, but I really can't help it. It just comes out.

He looks at me.

I don't think I have fully described him to you. He has these watery, blue, baby-looking eyes. Not a deep blue. Really, the opposite: a little washed-out looking. His face is childlike and unlined, 'cause he's pudgy. He looks guileless is what I'm trying to say, which can really be a problem.

I say to him, "No, Dad. No. No. No. You only take the *morning* ones, see? The ones right here." I point to the bottom compartment for Monday, thinking maybe I didn't explain it enough—about the slots. How the bottom one is AM, the middle one noon, and the highest one PM. He bends at an angle to see. He looks confused. It makes me feel just a little bit bad.

"Do you want me to go get your glasses?" I ask, sounding hopeful.

"Sure," he replies, hopeful back.

"Where are they?" I ask. "Do you know?" I don't have a great deal of faith in his knowing.

His eyes wander up to the ceiling, then he looks back. An idea has just come to him; I can tell. "Why, they're where we've *always* kept *all* of our glasses. In the kitchen cabinet, of course."

It's a joke, and he smiles to show me.

I'm not certain what I should do, so I simply look off. Patience is called for, I know, though it's not lightly won.

I sigh, and then I sigh again. Then I say, thinking maybe the pressure's been too much for him, thinking maybe I ought to adjust it a notch, "Tell you what. *I've* been asking the questions up to this point tonight. Maybe you'd like to ask *me* a question? To try and clear some of this up?"

"Ask *you* a question?" he says with a pondering squint. "Sure. What are you planning to do with your good looks?" he asks.

And that, as the saying goes, is that. I'll have to try again some other time. We'll wait till we have his old reading glasses safely in hand. I smile/grimace at him. He is my father. After all.

You've probably noticed by now that the relationship I have with my father is not going to break any records for being too deep—it's all on the surface. He treats me as if I am three, and I, in turn, respond like I'm three—pretty much. It's always been this way, strange though that may seem. I guess you could say I don't know him. I don't know the wildest dream he ever harbored in his life, or his deepest, most desperate fear, or even his greatest regret. I don't know any of the "meaningful" things, that's to say. It was my mother I felt I really knew. It was my mother I talked to. My father's a man. They don't talk all that much. This I know. Plus—and I know this might sound strange —we've never spent a whole lot of time with each other, just us two, so it's strange spending time with him now.

Maybe no teenage girl knows her father.

It's definitely strange suddenly finding yourself alone with a man you don't know.

BIG HEAVEN

Chapter 6

Anyway, all of that is okay—it's okay, it's okay, it's okay—'cause not only do I go over it again the next day, and set the alarm on the pill box, and even leave him a note as a kind of *double* reminder, but I'm going to a spiritual lecture tonight, so I'm psyched.

One of the reasons I'm so psyched is that immediately after the talks, we sit as a group and we meditate. This, it turns out, is better than meditating alone, though all meditation is good, 'cause of what's known as the "group-consciousness effect." That is, "the-whole-is-greater-than-the-sum-of-the-parts" phenom'. It is said that whenever more are assembled, God's blessings are greater. It is also said that in group meditations, like tonight's, a mingling of consciousness occurs —like a melding—wherein everyone's consciousness can merges with the consciousness of all the others, so that your own can be raised up. A single monk's consciousness can elevate everyone else's. I've felt this happen myself, by the way, and it's great!

Anyway, I'll try and describe it for you, 'cause this is key to my story—why I want to be a nun, pretty much—though I really should warn you: it's not easy. It's like a saying I read online one time: "From outside looking in, you never understand it. And from inside looking out, you can never explain it." It's also like the following quote by a German ministerial student when asked to describe an experience he had in the sixties while tripping on psilocybin: "A thought spoken is a lie," though I would change it to "An *experience* spoken is a lie," for that is more to the point. I think you get the idea.

All of that said, I still want to describe the meditations for you, but please keep in mind that when you're *in* the state I'm describing, you should never try to analyze it; you need to simply enjoy it. The moment you analyze, you're sunk, for then you've "stepped outside." And *that* said, of course we try and analyze—that's the very nature of the mind—though we shouldn't. And *that* said, here's my description.

At its best, it's like pure awareness, yet without thought. Pure peace and bliss. A feeling of nothing to move toward, or away from. A feeling of no more longing for anything, nor of repulsion from anything else. A feeling of nothing to do and nowhere to go. You are just *there*…it feels almost as if—when you're focusing right where you should, which is up in the forehead, at the point of the "spiritual eye" between the eyebrows—something is meeting you there, joining its signal to yours, picking up yours. It actually, honestly feels like that. When you're in the state, you never want to leave it, that's for sure. You wouldn't trade it for anything. It is pure well-being. It is God.

Unfortunately, "it" doesn't last all that long—not for newcomers like me. That's one of "its" tricks. But the more you meditate, the better it gets, or so I hear.

Anyway, achieving this state reminds me of what kids used to say when Officer Griffin used to come to our school for a D.A.R.E. session. When he was finally done with his talk, the kids used to say: "Officer Griffin has *left* the building!" It's a military—naval—saying that meant the captain had left the bridge, or something like that. It was supposed to be funny, as if now the kids could misbehave again.

Sometimes, when I'm meditating, I feel like this. Not the misbehaving part, but the other part: "Mo Proctor has *left* the building!" Your head is united with vastness somewhere else.

So that's the appeal—both of meditation and of being a nun, since they go hand-in-hand.

I hope it's becoming more clear now why I'm so looking forward to this session.

The bus drops me off early, and I find a seat near the front of the banquet room. The monk—a Hindu of the Swami Order—makes a joke as he's comes into the meeting place. He says, "On my way up here, I wasn't chanting, 'Om, God; Om, God,' as we're likely to do, I was chanting, 'Don't trip on the stairs, don't trip on the stairs, don't trip on the stairs'."

Everyone laughs.

Brother himself flashes a broad smile, then sits quietly down. Well, sits cross-legged on the floor.

So let me tell you more about the meeting: I'm at an open-to-the-public free talk, put on by the group for whom I want to be a nun: The Center for Spiritual Union. The talk is taking place in a ballroom the group has rented. About a hundred-odd people are in attendance, which is really not bad. It's the fourth week in a row I've attended such talks, so if you start to feel a little bit lost, just follow my lead.

That was a joke.

Sort of.

In any case, the speaker tonight is Brother Satnarada—you'll like him—and the title of the talk is: "Knowing Who You Are: It Might Be Better than You Possibly Think." Catchy, yes? Do *you* know?

Now we should shush. *Really.* If I'm going to be a bona fide nun, I really need to pay attention right now (this is another attempt at a joke, 'cause I'm the one doing the talking, not you).

"And so, good evening," Brother says. "It's so nice to see you all here. Tonight's topic, as you know, is 'Knowing Who You Are,' and I'd like to begin with a story, if I may. Once, around the time of the Korean War, Kirk Douglas picked up a military man who was hitchhiking. The man got into the car, not really looking at his driver, but then, when he did, and he recognized who his driver was, he said, very dramatically, 'Do you know who you *are*?!' Mr. Douglas said he thought about that one for years."

People laugh without restraint. There's a giddiness attending these talks that's hard to explain. You pretty much have to be here. But then, you are. Sort of. Well, you *are* sort of!

"So who are we?" Brother goes on. "Master," that is our guru, by the way: more on him later, "used to say that what you are is greater than anything and everything you are seeking.

"Think about that. I'll say it again. What you are is greater than anything and everything you are seeking. And Vivekinanda, another Indian saint, once said, 'The definition of an atheist isn't someone who doesn't believe in *God*, it's someone who doesn't believe in *himself.*' And Saint Augustine—always a favorite of mine—once said, 'Behold. You were in me, and I was outside of myself searching for You.' Not realizing who we are, not realizing we are a part of God, just as a wave is a part of the sea, can be compared to the donkey who goes around carrying a million dollars on his back, all the while searching for a dime."

He pauses.

He has a good point, I believe. Analogies, or so I have found, can be pretty effective, especially when the subject is God.

If I'm going too fast, I can slow his talk down for you. This is a power I have, since I am the narrator, and it makes telling all this stuff more fun for me.

Anyway, the idea that's propelling this talk is that stuff I already told you: How what we *really* are, are pieces of God, and how those pieces of God are our souls. How we're not our bodies, minds, emotions, as we typically think, since those aspects change, while what is "real" does not. How "divinity is stamped on our foreheads" as it were. So when Kirk Douglas stopped to ponder this question—who he really was—this was the answer he needed. So now you can skip the whole rest of the talk. Kidding.

In any case, Brother is telling a different story now. It might help to clarify things, so I really should hush.

"Once," Brother says, "there was an emperor who had four wives. The fourth wife was the one the emperor loved most, and, as a result, he tended to give this wife the bulk of his attention: the most food and love, the most beautiful of clothing, *et cetera*. He cherished this wife. His third wife he also dearly loved, though not quite as much as his fourth, yet this was the wife he took to banquets and such. This wife was his 'trophy wife.' His second wife he loved just a little bit less than his third, though this wife had been with him a very long time, and was a very dear friend, and his very closest confidant, *et cetera*. Whenever he underwent troubles and needed advice, this was the wife he first sought. And his first wife, who had been with him the longest of all, he loved the very least. He neglected this wife to the extreme, not giving her nearly enough love, let alone clothing or food, and, as a result, she was withering away before his eyes.

"One day, the emperor learned from the palace doctor that he was terminally ill, and that his time left on Earth was very short, and suddenly, he wanted somebody who would go with him to the beyond. So he approached his fourth wife and asked her. She told him, 'No way,' and promptly took off. So next he approached his third wife, whom he also quite desperately loved, and asked her. She said, 'I'm sorry, but the minute you're officially dead, I plan to remarry, so that tack won't work.' So then he approached his second wife, who had been his faithful confidant all of those years, and asked her, and *she* said, 'My dear. I will accompany you as far as I can—all the way to the grave, if need be—but that is as far as I will go.' Finally, having no one else to whom he could turn, he approached his first wife, who he had given zero attention for all of those years, and asked *her*. She said, 'Yes. I will accompany you to the grave and beyond'."

Brother smiles right here, for he knows what is next.

"Each of the emperor's wives," Brother says, "represents something. The fourth wife is the man's body, which he desperately loves and lavishes much attention on. The third wife is the man's status and possessions, which he also desperately loves, and shows off to the world at every turn. The second wife is the man's family, whom he turns to for help and advice, and who can accompany him right to the grave, but no further. And the first wife is the man's soul. And that is the one who stays with him through it all."

Brother now gives us a nod that says: "There it is."

He looks happy.

He is bald, did I mention? I have a theory about baldness. It goes that men who are not bald spend a lot more of their wakeful hours thinking than the men who are already bald, and that this thinking serves to mess with their hair follicles so that what hair they have continues to fall out until they're shiny bald. Think about it: A lot of professors and clergy are bald. A lot of astronomers, too, I would think. Thinking men…so Brother is a "thinking man." In addition to his baldness, Brother has small, even teeth that are yellowing, and a well-trimmed, low-profile goatee, and is really quite humble. If he were at a party, you wouldn't even know he was there. That kind of person. Believe me: in order to wear the long robes that monks wear —which are really just glorified skirts, if you ask me—you *have* to be humble. It's like this requisite monastic trait.

But returning to Brother's story. The point is that you're supposed to give more time to your soul. To God. I know you got that; I just wanted to bring it to your attention again. And hopefully, the story helped further convince you that I do indeed need to be a nun 'cause, if you believe it at all, wouldn't *you* opt to be a nun, too, so as to work toward your goal most efficiently?

You don't have to answer right now—I'll give you time to think about it. Ha! But I just want you to see the appeal of this thing. I just want you to see how my desire perhaps isn't so strange in light of these stories. And there's lot's more than stories to being a nun. Everyone bows to you when you come in, and you bow right back if you want to—this is about bowing-to-our-inner-God. Also, all of the monastics I've seen up to now seem blissed-out, so that is a draw. And then there's my prophecy that must be considered, which pretty much *said* that I'd become a nun at the age of sixteen…which is now.

Anyway, there's just a little more I want to impart before I move on. Not only are we in Cambridge, Mass, which is often referred to with love as "The People's Republic of Cambridge" to give you an idea of the city's, you might say, more "free-thinking" nature, but the group for whom I want to be a nun has traveled here to Cambridge just for outreach, is actually based in L.A. I mean, where else than "The City of Angels," located in "The Golden State," whose state motto just happens to be "Eureka!" meaning "I found it!" in Greek. "Eureka!: I found it!: I'll be based out of the City of Angels in the Golden State!" Hip-hip-hooray!

Anyway, The Center for Spiritual Union is only here for three months—doing general outreach-type work, as I said—then they leave. Which is another sign I've correctly deciphered my prophecy, and must make my big move *now*. At my age. This summer. I'll be seventeen in September. This means I must interview with them, gain acceptance, and fly back with them for my training if all goes well. Hey, it's all in the prophecy!

Anyway, here's some more you might like to know, or at least that I think would be helpful to know at this point: The group's already been here for roughly a month, which means I have only two months to act, or thereabouts. I first heard about their arrival via a flyer I saw at a bus stop. And I first saw the flyer *two days* after reading my guru's famed book, *The Call of the Soul.* Well, he wasn't my guru back then, but he surely is now.

All of this is cosmic: The timing of my reading my guru's book; the timing of the monastics' slated arrival from our lovely Bay state; my figuring out, not long after, that I should be a nun, based on the prophecy told about my life—I know, I know, but you're just going to have to trust me a little while longer regarding the actual prophesy.

There's a break before group meditation, and during the break I check my phone and discover three separate messages waiting for me in the loop—all from my father. I immediately think, *Uh-oh.* I immediately think, *Shoot.* I immediately think, *Darn.* He's not one to simply say hello on a whim.

The first message goes like this: "Mo?" Pause. "Mo?" Pause. "Are you there?" Pause. "It's your fa-ther." Then a *long* pause. "There's been an accident, Mo. Call me as soon as you're able." He sounds both confused and also pretty stern, like he's using his "father-role voice."

An "accident?" I'm forced now to think. That could be just about anything—right? An accident could range from spilled milk to a jet crashing into our house. Seeing no other real way around it, I play message two.

"Mo? Mo? Maureen…? This is your fa-ther, Maureen. It's the car. I'm not certain what I should do. I wish you would call me." There's a pause, and then: "There's an accident right here, Maureen."

What can I do? I *have* to play message three immediately, though I know it won't be good. Message three ends up going like this: "Maureen?" He's dispensed with the salutary "Mo" right off the bat. "I'm home now, Maureen. I haven't heard back from you yet and I'm expecting your call…it's your fa-ther," he tries to make that especially clear.

I think, *Ooooh-kay.* I think, *Maybe I can get someone else to pretend to be Maureen.* I think, *I* know *it's you, Dad.*

I call him back, but there's no answer, so then I start to wonder if he's all right. I hadn't really wondered this *before* he didn't answer, and now I begin to feel guilty over this. Then I wonder *why* I didn't wonder. Then I realize it's 'cause he *sounded* all right. A little severe in some places, a little bit aggravated there toward the end. Then, when he doesn't answer again, I think, *Ooooh-kay.* Then I think, *I hope he's all right.* And *then* I think, *I'm going to have to go home. I'm going to miss the group meditation—my favorite part—but I'm definitely going to have to go home right now.*

I was only at the frigging lecture an hour.

I take the bus. I catch it up in the square, which is "Harvard Square" to you, in case you didn't know, in case you are not from New England, or aren't incredibly tight with Cambridge Mass: the "Harvard" here obviously referring to Harvard University, which I bet you *did* know, though why they call it a "square" I don't know, 'cause it's not. Actually, I don't think most squares are. Though *some* are, like the one in Townsend, Mass, for instance. There really *is* a common there with four straight regular streets around it, forming a square, and that's the kind of place where the term got its name, I'd bet you. Though in Massachusetts, they're not really big on straight roads—things like grids, or order, or sense, or streets that are numbered—like they are in New York, 'cause in New York, you have streets like Second Ave., Third Ave., Fifth Ave., *et cetera*, while in Massachusetts—Boston in particular—the roads were originally byways for wandering cows. This is for real. I'm not kidding. Our roads are basically cow paths, and 'cause cows don't always go straight, a lot of the streets here are ziggy…that's why, I'm sure. And, yes, I know. I'm not thinking about my father…which I probably should…you must be wondering why I'm going on about *cows*.

Anyway, I catch the bus that takes me to Waltham, which is where we both live, then I walk from the center of town the mile to our house, even though it is dark, and I'm a girl all alone in the dark, walking at night. But let's not forget: I am motherless now. It's just my father and me left at home. I pretty much do what I want. Plus—Waltham is safe.

And speaking of Waltham—in case I haven't relayed this by now, and I don't think I have—they call it "The Watch City," 'cause back in the industrial age, they used to make watches, so someone came up with the slogan of how it is now "The City to Watch," 'cause of the watch-theme. So I live in Waltham, Mass. "The Watch City." "The City to Watch…"

Keep watching.

(And I know: I'm not really thinking about him, though I should…

I am actually kind of doing this on purpose.)

And yet, before long, I find that I must think of him, for the first thing I notice when our house pops into my view is that there's a dent on the front of our car, a Chevy Cavalier. It's this hollow space, with crinkles around it. It looks like a person took a baseball bat to it, or slammed the thing into a pole—I'd hate to see the other guy, I think, then I think how that's not funny. Not really funny at all.

I go in.

My father's in his usual chair in the family room, with the TV on, and the reading lamp on, and a bowl of pretzels on the table by his side, and everything else looking normal about the scene, except that the phone is sitting right on his lap. Right there. Right where he could just answer the thing.

I let this fact go and I ask, "Was anyone hurt?" It's the very first thing that I say.

"No…" my father replies. "I don't *think* so."

This answer's strange. Still: I try and stay calm.

"What happened? Are you okay? Does anything hurt? Your neck, your ribs, your back, etcetera?" And then, 'cause I don't want to give him ideas, I stop right there.

"Tell me what happened," I say. And then I discern that the TV should be off for this, and that I should be sitting, and that I should probably take in a few breaths. I turn the TV off. The saga unfolds. It would be agonizing to tell you word-for-word—agonizing for me anyway, and I don't think that pleasant for you—'cause of the pauses throughout, and the question marks studding the sentences—even midway through, where there aren't supposed to *be* question marks—and the weird circularity involved, or at least—the ellipses. So I'll just sum it up.

He drove—just as it was starting to get dark, I imagine—to Hannaford supermarket, which is right here in town, right here on aptly-named Main Street, and which isn't that hard in itself when compared to certain other kinds of driving, like driving in Manhattan, let's say, unless you're a man, age 65 who has something—plain old dementia, maybe, or is just-starting-to-manifest Alzheimer's, which has dementia as one of its symptoms— vascular dementia, caused by mini-strokes occurring in the brain, that kill parts—and it's starting to get dark, and your wife just died three months ago now, and you don't always take all your pills when you ought to. But miraculously, he made it to Hannaford, even *with* all those stumbling blocks, and with teenagers racing around, and drunk people racing around, too, who have maybe even had their licenses suspended, and a large population of seniors idly motoring, too—my father included in the bunch. Let's face it: No one in "The City to Watch" should really be driving—this is a joke, at least I think it is. But anyway, he makes it to Hannaford and—it's painful to even *retell*—but as he was pulling in and going to park, he hit another car. Luckily, the other car was parked. No one was *in* the parked car, thank God, still, he hit it. Well, he *slammed* into it is more like the truth, based on the damage I saw, though it must have occurred on the outskirts of the lot, 'cause nothing happened afterwards. No one yell, or came, or offered to help; no one moved. No one—not even the owner of the car—accused him. He smashed into an empty parked car, and then drove off.

"Dad. You left the scene of the *accident*? You simply *drove off?!*"

"You weren't answering your phone," is what he replied, as if it were *my* fault.

"Dad, let's not turn this around. You left the scene of the accident," I repeated.

"If you had answered your phone, maybe I wouldn't have left."

If I had been rational then, I would have stopped him right there. I would have said to myself, *Mo. This is a man, age sixty-five, who clearly has something wrong with his brain, and it was starting to get dark at the time, and his wife just died three months ago, and he doesn't always take all of his pills when he ought to. This is your father.* But instead, I got sucked in.

"Dad. I was at a *talk*. You can't have your phone on during a *talk*. Think about it."

And then *he* said, "Oh. You want to start an argument, huh? Is that it? Is that what this is leading to, Maureen?"

"Start an *argument?* Dad! You got into an *accident*! You hit another car and then drove off! It's a miracle no one was hurt!" And then, to belabor my point I declared, "Somebody *could* have been hurt!" And then I said—this wasn't the first sign of trouble between us; there have been others—"You can't drive anymore at night, Dad. You simply cannot."

And then *he* said, "Oh. I don't want to get into *that*. Don't you start *that*."

And then *I* said, "You can't. You're not thinking clearly these days. You're not responsible."

And then *he* said, "Well if *you* were around to drive me, *I* wouldn't have to."

And then *I* said, "I'm just *sixteen*! I don't drive!"

That stopped him. That finally shut him up.

Then he said, "Nuts."

At that, I left the room. I stormed down the hall to my room—which is not entirely true, since our "hall" is only three feet long. All right: *six!* I stormed down the hall, and entered my meditation chamber (a.k.a. my bedroom), which is where I'm at now. The only problem is: My guru is also right here, in my room, in a solid-wood frame. My guru is everywhere, of course, but even more so here in my room, 'cause here I can help but see him. I don't want to deal with him now, so I turn the other way, flop on my bed, plop a pillow over my head. But there's a question steadily nagging at me. I wonder. *Did Dad took his pills?* That is, was this an "accident accident," which means "for real," and something I'll now have to worry about, or just an anomaly from not taking pills? Before I left for the talk, I set the alarm, I left him a note, I went over it all again with him.

I wait, listening for whatever I can, which mainly is nothing is how it turns out—the absence of noise; I mean you'd think there'd be *something.* You'd think that if *you* were the agent of an accident, you would make noise, right?

Finally, I rise from my bed and walk to the kitchen. The pill box is there, on the table, and when I go to pick it up, check it out, I see that the switch is turned off. I open the box and—*voila!* There are the pills. In the PM compartment for Wednesday, where they shouldn't be. They're in the AM compartment, as well, where they also shouldn't be. Small little overlooked pills, happy as clams.

I almost want to take them myself…this shouldn't be happening!

I'm not even going to stop and *ask* about the pills.

Why didn't he take his damn pills? I reset the alarm.

My guru has an awful lot to answer for, I think.

Chapter 7

Actually, as I hinted, this accident isn't the first trouble my father's gotten himself into since my mother died. I never told anyone this—not even Janie, and she's my best friend as you know, who I end up telling *everything* to—but a good three weeks ago, I had just sauntered into the house from hanging with Janie, when CJ called. From CJ's Variety. Just round the corner from us.

CJ's the owner. I've known CJ all of my life. I've lived in this house all my life, and his store's always been on the corner, and CJ himself has always been in the store Anyway, CJ told me my father is there and how I should come get him—not good—and how he'd have simply "run him home" this once himself, but he had to keep the store open and all—also not good—plus even if he did "run him home," which would entail CJ closing his store, he wouldn't want to "drop him off blind" and leave him by himself—*definitely* not good. CJ got our number from my dad—good—but the reason for the call was that my father didn't have his wallet on him, and didn't know why he'd gone into the store in the first place, and was just in his slippers—I bet I don't have to spell out for you whether those details are good or not. He had already been in for the paper, CJ said, so he hadn't come in for that. "He seems pretty put out," CJ told me.

I went down. CJ nodded when I entered the store, and I nodded back. Then I convinced my father to follow me *out* of the store.

"You both take good care," CJ said.

Once on the sidewalk, my father turned to me, a bee-mad disgusted expression on his face. "Next time," he said, "don't send me out on a goose chase like that."

I hadn't a clue what to say.

Not a clue.

It was the first time my dad was so "off," and I know I was afraid. I surely didn't want to stand there and argue with him. All I really wanted was to get my father home, where we would be safe, where no one we might happen to know would chance to overhear him. I wanted to protect my father. I wanted to shelter us both.

Still, I remarked, "What were you *doing*?"—not all that helpful when a person isn't thinking clearly, though I don't think I was clear about my dad's situation at all back then. Still. I wasn't in any way "leading the witness." The question wasn't "leading" in any way. I was only trying to gather information at that point. I mean, I *didn't* say, "Dad. You're in your *slippers!*" Or, "Dad. CJ told me you didn't even know why you'd *gone in!*" Or, "Dad. You went into a store, and you didn't have your *wallet* with you!" I didn't say any of that. I just said, "Dad, what were you *doing?*" so no one could yell "Objection!" at that point.

My father just said, "I was…out."

He said it defiantly, like I better not ask anything else…

I asked something else: "Out doing what?"

He said, "Oh. You're not going to start now with *that,* are you, Maureen? Are you?"—which was similar, of course, to our accident-fight, and which is how he can get.

One really important thing about my father: He is a Gemini, which is the sign of the twins, which means he has two different sides. Most of the time, the nice side is the one that manifests, but sometimes, this other less-nice side shows up, such that you almost wouldn't think it was the same person. The other less-nice side gets mad, and kind of mean. Well—mean for my father, which isn't *really* that mean, but still, that other side isn't a picnic.

So I let it all drop and we went home, 'cause I didn't want to argue. Not on the sidewalk like that. Not with my dad in his slippers. Not after what we'd both been through.

And that was the night I found his pills. All three kinds. Aricept, Namenda, and the blood pressure one. They were in his night-table drawer, and were big news to me. No one had ever mentioned the pills. And that night, after I Googled them, I vowed he would take them.

Yet, still, I can honestly report that there have only been a couple such lapses: the CJ one, this new car accident being the worst. And back with the CJ one, he wasn't taking all of his pills as we now know, so this, once again, is my mission: To get him to take his pills. I just have to have to come up with a way to get him to do it…I just *have* to.

Oh, and you might be wondering what my father was like when my mother was alive: The answer is, he was fine. He would sometimes lose sight of a word here or there he probably would have remembered when he was younger, or he might have forgotten an engagement Mom made with him—but that, from my viewpoint, was it. So it was nothing that strange. Nothing like thinking his parents were alive, or forgetting why he went into a store. Nothing like *that*. Then again, before my mother died, I was a "typical teenager" I guess you could say, which is to say—I was the center of the world as it's known, which means there *might* have been some things that escaped my attention, or that my mother effectively shielded me from. Or maybe, 'cause he took all his pills when she was there.

What I *really* think happened is this: My mother's death is what did it. It threw him for a pretty big loop, I would say more than you'd normally expect.

Anyway, the last words I said to my father last night were, "I don't drive!" and today (surprise) I'm driving!

My father is safe in the passenger seat. We're on our way to our family mechanic who is right here in town. It's funny saying we have a "family mechanic"—sort of like a "family doctor" or a "family priest"—but suffice it to say that we *mainly* know Rick and his family, of Rick's Automotive and Auto Body Shop 'cause we've lived in this town all our lives, and 'cause my dad and Rick's dad were friends— members in the Knights of Columbus together for years, and 'cause Rick's mom and my mom both used to work at the bake sale held yearly in town to benefit the main public library. Waltham, though indeed a true "city" ("The City to Watch"), isn't incredibly big, especially if you've lived here all of your life, as we have. So that's how we know the whole family. I say "m*ainly*" though, really, neither of my parents were what you'd call "prize-winning" drivers, so having a "family mechanic" is probably not a good sign, after all.

Anyway, I called Rick up in advance to explain about our old Cavalier. He is the son of Rick senior and the one now in charge, having taken over from his dad, who is now retired.

Rick was extremely accommodating. "Bring her on down," he proposed, so I'm doing just that. And the reason *I'm* driving, as opposed to my father doing the honors—which is how these things are done when the child doesn't have her driver's license yet—is that we both feel a little bit jittery having him drive. We both, I believe, prefer me, which is overall disconcerting, seeing as how I don't drive. Still, the shop isn't far. Only a couple of miles, I'd say. And, luckily, I have driven *some*, which isn't to say that I "drive"; it's rather to say that we've driven—Janie and me—'cause of Cameron, who's a friend of Janie's, and who sometimes puts up with our driving. Still. I don't find it easy driving, but I'm not about to tell this to my dad.

My difficulties are mostly typical new driver ones—things like accelerating, steering, braking and so forth—no, I'm not going into detail—so suffice it to say, Dad makes these comments like: "Oh!" and: "Watch out!" and: "What was *that?!*" and: "Are you all right to *drive*, Maureen? You don't seem incredibly steady," and: "There's a car! There's a car! Right *there!*" and *I* come back with comments like: "I'm *fine,*" and "Dad. Please don't shout in my ear when I'm trying to *drive!*"

We make it to Rick's—minor miracle, but a miracle no less. He watches as I pull "her" on in—his choice of gender, not mine.

But I should back pedal for a moment: Before I ever set foot in the car, I had a list of excuses to explain why *I* might be holding the wheel instead of my father that unfurl like this:

One: My dad sprained his wrist. This excuse would've involved wrapping the "sprained" wrist, however, and my father might not have been thrilled about that.

Two: The medication my dad is now on prevents him from driving. This one is better as it's closer to the truth, which is good, 'cause it means that it isn't a lie—well, not completely—and people like me who want to be nuns really shouldn't lie. Anyone on a spiritual path who is in any way serious about it shouldn't lie. And I wouldn't have to specify *what* kind of meds. Still, the meds excuse could raise some tricky questions I'd rather not raise.

Three—and this excuse I thought was rather brilliant, which, by the way, is a clue as to the one I chose, though why it took me till *Three* to think this, I don't know: I only just got my learner's permit, and my father is letting me drive. Brilliant, as I said, and it *could* even be true, as I *am* sixteen—the age you must be to get your learner's permit here—though, of course, I don't actually *have* such a permit. Still, three is the one I chose. It's more of a "little, white lie" to an outright one. Three is the one I'm going to go with if Rick stops and asks me.

I pull "her" right up to the bay, and Rick saunters over. "You're driving," is what he remarks, and I very innocently nod, and there it is. So much for my excuse list and preferred choice. God works in mysterious ways.

Rick looks the Cavalier over, not asking what happened. "Family mechanics" are like that, I guess. "She driving rough?" he asks me.

"Not really," I say, like I know.

That's when he nods. "Okay. I'll give her a look-over. Now, can I run you folks home?"

And this is when *I* nod. *I* could easily walk the couple miles to our house, but I don't think my dad could. Or not at the conventional pace I would like.

Rick takes the keys and I'm "relieved" of my duty, so to speak—it is actually quite a relief—and we all head over to Rick's car, a '78 Mustang convertible with the top smartly down. Dad gets in front and I squeeze my way to the back. All the while Rick is driving us home, I chant *Om, God*—in my head only. "Om" is a cosmic sound—the sound the Creator emitted when He first went to fashion the world. It's the sound He continues to emit to sustain it—though it's not the "true" sound. "Om" is just something folks say to *approximate* the true sound, which is a sound that cannot be approximated, really, just as God cannot be fully understood by our small human minds.

It's supposed to be calming—this chanting of "Om." I chant it again.

The only reason I am chanting "Om," is that I'm feeling a little bit paranoid. The accident has me on edge. I don't know what to expect from my father.

Conversation inside the hot Mustang unfolds like this:

Rick: "So, Ed. I was sorry to hear about your wife. How are you making out these days?"

My father: "Oh yes, Rick. Thank you. It's been an adjustment, as you well can imagine. But Mo's been just great through it all. Just super."

I smile in case anyone sees, though I'm here in the back, and, I mean, Rick shouldn't take his eyes off the road. He doesn't. Really. Then I chant *Om God* some more.

We pass some condos that are fairly new to town.

Rick: "Those condos went up like greased lightning. I didn't even know they were planned. They're selling in the five-to-six-hundreds, I hear."

My father: "Something new is always going on."

Rick: "I'll say."

I chant.

Rick, going on: "Anyway, *my* father, he's pretty good. He doesn't come into the shop too much now. He's done with those 'headaches' he says. He's taken up golf as of late. It's a great way for him to stay fit."

My father: "Well that's a nice pastime to have." In other words, things couldn't *be* more normal.

I smile in case anyone sees, but, of course…

We drive past the new track on Bacon Street, and the new elementary school on Bacon street, and the rival automotive place next to the school, and talk progresses to jokes. This happens 'cause Rick is engaged in "mechanic-type driving" you might say, which means one arm is propped out his window, the other on the back of the seat, so he's steering with his knees—at least I *hope* he is. My father, noticing the feat, says, "I didn't know a famed stunt driver lived in our town."

Rick laughs.

I continue chanting *Om*.

Soon, Rick takes a sudden corner—too fast for me and my dad as we're thrown to the side—and Dad says, "People must take you for Mario Andretti."

I think: *Mario Andretti?!* That is so old school! Why couldn't he have said Jeff Gordon? Or at the least Dale Earnhardt? I want to melt right into my seat and disappear. Still, if that's all he's going to do…

Rick lets out a laugh. "All the time," he replies.

By rights, my dad could *complain* about Rick's driving—he's the elder here, after all, and Rick's driving *is* out-of-control—but my father's chief aim is to charm, so charm is what he does. Furthermore, it seems to be working. I think.

Finally, we pull up in front of our house and I think: This is it. My dad's going to blow it somehow. All of that nice drive for nothing: all of those *Oms,* he's going to say something like, "So. What time did you say you'd have the ladders delivered?" or: "So. Will we be seeing you again around lunchtime?" Something of that ilk. And I'll have to punt with a joke on the order of: "Dad, you *card*." And then to Rick: "He's always trying to get *someone* to come wash our windows"—regarding the ladders, if that's what he says—or: "He's always about mooching lunch invitations"—while Rick simply sits, looking on.

Instead, Dad extends a hand. "It's been a real pleasure," he says. "We'll have to do it again some time." That's, of course, another joke. It's not for real.

Rick laughs, and I breathe a sigh of relief and stop chanting *Om* for a time. Mrs. McClancey looks out her bay window, and I start saying *Om* once again, but by then we are out of the Mustang and moving up our own walk straight toward our house, and then we are in, while Mrs. McClancey remains where she is.

So maybe I was just being paranoid all of that time.

Maybe my father *is* fine, though later I think—and I know this is peevish on my part—but I think, *Why is he normal when* others *are around? Why can't he be that way with me?* I know that's being babyish and peevish. And I know what you're thinking.

BIG HEAVEN

Chapter 8

Anyone could get into an accident, I realize. That is a given. Still, it wasn't just some "anyone" who got into the accident, it was my *father,* so I'm thinking he just shouldn't drive. Not until I can get him to take his pills regularly. Not until he seems "stable" for days at a time. More like months, ideally.

Driving's a really big deal when you sit down and weigh it, but I don't think I need to tell *you*. I am going to have to get him sorted out. And yet, in the meantime, I have to set things up so he doesn't drive.

Which isn't to say I don't feel a little bit guilty about this decision —I do, not to mention a little bit worried as to how I'll pull it off—yet, to alleviate my guilt, I think this: *He doesn't really need to drive.* Plenty of people don't drive and still lead normal lives. They take buses, trains, have friends give them rides. Plenty of people— especially ones who are older—never even *learned* how to drive, and they seem to manage just fine. Granted, my dad doesn't have any friends, so there goes the friends-giving-rides idea. And granted, the bus might present a challenge till he's taking his pills regularly, but Rome wasn't built in a day. And anyway, any *not* driving done on his part will only be temporary, and there are always taxis.

But all this hinges on his taking his pills, so I come up with this: He takes his pills if I hand them to him. And he took them, I bet, when

Mom was alive and handed them to him. But 'cause I can't always be home, I'll have to do the second best thing. I'll call him and wait on the phone while he takes them, then have him report his success. If that doesn't work, then there's a block, like it's more than "forgetting" on his part, 'cause the night of the accident, the pill box *must* have gone off, and he *must* have then shut the thing off, which means he *must* have made an actual *decision* to not take his pills, even if it was a subconscious one. It's as if he's acting out. It's as if he's protesting my mother being gone, at least in part. What I'm beginning to think is that he wants human attention, so I'll see that he gets it by calling. The only thing is—he'll have to pick up the darn *phone*.

It's too bad our neighbor Mrs. McClancey can't somehow help out, but I deem that a no, not only 'cause she has her own life—don't forget those sad destitute orphans I made up from a really poor country in Africa somewhere—but also 'cause, as I said, we can't let any outsiders in—who knows what would transpire then? Of course, once I get everything sorted, we won't *need* to let anyone in. But that in a nutshell is life for you. Right?

What I do next is I call Rick, and tell him that I'm a little bit worried about my father driving—at least for now—'cause he needs to have his eyes checked—he *might* need a new prescription—and 'cause he's on these new pills for high blood pressure, and we want to wait until he's stable on the pills before he drives, and 'cause, well, he's just getting *old*, so we're reassessing the driving stuff, so if Rick could just wait for right now on the car, that would be really helpful. Maybe he could make some dumb excuse if my father calls.

Rick tells me, "Sure thing." And so *then* what I do is simply not mention the car to my father in hopes that my father will forget about it.

He mentions it almost immediately.

"Mo. Have you heard any news about the car, 'cause I haven't."

This exchange happens in the family room. My father hijacks me as soon as I come in. Dr. Phil's on TV.

"Oh, yeah. Rick did call me, Dad. Bad news."

"Oh?"

"'There's some trouble with the engine,' Rick said. 'Something to do with the carburetor and radiator and engine block, from when you hit that other car'." I have no idea whether the carburetor and radiator and engine block are even *near* one another in a car—near enough to be hurt by a solitary blow. I have no idea if "engine block" is even a "*part*," but my dad doesn't know engines either, so I leave it at that.

"Gee," my father replies. "That's too bad."

"Yeah. It is. I know."

"Gee."

He pauses. I'm about to book it to my room—I have some major praying to do, given all the lying I'm doing. Then my dad gestures towards a chair and says, "Did he say how long it would be?"

I am still standing. There's no *way* I am taking a seat for all this. "Well…He seemed to think it might not even be worth getting fixed, considering the mileage. He said he'll take a look. He won't charge us for looking."

"You don't say," is what my dad says. "I really didn't think it was that bad."

"I guess it is. I guess you never really know with these things."

"So we'll be without a car," my dad says.

"It sure looks it," I answer.

"Well. We'll have to keep right up with that, won't we?"

"We sure will."

"Let me know what he says. Won't you?"

"I will."

And that seems to be about it.

I book it to my room. Still, this hasn't achieved the larger goal. Dad thinks Rick will call back most any old day. I wish I could simulate a phone call right now, which I would rush to my bedroom to "take," and it would be "Rick," and he would "tell me" things weren't looking good. How the Chevy indeed might be "totaled," considering the mileage. But how there was one more thing he should try before he gave up, and how that would, of course, "take some time," since he was currently "pretty backed up" with some other planned jobs…so in the meantime, we should both just "sit tight" per our family mechanic.

But there is no simulated phone call since I hadn't worked any of that out until now—which means I'm stuck.

It figures he'd be lucid when I lie…Still, he's lucid. That's good, and we can't not appreciate *that*.

The car issues aside, you might be wondering if I always run from my father the way I just did. You might be thinking that it's really not nice—it isn't—and I don't *always* run—I was hiding information about the car just now—though I do run sometimes.

The reasons for this are obvious: Teenage girl. Father in his sixties. Not a lot of common ground there. Girl doesn't really feel she knows her father. The typical.

Still. Soon after we buried my mother, I did sit and "visit" with Dad. This was occasioned, at least in part, by his making his usual statements like, "Mo! To what do I owe the honor?" the minute he saw me come in, like I *was* about to visit with him. Or, "You're going out *again*? I thought you might like to join me for a round of Sudoku!" this being his joke.

So one time, I did "visit"—though I might have actually been on my way out. The TV was going at the time, and to conduct our "visit" properly I figured that it should be off, so I turned the thing off, then sat down. We kind of sat just looking at each other. You could feel how Mom wasn't there—puttering in the kitchen, asking about our days, telling us a humorous story about an odd neighbor…

Something.

Soon, my father said, "So. What would you like to talk about?"

This was a cringe-worthy opener if ever there was one.

"I don't know. I thought I would leave that to *you*."

We were both being "charming" right then.

He replied, "Oh. You're not going to get away with *that*." He was making a joke, sort of—well, he was trying at least—so I smiled. I was thinking it would have been better with the TV on, but we'd already ditched that idea, and he watched way too much TV as it was, and I was there now to "visit" after all, so I suggested a game.

That was about the extent of most of our "visits."

Of course, he liked that. But then there was the question of which one.

"I could beat you in chess," he remarked. This was another joke, 'cause my father is quite accomplished at chess and I don't play.

"That you could," I said right back, being "charming."

"Or, we could play…Scrabble."

"Okay."

I should tell you something about Scrabble. It was my mother's game. She loved it, and was also quite good at it. Probably the only reason my father and I ever played Scrabble was 'cause of my mother, so it was strange we'd decided to play then. Or maybe not. All I could hope, now that Scrabble had been brought up, was that my father wouldn't bring up my mother.

That we wouldn't have to talk about her.

It was the one thing I didn't want to talk about. It was always like putting alcohol on a wound. To be completely honest—I should be, I'm *almost* a nun—my father and I *never* really talked about my mother.

I went and got the Scrabble game. While I was arranging the tiles, Dad said, "My little girl is paying me a visit!" which of course made me cringe.

I put down CAGE for seven points. Dad put down CAT for five points. Then I put down TOY for fourteen points, with the Y on the triple-letter-score, which had meaning is how it turned out, 'cause Mom always got the triple scores. It always just seemed to work out that way.

Dad said, "Your mom was a great Scrabble player."

There it was.

I answered with, "Yeah," but inside I was really thinking, *Stop! You're breaking the rules! We don't ever talk about her!*

Then he said, "You must miss her."

All I could do then was nod. I was figuring he was being a parent, doing what a parent had to do: checking in with his child. Not that I wanted any part of the thing. Then he said, "She loved you very much, you know."

That was the moment I wanted to bolt straight-away from the room and burst into tears—though I didn't. I stayed where I was. I was brave. For him. Still. He must have observed my reaction, for he said, "I miss her, too." And *then* he said—trying to sound more upbeat, 'cause he didn't really want me feeling sad—"But I still have you. And now I can get to know you *better*." And then he added, "Ope!"

He played the "Ope!" game with me, where he touches me, just with his finger, and then exclaims "Ope!" I smiled in return like I was three, but it was a sad smile. In truth—there it was again—we hadn't a clue how to relate to each other.

He said, "We'll be all right. Right, kiddo?"

He was putting on his brave face, so I simply answered with, "Right."

We played some more Scrabble. I don't remember the words we put down; it's all a blur. And after awhile, Dad started looking kind of lost, like he might have *again* been thinking about Mom, till he said, "She really was quite good at Scrabble."

Tears fell.

I couldn't go on.

I looked away and wiped at the tears with my sleeve. I swallowed. Then I blurted out, "You should date." It just came out. It wasn't even *close* to what I meant. I had never even had a single thought about that.

My father looked at me with wounded puppy-eyes, like I had pierced him right to the core. Like I was trying to just pawn him off on someone.

"Or not," I immediately added.

I remember thinking at the time: *I'm* sixteen. *Why am I even in this position?*

It wasn't much of a visit. They never were.

I very much wished the TV had been on.

Anyway, the very same day as our car conversation, I have to go to work. I work at the Embassy Cinema, which is right here in town. I can walk there, yet 'cause my hours are four to eleven, I'm going to miss being there for Dad's pills, so I decide this is D-day. Test time. Zero-roger-hours or something like that. At nine o'clock that night, I call my father up about his pills—I don't leave a note on the table; I don't use the very largest notepaper we have; I simply call him. It's my break, so I call from outside. The pills are in the pill box on the table —the *alarmed* pill container—though we really don't have to rehash all of that. The good news about the box is that when I get home, I can check if the pills are both gone. The time-slot is Thursday, PM, the upper-most one for that day, the one with PM printed on its top.

"Yes?" his nighttime voice says.

"Dad?"

"Maureen?"

"Yeah. I'm calling 'cause it's time to take your pills. I'm calling to remind you of this."

"Is that right?" is what he says then.

"Yeah."

"Okay." Pause.

"All right. So what I'm going to do is hold while you go and take them. Then come right back and tell me you've taken them, okay?"

"Really?" he skeptically says.

"Yeah."

Pause. "I don't know. It seems like a pretty big rigamarole to me."

He's the only one I know who really uses this word. I'm not even sure it *is* a word. "It's all right, Dad," I continue, trying with my voice to both encourage and soothe him, like it's no major deal. Like, yes, it *is* skin off me, but like I am agreeing to part with the skin. Like, for *you* I am happy to do it. I try and keep it light for him. He loves lightness.

"If you say so," he says pleasantly.

"I do," I say, doing my part.

"All right…I'm going…I'll be right back. Don't take any wooden nickels while I'm gone."

This is one of his stock jokes. "I won't."

It takes a long time. Finally, I hear him pick up the phone again.

"I'm ba-ack," is what he next says.

"Oh good. How did it go?"

"Fine."

"Yeah? You took *both* your pills marked for Thursday?"

"Yes."

"Okay. Good! Great! I'll see you tomorrow then, Dad. Sweet dreams."

"And sweet dreams to you, dear, as well. Be safe coming home."

Be safe coming home, I think. Exactly what any dad would say. Perfectly fine.

Oh, and since you might be wondering about my job at Embassy Cinema, it's good. I like it. I'm a "concessions attendant," as I said, which is relatively enjoyable, overall. It's also my very first job, as I mentioned.

The movies that are playing right now—at least the ones I am interested in—are *Tammy*, *Sex Tape*, and *Wish I Was Here*. As employees, we get to see one film for free every week, and I'm going to treat Janie to a movie—pay the admission just for my ticket. We've narrowed it down to the first two titles above, and of course, Janie wants to see *Sex Tape*, which of course figures—she probably thinks she'll learn some new positions—while *I* want to see *Tammy*, since I totally *love* Melissa McCarthy. But since I'm the one doing the inviting, I'm leaving it to Janie. That's just plain "being nice," which monastics should be.

The only other news regarding my job concerns the male lamebrains who work here. They're my age or older, I'd say, but just to give you an idea, when it's time to clean the butter machines out, it's pretty gross—they call the hardened, rancid butter "smegma" to elicit a rise from us girls—I didn't even know what smegma was, though I had an idea: old dried-up semen or something. But it turns out it's more than just that. Or, not that exactly. I Googled it and found the following: "the secretion of a sebaceous gland; specifically: the cheesy sebaceous matter that collects between the glans penis and the foreskin, or around the clitoris and labia minora"—major league *yuck* —so it seems my "semen" guess was wrong, though close. But anyway, that is the level of "maturity" we are talking about here. That is how these guys get off. When they say the word now, I give them my *uber* "disdainful" look. I don't believe nuns are supposed to be disdainful—but I'm not *quite* a nun yet. Oh, and in case you are wondering, I've kissed a boy—tongues—but that's it.

Boys I find are pretty immature overall—except, I guess, for Cameron—so it won't be *that* hard giving them up when I'm ordained.

Sort of…maybe…for the most part.

I'm careful going home, as Dad advised, and the first thing I do when I get back is I check on the pill box on the table. For the compartment marked Thursday, PM. Both pills are gone. Hooray! Of course, he could have stashed them in a drawer; or wedged them between the plump cushions of the couch; or flushed them down the toilet; but why would he do *that?* No. I have to have faith and stay positive. It's what a nun-wannabe does.

Chapter 9

Today is the next day, Wednesday, and I don't have to work today or tonight. Dad seems just fine. It's a really incredible day, so Janie and I decide to meet at our usual spot. We wait until two-ish to meet, 'cause nobody does stuff till then. Let me fill you in.

First off, we meet at "the Charles"—the Charles River that is—which should definitely mean something to you, seeing as how it's historic and famous—a "classic" place, at least around here. We meet on a bench "along the Charles"—the Charles River Reservation Riverwalk to be specific—a load for one mouthful, I know. The walkway is relatively new—Waltham: we're watching—and pristine granite pillars mark where it starts, and on the granite pillars is a heron in black silhouette, standing amid waving grass in a marsh to give them that uppercrust nature-ey look people like.

They really are nice. And you've got to love *this*: Farther down the walkway is a tablet that reads: "In Memory of Arthur and Sidney Barnes, full of unbounded faith in the essential goodness of all people, who thoroughly enjoyed adjacency with the Charles River ecosystem"—you have to love that word, "adjacency"—"while living their fun-loving and fully-accepting lives in Watertown, Waltham, Newton, and Needham. It is through their foresight, generosity, and love for this ecosystem that the proper stewardship of the entire Upper Charles Greenway is now secure in perpetuity"—I am *not* making this up—"unbounded faith in the essential goodness of all people"; "fun-loving"; "fully-accepting"—it's just too good to make up—I love Waltham.

Anyway, some of the stuff that we do by the river is we talk.—Duh —we eat (when one of us thinks to bring food)—we grab each other's iPods and listen to the tunes the other has downloaded, typically dissing those tunes…in other words, we have fun.

Today, when Janie shows up, she has her reliable sidekick in tow, that guy I keep mentioning, Cameron. She's bringing him on purpose. It's part of her blueprint to foil my imminent plans…I know how Janie's sick mind works.

I know Cameron through Janie, as I said, and Janie's known Cameron forever it turns out, since he lives on the very same street, and since they played with each other as kids, and since their mothers are fast friends. In fact, not to be *too* graphic here, but there are pictures of them naked in a kiddie pool together when Janie was two and Cameron three. Janie's mother proudly showed me the pictures. Janie, of course, wanted to die. I liked them. But anyway—just as Janie's known Cameron forever, I feel I have, too, though Janie and I didn't meet till third grade, so I didn't really know Cameron before that time, though he's always sort of been on the "periphery" you'd say, like I'd say hi to him at assemblies and stuff, 'cause Janie would. But then, when we all became juniors last year, he started hanging out with us more and, it was weird, 'cause the year he finally *became* a junior, he became like this "man" all at once. I don't know how else to describe it. He went from being a "boy" in the back folds of my mind, to being a "man." And now he's like this *uber* man. He let his curly brown hair grow out some, and he's got these long sideburns now. And he shot up, as they say, "overnight," so he's really quite tall—six-two—and broad looking. And though he isn't *incredibly* broad, he's still broad enough to acquire the label of "man." Another way to think of it is this: He's not like those rock stars you see, who are really much older than Cameron, but who are also quite skinny, and who, as a result, will never look like "men" in my mind, no matter *how* old they get, 'cause their bodies are just like Anthony Kiedis' of the Red Hot Chili Peppers. That guy will never be a "man" in my eyes. Not in a Cameron-like way.

Unfortunately, I love Cameron's neck—his thick, smooth, beautiful neck. It's beautiful! And I love his arms also, unfortunately. They're spiked with brown hair, which is great—I stare at his forearms a lot. And, I have to admit that I love his shoulders, as well, even though I've never had a look at them directly. Still—I love them. And I'm sure I'd love some other parts of him, as well, if I could only see them.

You get the picture.

He kind of just sort of "hangs out" with us. Janie says he does 'cause he likes me. It's definitely not that he likes her, she tells me, and it's definitely not that she likes him, 'cause they've known each other forever, so that would be like "liking your own brother," as Janie has said, and that's "not going to happen in this lifetime." Besides. Janie's set her sights on someone else, though I can't tell you who. Not that you know him from Adam, but a promise is a promise (It's Ian Burchill).

By the way, I asked Janie once if Cameron ever *told* her he liked me and she said no. "But women intuitively know such things." And then she winked. Actually, it's not really going to help if I like him. Not if I want to be a nun. And I want to be a nun.

Anyway, we're sitting on a bench along the Charles, and Janie starts right out by bringing it up—I wasn't planning on mentioning it yet. She says, "So. Cameron. I don't think we've told you the *news*. Mo is running off to join the circus. Isn't that right, Mo?"

She grins at me, trying to be funny. Heck—she *is* funny. One thing you should know about Janie—she's got that whole, wry, tough girl thing going on—it's 'cause her father left them—but, really, she's a doll. Plus, she loves me. Trust me on that.

Cameron takes the news in stride, but then, he takes everything in stride. "Oh?" is all he replies.

"Well it's not *really* the circus, now is it? Or is it?" Janie remarks.

"Very funny," is what I reply, which is not the cleverest comeback around, but then, I'm not good with quick comebacks, so this one will have to make do.

Janie says, "Well she's *really* planning on being a nun, though it might just as *well* be the circus."

"My good supportive friend," I mumble. This is a better retort. At least it employs the raw sarcasm the two of them like.

"You're going to be a *nun?*" Cameron says.

"Yes."

"Huh." He seems to take it "in stride" though his eyebrows inch up.

Janie explains how it isn't a Catholic nun, but an "Eastern one" as she calls it, though they all still take vows, she explains, "so a nun is a nun is a nun," she tells him. Then she tells him how I've hooked up with this group from L.A.—the "Something for Spiritual Something"—and how they've sucked me right in, and how I'm planning to "leave all I know" to become like this…"*nun.*" How I "thought the monastics looked happy," so now *I'm* about to do it.

"Do what, exactly," Cameron asks, inching his eyebrows up more, a glint in his eye.

Janie laughs. Then she says, "No. I mean she's thinking of doing it —becoming a nun—like *soon*. Like…*now*. Like not even finishing high school first."

"You're driving me to it," I say. This is good.

"Why the rush?" Cameron asks me. And though he asks *me*, Janie answers.

"'Cause she had this supposed 'prophecy' when she almost died that said she had to be a nun at sixteen. And 'cause this group is leaving soon to go back to L.A., and Mo wants to go back with them when they go."

There's a little more to it than that, though I just let it be.

Then Janie says, "Do you think we should run an intervention? Deprogram our gullible friend? We could play her a tape that says, 'Nuns are bad. Not for you. Nuns are bad'." She smiles at me.

Cameron says, "I don't think we need to. Maybe she knows what she wants."

"Thanks," I reply, actually looking at Cameron and nodding.

"Poppycock," Janie next says.

"'Poppycock'?" Cameron and I say at once.

Janie grins. "I heard Mr. P. say it once." Then she says, "Listen, Mo. I know that you've been through a lot. I know that your mother just died. And I feel *horrible* that that had to happen. It's something no one should ever have to go through. But you *can't* be a *nun*. You just can't. You'd give up all the good stuff! Besides. You'd leave *me*."

She makes her sad, puppy-dog face.

Cameron makes one, too.

Then Janie says—snapping right back: "Instead of becoming a *nun*, why don't you try a more traditional escape method first, like…driving cross-country. Help me out here, Cameron."

"The circus is good," Cameron says. He's not taking this seriously at all—just purely "in stride."

"Okay. Take a hot air balloon ride. Then sail around the world. Become a singer in a band," Janie continues.

"Or at least the tambourine player," says Cameron.

"Join the Peace Corps."

"Do they even still *have* the Peace Corps?"

They come up with more, like I'm not even physically here: work in a soup kitchen; write a book (even an e-book is good); volunteer for a cutting-edge medical experiment, or at least give blood. "Have you ever even *given* blood?" This from Cameron.

They're not going to stop me, is what I think, just 'cause I'm going to be a nun, though I'm not going to dwell on this further.

"*I* know. You could train to be a sex therapist."

I give her a "buddy" a look.

"Well. You could. Just in case you want to experience *sex*, yet still do *good* at the same time."

This doesn't merit a look. We all sit in silence awhile. Finally, I call upon Cameron to somehow weigh in. "What about you? Are you *with her* on this? You said I might know what I want."

I'm expecting him to give it to me straight, without all the antics involved, since Cameron's a pretty straight shooter you could say, though reserved in his manner and speech; still—he gives it straight, though I know he doesn't like to offend.

He thinks for a minute. He's as calm as the slow-moving Charles as he thinks. Then he says, "I just think you might be a little young to commit the rest of your life to a religious order. Like maybe you should check out some other stuff before you decide."

"You offering?" is what Janie says.

Cameron looks away. I blush. I have a feeling that Cameron's blushing too, though I'd never dare check that right now. I can't *believe* Janie actually said this.

"Your stomach's showing," I say, to make Janie look. Janie hates it when her stomach shows. Sometimes I say it when it's not even partially true just to get her to look, like right now (her stomach isn't *really* showing. And it's not how a nun should behave, but as Cameron pointed out, I'm not a nun yet.

Janie predictably looks at her stomach. And with all of her wry goings-on, I never get to stare at Cameron's neck.

Perhaps I should pause, to clue you in on how Janie and I became friends, since it might seem to you like we're so totally different (which we are).

The story unravels as follows: We were in the same dance class in third grade, which means we must have been just about nine. We didn't know each other from school at that point, 'cause we didn't go to the same school yet, so it was at dance that we met. Anyway, one day, we had to line up in front of a mat and then do a limber. This is a handstand into a backbend and then to your feet once again. I was afraid of doing handstands back then, never mind limbers, 'cause once, when I was practicing them at my house, I fell on my head, and it really really hurt and really frightened me. After that, I never did a handstand again, but now we were being directed to do them.

One other key thing you should know to help with the story: For any of the girls who had trouble doing limbers, or who seemed in the least bit hesitant in their approach, they actually had a harness they'd use to flip you over. It was an old-fashioned method of "spotting," I guess. They had to use it on one girl, though most just did their limbers on their own. Clever them. Me, I didn't want to do my limber at all, and I *definitely* didn't want to do it with a harness. The instrument looked like a torture device from the grim Middle Ages. So when it was my turn to go, I simply uttered, "No thank you," then turned right around and bumped into her. That was how Janie and I became friends, 'cause Janie thought it cool—my refusing to cave to "authority figures;" my being my "very own person," so to speak—but, really, I was plain petrified. I couldn't think of any other choice, so I simply said no. Really, I'm nothing like my "very own person." I never stand up to "authority figures." I'm a people-pleaser, in case you couldn't tell. But Janie hadn't discovered that yet, so that's how we first became friends.

At some point, of course, Janie saw how I wasn't what she thought, but by then it was too late: our friendship stuck. Plus, if you think about it, a goody-two-shoes and a sarcastic person work nicely together. It gives the whole structure some tension. It helps to make Janie *more* Janie—having me. Janie, when you think about it, *needs* me.

And before we officially move on, I want to describe her to you, to ensure that you have a good picture of her, though I suspect you already do: Janie is big-boned (I'm average), and she's tall (me, again—an average five-six or thereabouts—all right, five-five-and-three-quarters). Her hair is long, with bangs, and frizzy—don't breathe a word that I just said—and she wears it like Zooey Deschanel from *New Girl*, ironing it first. This is how I wear mine, too. This is how everyone we know wears their hair…we all *like* looking like Zooey Deschanel. Anyway, Janie's got large, wide-set eyes that are green—a sure indication of wisdom, she frequently reminds me—and her nose is a little bit big, but not in a bad way. More in a cool Lorde way, you'd say, which is really to say sexy. Also, it shows she has character—her nose. That's one thing my bud has in spades: plenty of "character."

I, by contrast, am more "average-looking," which is to say that my nose isn't nearly as big, but which is also to say I'm not as unique-looking. I'm more petite than Janie, more "average-to-pretty," perhaps, more "what boys would typically go for," as *Janie* would say. She says I look like Taylor Swift with my "cute upturned nose and nice cheekbones," but I don't believe it. No way. Janie's always being nice. Well, not always. But…

Anyway, 'cause Janie *is* taller and larger, her personality matches, as I'm sure you can now see. Maybe this is 'cause if you're bigger, people expect greater things, and if you don't deliver, they notice, so Janie delivers (plus, her father left when she was just three, and I don't think that's a thing you get over too quickly).

Janie's a red-head, by the way, though she calls the color "auburn"—It's red. Also, she's added some streaks to her hair that are blue. Blue, however, is a euphemism. They're actually more indigo and turquoise and purple mixed together. Also, she's got all these freckles she covers with make-up till they're just little specks…but don't breathe a word of what I've just told you—or that you know.

BIG HEAVEN

Chapter 10

For days and days on end my father is fine. I go to work, visit Janie where she works—at the Wendy's right here in town, and hang by the good old Charles River with Janie. Fine. I'm not always home is what I am saying, and I call when I must about his pills, and he always answers my calls, and he always takes his pills, 'cause they are gone by the time I get home. And nothing even the slightest bit strange comes out of his mouth. As a result—I'm pretty darn happy about it all. As a result—I feel pretty bad about my father not driving.

A couple of times, he's asked if I've heard from Rick. And at least that many times, I've seen him go to the large bay window that looks out on our driveway, as if he could magically conjure the car. He still goes to CJ's most days for the paper, and he then sometimes goes for a walk instead of coming right home—it's summer; he should be out; I don't like to see him with the TV always on. He looks sad. Yes, I know I sound like a typical parent fretting over a kid, yet I think about the places he used to go, the places he went when he drove, and I wonder if he still goes to those places? I trust him to be more on his own now that he's acting so stable.

With this in mind, I jot down a list of his places:

Hannaford Grocery. Okay. It *is* the site of the accident, but it's also a place that he really likes to go just to browse. And I know that sounds strange—food-browsing"—but it's what he likes to do, unless it's the models on *Cosmo* that get his attention, though there's nothing wrong with that is what I think. Nothing at all. And I know he can stand in the nut aisle for hours on end, engaged in—I'll say it—nut-browsing—and what harm can there be in that.

The bank. That's "The Bank of America." For now. Don't hold your breath.

Maria's Home Cooking. A restaurant, obviously.

Blockbuster Video.

Peking Garden Chinese Restaurant. He always gets the Moo Shi.

Davio's Barber Shop.

After those, it's a pretty big blank. Then I remember Home Depot, but that requires a car to get to, so I cut it from the list. Besides. The house looks pretty well-tended right now.

I decide to draw him a map, so at least he can walk to some places. I start with our house—which I stash way down in the bottom, way to the left—then I map out the five streets into town. Everything, except for Maria's, is on the main drag, and Maria's is not very far from this drag. Yet even with our house at the bottom, I still can't make everything fit, so I have to start over—three times—shrinking and shrinking and shrinking, learning something different each time. This I do in my room. My father is in the family room, of course. He never hangs out in his own room, maybe 'cause it's a "teenager-thing"—spending one's time in one's room—or maybe he just doesn't need to, seeing how *I* always do. Anyway, the minute my drawing is done, I leave my cocoon.

He's sitting in "his chair" so I sit kitty-corner to him on the couch. *The Price is Right* is on.

"Mo!" my father exclaims. "You live!"

He's a regular laugh-riot, that man.

"I drew you a map. Look."

I hand the thing to him. It's on legal-size paper, and I highlighted all the significant places in red; then I highlighted the street names in red ink as well, since they, too, are significant I figure; then I highlighted our house with the red pen as well. For all of my diligent highlighting, the map might as well have been *done* in rich red, but then I would have needed another shade for the significant parts…

I'm thinking all this as he draws the map close to his eyes.

"It's 'cause we don't have a car," I put in. "It's so you can still zip around, like you do."

This is a joke. My dad doesn't "zip."

"Anyway, here is our house," I point out. "And this is the street where we live…"

He stops me. He breaks into song. This is something he does. I may have neglected to mention it to you.

"'People stop and stare…'" he sings. This is from *My Fair Lady*, the Lerner and Loewe song, *On the Street Where You Live*, in case you didn't recognize it. It's about this guy who has to be on the street where his love lives, no matter how much people stop and look at him. I know the old ditty by heart, 'cause Dad used to sing it when I was young, plus—we have the old vinyl. I'm a little bit loathe to admit it, but I like that song. I also love those composers, who Dad always talks about.

"That's good!" I extol. "That's good! So anyway, here is our street. And the next place we come to on the map is…" and that's when I see what will happen, but it's not like I can alter the *name*. The name is the name is the name. It's written right there in bright red.

What am I supposed to now do? Erase it? "The next place we come to on the map is Maria's Home Cooking," I say.

Too late. Even if I *was* going to change it.

"'Ma-ri-a'," he sings. "'I just met a girl'..."

This is from *West Side Story*, the Sondheim and Bernstein song, *Maria*, in case you didn't recognize it, though I could bet money you did, 'cause it's really quite popular. And my dad, it turns out, is quite musical, so it's sort of a real treat. Well, sometimes. Okay, not always.

I smile at him.

"Okay. So place A is here," is what I say—I am not about to repeat my mistake—"and places B, C, and D are here. These are all places you like to go. And most of them are right there on Main Street, see? And that one that isn't—let's call it 'Place E'—I circled it in red for you, see?"

He takes the map. He reads. Then he quotes, "'Bank of America...'

I'm not quite sure I know that tune." But this is his joke, so I smile. He likes it when I smile. He touches me and says the word "Ope!" I smile again, reminding myself that I'm going to be a nun, and then, before *too* much more time passes by, I go over the route in reverse that would get him back home, and then I think to test him.

"Time for your test," I sing out, to make it a game. He likes games.

"Will I get a gold star?" he replies, joking back.

I smile, but it's really an "I'm going to be a nun" smile.

"Okay. Now do you remember how *long* I said it would take to get to Hannaford Grocery?"

He looks at me, his eyes their watery-blue, his lips scrunching up. "No. But if you hum a few bars, I can fake it."

I nod and put down the map. I am thinking we might need a new routine—that this one's getting stale already. But for now, *The Price is Right* is on.

For real.

Anyway, I know. I'm not exactly whipping through my goals regarding my father; the thought occurs to me that I might need to be a bit tougher with him. Once that thing about me being three begin, I can seldom break through it.

It's not easy being tough with my dad. He's sweet, and that's the problem.

Oh, and there's one more thing you might be wondering about: just *why* my dad is so pleasant, considering the fact that his wife just died.

I think it's like this: He's a man. He wants to be strong for his "sweet little girl." He was taught that you don't show weakness in front of your child. He was raised to be pleasant, or else maybe he naturally is.

For example, at Mom's funeral, we were sitting in the church, side-by-side, and every so often, Dad would take hold of my hand like to say: "Are you all right?" Like to say: "It's all right." Like to say: "I'm here if you need me." He never did *say* these things, yet they were communicated the best way he knew: through the solicitous hand-squeezing. So he's quiet, private, reserved, yet you know that he cares.

I can also report to you this: One time, I walked past his room and peeked in, and he was sitting on the edge of his bed, holding this eight-by-ten picture of my mother. It's one that he's always had, sitting front-and-center on his bureau in a silver-plate frame. A glamour shot of her, you'd say, or that's how it's always seemed to me, though in reality, it was her high school graduation picture, though she looks a whole lot older in it than eighteen. She looks like a Hollywood starlet to me, with very dark lipstick on very large lips, and arms crossed perfectly so, and a trim, tailored suit with black piping. And there's this look on her face, as well, like she'll conquer the world one day.

I've always treasured that picture, and I've always been in awe of it, too, just a bit. And, on this day, my father was sitting on his bed, holding that picture, and talking to my mother. The words that came out of his mouth were: "I know, dear...I know...I know." So even though our relationship's not incredibly profoundly "deep," I do know there's more to my father.

I do know that.

Anyway, the very next day, I decide to test my father for real by sending him on an errand. We're out of skim milk, I declare, and the walk will do him good, I go on, and besides—he can't just sit there in his chair all day. While he's out, he can stop by the bank, I further suggest and hand him the map. So in a way it's like a double test.

An hour or so later he comes back. With the milk. *And* a fresh packet of cash in his wallet—I check—*and* the latest issue of *Playboy*, which he tries to keep hidden in its bag from me. Nothing wrong with that, is what I think. Nothing at all wrong with that.

Chapter 11

What with Dad's accident and all, and the pill-monitoring, and the lying to Dad about the car, I haven't been as free to sit and meditate as I'd like. You have to make God Number One is what they say, and on this I have recently become lax. They actually have an analogy about this that goes that giving your energy to, or honoring or what-not, both the material world *and* God, is a lot like trying to cross a lake in two boats, with one foot in one and one in the other: you're not going to get very far. It's also like that Bible saying that goes, "You can't serve God and mammon both." It really *is* an awful lot like both analogies, so much so, I was *determined* to attend the spiritual lecture tonight. I arranged my whole schedule around it. I mean, I *have* to get to know this spiritual community if I want to fly back with them to L.A. And Dad really seems to be better. He actually came home with milk!

The last time I attended a talk was last week, and that was the night that I left early 'cause of Dad's accident. But that's a blast from the past. Water under the bridge and all that.

Tonight's lecture is entitled, "Making the Effort to Find God"—it's like he's speaking directly to me in my situation—and about a hundred-odd people will be there, some of whom I recognize as "regulars." They hold these talks in a huge ballroom, as I have said, which means the first several rows will full quickly.

I come early and sit up front.

Anyway, the introducer for the night's talk is Brahmachari Paul, who is an associate monk, you might say a "monk-in-training"—a "student of the *Vedas*" as they're known at the center—that's what *brahmachari* literally means in Sanskrit. He is also quite funny. He says, "Tonight's talk is on 'Making the Effort to Find God,' and I'd like to start out with a story if I may. A survey was once given to some college students concerning God and whether they believe in Him or not. One student answered, 'Sure I *believe* in Him. But that doesn't mean I'm *crazy* about Him'."

People laugh. We are a bubbly group.

It's not incredibly hard to make devotees laugh.

Brother goes on.

"To tell us not only why we *should* be crazy about God, but how we can *achieve* this beatified state, our speaker for tonight's public talk is Brother Satgovinda."

Brother comes to the stage in his long ocher robe. I'm not going to tell you his *entire* talk, 'cause that might be tough to sit through if you're not planning on being a nun real soon—but here's the high points:

He starts by telling us things we already know, and that I likewise told you, like how only God can satisfy us, and how God is what we *truly* seek. Like how, once we experience God's bliss in meditation, nothing on this earth can compare. Sensual pleasures pale in comparison. Like how the world was intentionally modeled this way, 'cause we need to go back to God. God wants us back.

Next, he gives examples. I really like these, 'cause then I can tell them to you! Ha! But really: they help make what's lofty more real—bring what's sublime down to earth. They make it way easier to relate.

Brother tells us how there used to be this old Camel commercial with the slogan: "Are you smoking more, yet enjoying it less?" He pauses to let this sink in, then he says, "This is what happens to us as we merely continue to *live* on this planet. We enjoy pleasures less; we become rather sated by life. Yet this is also what draws us closer to God."

He then says how trying to be content with earthly pleasures is like looking for a diamond among glass—not at all satisfying.

He *then* quotes Sri Ramakrishna, an Indian saint who said, "When the bee is outside the flower, it buzzes around, restless. But when the bee is *inside*, the sweetness has silenced it." That's what the bliss of God can do. In other words, when you're in that bliss, that peace, it silences all of your other desires. Brother says, "In the stillness, there aren't any questions. We're just happy to be there." I jot this down to store away and somehow use on Janie.

When Brother speaks, there is so much heartfelt emotion on his face, almost entirely centered in the mouth, it's as if he is *feeling* every word before it comes out: as if each has been given a weight and he needs to express its set weight. You can practically feel for yourself just how much Brother tries. His eyelids press down as he speaks. It is all deeply sincere. It's 'cause he wants us to deeply love God. You can't help but get that from him.

Brother tells us that the more we experience God, the more we'll *want* to experience God. He says that the more we meditate, the more that we'll *want* to meditate, and the more we'll be able to retain the resulting consciousness in our lives. He says that once you start to forge a relationship with God, you won't be happy unless you continue to do so 'cause nothing on this earth can compare.

It all sounds pretty darn good. It makes me want to sit and meditate *now*—do nothing *but* meditate.

Really.

There's a flip side to the cheery coin, however, and that is that we must make the *effort* to come to know God—that we must actually *work* at the relationship. There's a saying that goes, "To know God is to love Him," but we must work to know Him and it's not always easy. Brother tells a story to illustrate this.

"One night," Brother says, "a woman went to pick up her friend at the Burlington, Vermont, airport. The friend had never been to New England before, and was very excited to come. On the lengthy ride home, the woman attempted to give her friend a tour, even though it was dark outside.

"'And over there,' the woman remarked, 'if it was daylight now, you could see Lake Champlain. It really is something, the way the water reflects the blue sky, the forest-green islands that dot it throughout, its venerable size. And over there—to your right—lie the Green Mountains. They're a real sight to see in the autumn—simply *ablaze*! And now, to our left, is an original red-covered-bridge! They're *really* a find.' The friend replied—wait for it—'Oh! How *theoretically* beautiful'!" Brother then gives us a grin. "Believing in God, yet neglecting to *know* Him, neglecting to put in the work that's required is the very same thing as these sights: beautiful in theory only."

He looks at us. Everyone there can see how much he cherishes God—you can just tell—and he wants us to cherish Him, too. I guess when you're happy, you want all of the world to be happy with you.

He gives us a few more inspiring words to help us along. He quotes Will Rogers: "Even if you're on the right path, you'll get run over if you no more than sit there." He quotes Saint Teresa of Avila: "A saint is a sinner who never gives up." Lastly, he tells us that *our* job is just to make the effort: that God and guru are in the "results department" as he calls it. The stillness, the bliss, will come of their own accord, he tells us. "Effort *is* progress," he says, as my guru used to say.

And then, all at once, he's done. He bows to the picture of our guru on the stage, then he bows to us. We, as a group, do it back.

Afterwards, we meditate.

Brahmachari Paul leads the meditation. Together, we sing a chant directed to God, and then fall still.

I'll try once again to describe what results, but please keep in mind that it's beyond words. It's like that quote I told you before, by the German ministerial student: "A thought spoken is a lie." And meditation is beyond thought.

Anyway, keeping such caveats in mind, here goes:

It's peace, it's bliss, it's no-thought, it's non-desire, it's perfect complete contentment, it's total awareness, it's no lack, it's no need. It's the alpha and omega in one. It is all that that there is. And remember, it's far more intense when you do it in a group. It's as if your consciousness is somehow lifted up by everyone there. Made exponential, as a real math geek might say.

Basically, having this kind of experience makes me feel invincible, like I could tackle any problem, win any struggle at all. Any at all. Like, what was I ever worried about in the first place?

After the meditation, Brahmachari Paul heads to the podium again, and makes the following announcement: "For those considering monastic life, The Center for Spiritual Union will be hosting a one-week retreat, from July twenty-first to July twenty-eighth, at The Espousal Retreat House in Waltham. More information on the retreat is available in the foyer outside the ballroom. Monastics will also be present in the foyer directly after this announcement to answer any questions you might have regarding the retreat, or regarding any other topics we have covered in our talks. We warmly invite you to speak with us."

Waltham, I think…*retreat*…*monastic life*…if anything was more "up my alley," I couldn't think what. Like I said, it's like God's speaking directly to me in my situation.

I'm *thrilled*.

Before I leave my seat to head to the foyer, however, I say a short prayer to God, asking that if it is really *meant* for me to speak to the monastics, *meant* for me to attend the retreat, *meant* for me to indeed become a nun this summer as my prophecy states, that He will help me do so. Take action. Start the work.

I get up.

Once in the foyer, I see there's a crowd—more than usual. Most of the time, people leave right after the talk, but not tonight. People want to speak to the brothers. They're both in attendance, I see, looking as earnest and sincere as ever: Brother Satgovinda in his long ocher robe, and Brahmachari Paul, the monk-in-training, in a long ocher shirt and tan pants…I love ocher.

I really *should* go up to them—tell them my intentions, get the proverbial ball rolling right now—but there are crowds surrounding them both, so I go to the table that offers literature. Most of the pamphlets I've already looked at and actually memorized. In fact, there's a lot about being a nun that I already know that I haven't told you. For example, the minimum age is eighteen—which I'm not—so I'll have to figure a way to get around that. There's such a thing as made-up birth certificates, of course. You can buy them. I could do this in L.A. but it's not the best way—which is to say, lying—to start on the path, but zealous goals call for zealous measures, I believe. I also have come to know that there are actually stages to being a nun, which means you're not a nun right away. They make you jump through hoops. First, you're a postulant, which lasts one to three years on average; then you're a novice, which can last three to seven years, or so I've heard; then you're a *brahmacharina* (nowhere does it state the length of *that* advanced stage); then finally they make you a nun, where you get to wear the ocher robes. I also know you have to pass interviews before you can start, and that you have to take vows.

But what I *don't* know is anything more about the retreat , so I pick up all the new literature and look it over. One gives a basic intro to the week, another a detailed schedule for it all. Basically, you get up at six —ugh—to gather as a group at six-thirty for morning meditation. After meditation, there's breakfast, then there's a monk or nun talk from eight to nine, then it's "quiet work time" straight until lunch, which happens at noon. I'm guessing quiet work would involve food prep, cooking, light housecleaning, gardening, *et cetera*. After lunch, there's more "quiet work time" from one to three, then there's scheduled free time from three to five, during which it's suggested you "practice the presence of God" while strolling the grounds. At five, there's group meditation. Dinner is at six. *Satsanga* takes place every night from seven to eight—that's "spiritual discourse," in case you didn't know. And then from eight to nine is another monastic talk and closing prayers. Everyday, the same. That is your week. You live like a nun in other words. During free time, monastics are available for counseling, in case you'd like that. And bedtime is pretty much ten, which is pretty early, but considering when you get up…well. Still, I'm thrilled.

After I've looked the tract over a few times, I check out the monastics again. They're still surrounded by people, which makes me annoyed. *What's everybody got to say that's so frigging important?* I wonder. What are they flapping their gums about? *I* have something quite crucial to say, since *I* want to become a *nun*, and that's what the retreat is about. What are *these* folks about? It couldn't be they all want to be monastics 'cause you're supposed to be under forty for that, and most of these people here are *not* under forty, trust me. For another thing, you can't have worldly ties that would serve to hold you back—like, you can't have a spouse or kids—and most of these folks I'd say do.So—*What's up?* I wonder. *I'm* the one who needs to be heard.

As to what I actually would say, I imagine it being something like this: "Here I am! I'm your girl!" Or, "Just give me the go-ahead nod—I've already packed my bags!" Or, "So how do you think I would look in ocher robes?" I don't know. I sort of just have this idea that they can just *look* at you and tell just from the sound of your voice and instantly know whether you'd make a good monastic or not 'cause the way a person appears tells you an awful lot about that person—right? So, what I really think I want is confirmation. I want to hear the brothers exclaim: "You're just what we want. You're the one we've been looking for. Where have you *been* all our lives?!" I want so badly to know what they think. But when I look over at them again, there are still all those people around them.

Finally, one of the brothers—Brother Satgovinda, the one who's devoted beyond mortal words—is standing alone by himself. He sees me look over, and nods. It's the exact perfect time—sort of. The very exact perfect time to make my way over to him, to utter that whole "Here-I-am!" speech of mine, to look up into his eyes, but something stops me.

Maybe it's that he looks tired after talking so much.

I think, *I'll just leave him in peace for a time*.

BIG HEAVEN

Chapter 12

It's funny, but ever since I left the hotel, I haven't once taken my hands off the retreat pamphlet. Now, back home, I study the schedule once more, even though I have the whole thing memorized.

A retreat…to see if you're interested in the monastic life…who would have thunk it? The stars seem to be lining up just for me, as if somebody was trying to tell me something. Those statements are rhetorical, by the way, 'cause things *are* lining up just for me, and someone *is* trying to tell me something. That's what having a guru is pretty much like, by the way.

A week. Just think. A week. A week of doing nothing but focusing on God with like-minded souls all around you and everyone working toward the very same goal. What with the meditations, and the talks, and the *satsangas*, and the presence of monastics about, and the counseling sessions with the senior monastics, you'd be reminded of God all the time, even at meals, or when walking the grounds or engaged in day-to-day work. Keeping God in mind—"practicing His presence" they call it—would be so much easier to do on a spiritual retreat 'cause you wouldn't have the pull of the world distracting you, and 'cause others would be doing the same thing, and 'cause all of the week would be just for this, which is why I *have* to go.

Oh, and there's this: On retreat, you'd have the benefit of group meditations, which include the "group-consciousness effect," and you know just how much I love that. I'd get to have that *twice a day* for seven days!

Plus there's this: I've worked up a plan for being a nun, which is to talk to the monastics while they're here, tell them my intentions and get their approval—get them to accept me as a new postulant *before* they go back to L.A.—so I can hopefully go with them when they leave—and the retreat is the *perfect* time to act, since that's the whole purpose of the retreat! I could use an on-site counseling session to start. It could maybe even count as my first interview…it's like God's setting all of this up just so I'll fulfill my prophecy.

Plus, even if I didn't have a prophecy—which I do, and which I'll tell you about soon, I promise—I'd still want to become a nun 'cause, let's face it: the world needs me. The world is in pretty rough shape, you might say, and could use extra light. I mean, suicide bombers exist, can you even *imagine*? Gunmen make their way inside schools and then shoot students dead. There was that man in Amish country, who used little schoolgirls as targets, lining them up against a wall! It's a perilous time. The whole world needs help, and I, myself, can best help by being a nun and really truly changing *myself*.

"If you want to change the world, change yourself," it is said. My guru has put the thought thusly: "Change yourself, and you will change thousands." It's all 'cause of one's vibes. It's 'cause of the energy a person puts out. It's 'cause of one's feelings and thoughts, which are tangible things that act on and influence the world. If I were a nun, I would put out really good thoughts. In fact, I'm thinking that maybe God even had my mother die to help me to make this rather radical decision and give Him my life.

Well, maybe.

Actually, I don't really know…who *does* know?

So those are all of the reasons for why I *have to* go on the retreat and become a nun.

I just need to square it with Dad.

But before I actually "square it with him," I make up a list of all of the things that will have to be in place before I can leave my dad for a week:

1. Stock the fridge. This one's easy. I'll go shopping the day before I leave, then give my dad a tour of the kitchen;

2. Put a hold on our mail. This one's also not hard. I just have to go get the form and have my dad sign;

3. Make sure that Dad takes his pills. This one's hardest of all, but as I think about it, I come up with this: I could have Janie call and gently remind my father; I could have Mrs. McClancey drop by once or twice, perhaps with a stew; I could call him myself—they probably don't want you making *too many* calls on retreat, but I bet during a "walk on the grounds" I could call—I mean, who is it really going to kill? I *have* to go on the retreat, so God will just have to be mellow.

And then I think, *Hey, I can do a trial run.* I'll stay at Janie's a couple of nights to see how things go—stock the old larder for that. Dad should manage that just fine.

Now that I've got it all settled, I sit in my room in front of my altar and meditate. The minute I find I am finished, I evaluate.

It was a good meditation. I mean, it *was* good. But, of course, it was nothing like group meditation, where you reap "the group-consciousness effect." Nothing like what it would be like meditating in a secluded ashram as a bona fide nun—or on a retreat.

Sometimes, in fact, when I'm meditating—like just now—I see Cameron's neck in my mind. *And some other parts of him, as well,* my third eye asserts. That's never good.

Anyway, later that week, we're all hanging out by the river again. We're doing this, at least in some part, 'cause Janie chose to bring her secret weapon along with her—Cameron—and I've never once yet had a boy to the house. I guess I've been sheltered, so there goes the having-people-over idea, and also 'cause we *like* hanging out by the river. Other kids tend to hang out downtown, or in the fields that border the high school, or at Cavanaugh Park—places where they can be *seen*, in other words, whereas hanging out by the banks of the Charles is making a statement—kind of—that we three don't need to be "seen"—that we hang out to be with each other and watch the *real* world. Granted, you can watch a pretty real world by hanging on Main Street, too, like at McDonald's, or Wendy's, or Joe's, or whatnot, but if you're hanging out waiting to be seen, you're spending most of your precious time posing, so how can you really watch the world? Besides, we three like nature.

Anyway, 'cause *I* am the one with the stuff going on, I start in telling my buds Janie and Cameron about the retreat. How you go for a week. How it'll be like a regular, intense Wednesday night meeting doing group meditations, except for a week instead of an evening.

I describe it like this: Say you've taken a drug, and the drug makes you really really high, and say you could stay on that drug for an entire week. Wouldn't you *want* to?

And I know. I'm not *totally* inured to my audience. I know that they're wise asses, but I'm going in pretty sincerely to see what they'll do. I'm giving them the benefit of the doubt, you might say.

I shouldn't.

Janie—who never lets things sit for long—says, "Retreat? Is that where you wave a white flag while you flee on your horse?" She winks at Cameron.

"No. But I *do* get to leave you and Cameron behind." This is good.

Janie just whips out her iPhone, looks up the word, "retreat." Her "flag" comment must have inspired her.

"'Retreat.' Here it is: 'An act or process of withdrawing especially from what is difficult, dangerous, or disagreeable. Two: the process of receding from a position or state attained. Three: the usual *forced* withdrawal of troops from an enemy…' Doesn't sound blissful to me."

I smile through it—even Janie flashing her iPhone around—I'm planning to smile through it all.

Except, I *don't* simply smile through it all, I say something else: another key part of my plan. I tell Janie how I'm planning to leave Dad alone for a couple of days to get him ready for my being on retreat, and how I plan to spend those couple of days hanging out with her. "Kind of like a trial-run," I say. "And also just to give Dad time alone, which I think would be good, since it can't be that easy with a *teenager* always around." I'm spinning the story for Janie, in case you didn't know…I bet you know.

Janie says, "Oh, good. A *sleepover!* We can make popcorn, and put curlers in our hair, and make prank phone calls. And—I know! Why don't we also invite your old man? I don't think *he'll* have anything to do for either of those days."

I give ole Janie a look.

She looks back. Then she says, "C'mon! He'll be *lonely* without us around! He really likes our company!"

"That kind of defeats the whole purpose. Wouldn't you say?"

Cameron just stays silent through it all. But then he stays silent through most of our riffs.

I say, "Listen. Really. He's fine. He's taking his pills. He goes into town. He's even gone out on some errands for me. I'm not going to be with him forever, you know. I'm *sixteen*."

"A woman of the world," Cameron all of a sudden pipes up.

I try to ignore him. "Listen. My father has got to branch out—make friends—now that Mom's not here. I mean, I'm his daughter, sure, but I'm not his *peer*. He needs to have *peers*. I'm thinking of having Mrs. McClancey drop by while I'm gone."

Janie says, "Great. The man's been a widower for what—three months—and you're already getting him hitched?"

"No. I just want him to have a few peers."

"I know," says Janie. "Why don't we add some Viagra to his pills? Then you'll have trouble trying to *keep* Mrs. McClancey away. She can move right in." She winks again at Cameron.

Cameron, her ally, winks back.

I say, ignoring them both, "I'm planning to stock the refrigerator for him, and stock all his pills, and I'm even going to whip up a casserole for him to just nuke, but he's got to learn to do more for himself. This will help." And then I say, steamrolling on, for we've talked about my father to death, which wasn't my intention, "Anyway, that's all the stuff that *I'm* going to do. And as for you, Janie McCrae. What *you're* going to do is clean your room, 'cause I've seen nasty dust bunnies there and I *don't* like to sleep among dust bunnies. You're also going to notify your mom about my coming, and make sure your own fridge is full. I like cake, by the way. Chocolate Entenmann's will do very nicely."

Cameron says, "I'm not sure that ashrams are known for cake. Especially Entenmann's"

Why is he all of a sudden speaking up? Maybe he really likes me? I wonder. "Well then, I better get my fill of it now. Hadn't I?" I reply.

There's a pause, where Cameron gives Janie a look, and Janie gives Cameron one back. Then Cameron says, "She's not as docile as she was."

Janie replies, "It's the brainwashing."

And *Cameron* replies, "So the time for intervention is now?"

And Janie says, "It should have been started last week."

They're wise asses, the both of them. They could never be "together" 'cause of that. They need me. I'm the one they oh-so-merrily play off of. I am *not* a wise ass—surely you've noticed that about me, though sometimes I gamely join in.

Anyway, I let my lame friends have their fun, 'cause *I'm* the one going on retreat. Hooray! Besides. I know they only do it 'cause they like me. 'Cause they don't want me becoming a nun without them.

Finally, I say, "*You* can say whatever you'd like, but regarding 'the teachings,' I *know*. Just like I know Chris Cornell's the greatest singer alive. *Way* over Maynard James Keenan of obsolete Tool."

I smile at Janie, victorious.

Cameron says, "She's really got it all figured out, huh?"

Janie shrugs. "You know what they say. If you want to give God a good laugh, tell Him your plans for the future."

She got this line from me, and I got the line from the teachings. Cameron thinks it's great, you can tell. He smirks broadly.

Too bad I lust for his neck so much.

And pertaining to Cameron, I'll say this: Scientific studies have shown that romantic, passionate love—the kind where you lust for somebody's neck, I imagine—is akin to mental illness. This is for real! I'm serious. There was a cover article in the February 2006 *National*

Geographic all about it, citing various studies that back up this thesis. In "From the Editor" at the front of the issue, Chris Johns aptly put it like this: "To be madly in love could be exactly that—madness. The term 'lovesick' is surprisingly accurate…People experiencing romantic love…have a chemical profile in their brains similar to that of people who suffer from obsessive-compulsive disorder. Love blurs the line between mental health and psychopathology." I kid you not. It really says that.

Johns goes on to say, "Still, we can't resist the siren's song, and science has an explanation for that, too. Love, it seems, lights up certain areas of the brain and releases chemicals that provoke hyperactivity, recklessness, and exhilaration. That's why spellbound lovers stay up all night to see the sun rise, take extraordinary risks to see each other, or, as Britain's Edward VIII did, throw a whole country aside for 'the woman I love'." In short, love can be dangerous, Chris Johns concludes.

That about sums the thing up, though I will cite some studies for you, to make it even more concrete. They are all culled from the same magazine article.

At the University of Lausanne in Switzerland, Claus Wedekind had forty-nine women sniff different men's smelly sweaty T-shirts. The women tended to prefer the smell of T-shirts worn by men whose basic immune systems were different than their own, since this produces healthier children when you mate. In other words, you might end up falling in love based on somebody's *sweat*.

Donatella Marazziti, a professor of psychiatry at the University of Pisa in Italy, measured serotonin levels in the blood of twenty-four subjects who had "newly fallen in love," and who reportedly obsessed about their beloved several hours a day. She and her colleagues found that the subjects' serotonin blood levels were most similar to those suffering from OCD, and least similar to a mentally-healthy control group.

And get this: Basically *all* researchers agree that romantic love dies out—usually within four years, states one researcher—as that is how long it takes to raise a child through infancy. Imagine if it took *six months* to raise a child through infancy. Love might expire in *that* amount of time. Or, it could all just become way too much, some scientists say. Per brain-imaging studies, an excess of dopamine in the brain accompanies passion, and makes us feel like we can fly. But cocaine users, who also experience this effect, report a phenomenon of tolerance after a time. The high dies when the brain becomes desensitized to the cocaine, the theory here being that the brain can't maintain the intense neural activity required for either a cocaine high or for being in love.

Regardless of the reason, it means love always fades. Now I ask you: Would you rather be *mentally ill*, jerked around by somebody's *sweat*, experiencing a false kind of "drug high" that fades, or would you rather put your money on God?

Not that I'm saying I'm "in love" with Cameron, madly or in any other way. I'm only saying that if I *do* tend to think about his neck, it's only normal…okay, it is also a bit insane.

And note: "Obsess about his neck" is only the half of it, but I'm sure you've already picked up on that.

BIG HEAVEN

Chapter 13

My father's in the family room watching Jerry Springer on TV, a show with the title "Springer Secrets" in which a man has been cheating on his girlfriend—not on Jerry Springer, gasp! Springer asks how *he'd* like it if he found out his girlfriend was cheating on *him*, to which he says he wouldn't like it, and Springer then says, "So maybe you can see how your girlfriend would feel," after which the guy says, "She should just get over it and not stay angry forever." The next thing you know, the girlfriend who's been waiting backstage—of course— comes out—of course—and starts swearing at her boyfriend—they bleep it—and shoves him, then shoves him again, so I take the all-powerful remote from my father and change it. My father is way way too good for crass Jerry Springer.

It's mostly soaps on right now, and I know my dad despises soaps, but I find Montel Williams before long so the two of us start to watch that. Montel features a woman who went from 527 pounds to 162 pounds, mainly thanks to a book by Bill Phillips called *Body for Life*—previously featured on Montel's show, of course. It turns out that the theme of today's show is People Whose Lives Were Changed by Watching Previous Montel Shows. *Pretty good marketing*, I think. Anyway, this woman, who heard Phillips on Montel up and changed her whole life. Witness the hundreds of pounds lost. The next thing you know, the author comes out—of course. He's been waiting backstage—of course. He hugs the changed woman, then he says how the best part of her whole story is that now she can be an inspiration to others. She looks pretty darn good, I admit. We saw the "before" photos, too.

Anyway, at first I want to turn the TV off 'cause it's garbage, and *then* I want to turn the TV off 'cause it's riveting. I finally just turn the TV off. I have something to relay to my father.

"Dad," I declare. "I have something to tell you"—this is a definite, good start. "I'm planning to go to Janie's for a couple of days —two is what I'm thinking—for a sort of like girl-only sleepover, and following that, I'll be going on a spiritual retreat for a week."

Two new things you need to know at this point:

1. I was "raised" Episcopalian, though we didn't often make it to church when I was young, and my father doesn't go to church now, and I don't go now, yet my father believes in God—and actually *likes* God—so his swallowing this idea about the retreat will be easier, I think. I mean, it's better when a person likes God, right?

2. He knows I've found a "spiritual path" as he calls it. He knows I go to "spiritual talks," but he doesn't yet know about my nun aspirations…one baby step at a time. My overnight visit at Janie's is one.

Anyway, I stop to assess how Dad is taking the news.

He seems fine. If there's any reaction at all, it's that he's happy to see me. These days, just FYI, all I really do is tell my father what I am doing, where I am going, and he goes along with my plans. I haven't heard him say no to my face since Mom died, and not a whole lot before that. It's a good thing I'm a good kid, 'cause a person could really take advantage of this.

I tell him more about the retreat, though I probably don't have to: How it'll be a great way to "spend time with God and totally focus on Him." How it'll be incredibly healthy. All vegetarian. How my meditations will improve by leaps and bounds. Then, 'cause he still isn't speaking, just looking at me with a "smile" you might say, I inquire, "So will you be okay here without me?"

"I'll give it the old college try," he replies, which is one of his lines, then adds, "though I'll miss you."

This I hadn't quite counted on…it gets to me.

"I'll miss you, too," I offer.

After that, I decide we need to hang out together awhile, which is another precipitate thing I hadn't quite counted on. The thing is, it's totally quiet at first when I do. Neither talks, and I find myself wishing Montel was on.

We stare at each other, Dad and I—Dad in his usual chair, me on the couch that is cater-cornered—till he says, "So. My girl is really growing up, huh? Going away overnight?"

I nod. I have no idea if my father knows how old I am.

Next he remarks, "Well this *is* a definite treat. A father-daughter visit," looks softly at me and smiles.

What I do then is I notice that he looks a little…parched, sitting all expectant in his chair. I mean—I know *I'm* here, but root beer would make it better.

"Would you like a glass of root beer?" I ask. "With ice?" My dad's got this thing about ice.

"Why, that would be *delightful*," he says.

I get him the root beer—with ice. Then I end up thinking that he *still* looks a little bit off, without any snack to go *with* the root beer so

I say, "And maybe some microwave popcorn, as well? We have Newman's."

"How do you read my mind?" is what he replies. He smiles, my sweet, corny dad.

I should probably explain just why he's the way he is, or at least why I *think* he's the way that he is. As you've probably noticed, he's "different:" He's corny, refined—well, he's from Maine—that's my excuse—but really what you see is what you get with my father, which is to say that he really *is* just as corny as he seems. He really *is* as refined. He really *is* far too good for this world—and not really "of it"—and there's a very clear reason for this: his agrarian roots. He was sheltered from a lot of crummy stuff—not quite as much pukey garbage goes on up in Maine, I think. Another definite cause is the era he grew up in: the fifties. A time when "the King" was around. A time when people brought your burger on roller skates, and when sock hops and bobby socks were in. Guys "pinned you" back then, whereas, today, guys typically F you. It was a much sweeter time is my point, which is why Dad's so corny. It was a kinder, simpler time back then.

Anyway, I bring him the popcorn, in a bowl, and I have some too, in another bowl, and we "visit" as we eat, my dad making comments like: "Gee. You're a pretty good cook!"—a joke—and, "We should do this more often, I think," and: "You're not half-bad company. You know?" Not only does he live to be charming, he seems to be charmed by *me*, though I'm not really doing that much.

After more endless time passes by, I ask if he'd like the fan, 'cause I'm thinking he looks rather hot in his chair, and he says yes. Actually, he says, "Why how very gracious of you," so I bring it over, turn it on, and aim the symmetrical blades toward his face. I'm waiting on my father, which is the opposite of what I've been *telling* him things will be like—the opposite of what I've been telling *myself* things will be like—but that's what this thing called life is about. You know—duality. So I'm fitting in.

He says more cornball stuff as we hang together, like: "She makes popcorn *and* she gets fans. What a girl!"

Finally, 'cause it seems like our "visit" is not done, though our popcorn is, I ask if he'd like to play a board game with me. He says yes. Actually, he says: "Well that would be quite the nice treat." I go and get Tri-Ominos. We end up playing three mind-numbing games 'cause we tie the first two.

All this takes time. Lots of it. That's the trouble when you hang out with my dad. You get sucked in. Anyway, mind-numbing board games or not, I am going on retreat soon. *Hooray!*

I sort of have this feeling, as I said, that my guru's behind some of this, so now might be the perfect time to tell you about him. Like, what a guru is. How I came to have one. How I know he is mine.

First, let me give you some background. The term guru is Sanskrit and means "one who dispels darkness." It is said that when a person starts searching for God, God sends books and teachers to help, but when the person's yearning is deep enough, God sends a guru. A true, God-realized guru. That is what happened to me. Furthermore, it is said that God ordains the relationship between guru and disciple—that is, the guru sent is meant specifically for *you*—and that this relationship is eternal, which means that the guru will guide you, and work with you, and stay with you for as long as it takes for you to reach emancipation. You, for your part, are expected in turn to be loyal to your guru.

My own guru is no longer "present in the body" so to speak. In other words, he is "dead," though that doesn't actually matter and can even be good, 'cause one of the aspects of a *true* guru is that they are omnipresent. It's a lot like the idea of Santa Claus. You know, "He sees you when you're sleeping, he knows when you're awake" and so on, or, if you prefer, it's a lot like the concept of *God*, for that's where the whole idea comes from to start. Anyway, I can talk to my guru at any time 'cause he is always there to hear me. He's always "tuned in." And just in case you're interested, every true guru was, at one time, a person like us—knowing the same struggles and joys, the same heartaches, but having lived many many lives, until eventually attaining liberation which means that there's hope for the rest of us schmucks. *Ha!*

But anyway, the way I *know* that *my* guru is *mine* is that soon after my mother died, I read a whole bunch of spiritual books which all seemed pretty much "true," and said the same thing—my guru's book being just one—so then I was stumped. I'd read all the books, yet I still didn't know which teacher was mine, and I very much wanted to follow *a* teacher. So what I did then was I prayed—pretty hard—and asked for God's guidance. And the next thing I knew, I saw a flyer on a bus stop, promoting my guru's group and announcing their arrival the very next week—the last time they had been in our area was more than a decade ago. If ever there was a sign he was just for me, this was it!

Since then, I started praying to my guru, and accepting him as my very own, and I've felt his steadily growing presence in my life, guiding and directing me. So that's how I know my guru is mine. That's how I know our tie is "ordained." Of course, there's a lot more to it than that, but for now, that's enough.

Anyway, my "trial run" consists, to start, of packing my bag with my summer pajamas, and my pillow, and my slippers, and a wallet-sized picture of my guru, and other hanging-out clothes—for "The City to Watch"—and my vintage Dunlop tennis racket—'cause Janie and I might get in some tennis—and even my sunblock, bathing suit and towel, in case we swing by Walden Pond in our two days, and, of course, my trusty old Red-Sox hat for the sun. I feel more like I'm going on a vacation than a sleepover!

It also consists of walking to Janie's, bringing a coffee cake along for her mom, and baking sugar cookies while there. And no: she *didn't* go buy yummy Entenmann's like I asked, but she did get those kind you just break apart then stick in the oven, so we *felt* like we were actually "baking." For real. "Who *says* that we don't cook?" Janie asks, as one sugar cookie after another melts in our mouths.

Later, it consists of spreading out my army-surplus sleeping bag next to Janie's bed, then grabbing her favorite stuffed animal and holding it close—"You want to be chilling in *my* bed tonight, don't you Mr. Piggly Wiggly, dear?"—and of Janie snatching him back. And it consists of going up to her Maynard James Keenan poster and french-kissing the rock star right there—right on the paper—well, actually only *pretending* to french-kiss him—and of Janie declaring me "ew, gross," while wiping my ersatz "saliva" away. We're on Janie's home-turf, so I explain I'm sorry, but I have to get it all done now before I become a nun.

Later, it's made up of rummaging through Janie's desk and extracting a notebook, then pretending that the notebook is her diary. "Dear diary," I pretend to read. "Today I decided I'm *in love* with Ian Burchill. Yesterday I think I loved him, too, and the day before that day as well, though I'm having some trouble remembering that far back."

"Give it!" a stony Janie says, not liking me mentioning Ian Burchill. Then: "That's my organic chem' book, if you really care to know, though I'm sure it's Latin to you."

"I was taking organic chem' before you were *born,*" I reply.

"Give it!" Janie repeats, "or I'm telling our good buddy Cameron you're madly in love with him. That you're thinking of giving up the knighthood for him"—it's "nunhood" as Janie well knows; Janie is just being Janie.

"Very funny, and I really don't care."

"Aren't you supposed to yank some sort of *sword* out of some sort of *rock*, like is done in Excalibur?"

I ignore her and move to her closet, sifting through her clothes. Gold mine! "Seen it a million times. Seen it a million times. Seen it a million times." Then, to a skirt that looks pulled from a grave and that I've teased her about before, I say, "Right not to wear it," immediately replacing it back on the rod.

"You know Cameron likes you," she says.

I pause, but just for a moment. "So you've hinted," I say, casually examining her stock of shoes.

"No, really. He does. I know."

"Has he said so?" is what I ask next, rejecting some shoes for others.

"It's not like he has to," she says.

"So you've hinted," I tell her again.

This time, it's Janie who pauses. "So let's say he does," she goes on. "Let's say he really *really* likes you. Let's say he even asks you *out* before we die. Could you *really* say no to that *neck*?"—I had told Janie I liked Cameron's neck...big mistake!

"I'm going through with being a nun, so I'll have to say bye to that neck."

"Wouldn't you like to have sex before you do?"

This is smack out-of-the-blue shocking, especially seeing how *Janie* has never had sex.

"Like *you* really know about sex."

"More than you. At least I've fooled around with some guys, and I've come…have *you* ever come with a guy?" Then she says, "Don't answer. I know your answer is no."

"I've come," I say.

"Just not with a *guy*," she repeats.

"No. Not with a guy," I admit, 'cause otherwise she won't let it go. Then I say, "Piggly-Wiggly doesn't *like* this kind of talk. *Do* you Piggly, dear?" I pick the stuffed animal up and look him in the eyes.

"You should definitely come with a guy," she goes on.

I think about it, but don't give an answer. I really can't imagine the act. Then I can.

Right then, my cell phone goes off, and my "trial run" now includes this: my father asking where the jam has got to. My coming with a live, breathing guy will have to wait.

Anyway, after the bothersome call, I'm tempted to turn my phone off and shove it in the bottom of my bag beneath my socks. After all: who *knows* where the jam has got to? It could be orbiting ring-enclosed Saturn by now, what with my father in charge. But if I really *did* turn my mobile phone off, I'd feel pretty bad. And it wouldn't be 'cause I am worried about him—I'm not—for what is there to worry about? He doesn't have a car. He's taking his pills. My glorious "trial-run" is only for a couple of days, so what could go wrong? My father is fine. Like my guru says, you have to think positive thoughts. The one thing that *does* have me *slightly* concerned, however, is that he might be a little bit lonely without me around. *Still, I can't be his babysitter,* I remind myself. *I'm the daughter. I'm the one who should be taken care of! Let him go look for his own jam!* though, of course, I duly told him where to look.

So now, anyway, it's time we engage in *my* activity. We've already massacred Janie's. We made this cool deal where we'd each get to pick a single thing, and the other would have to take part in that thing. We tackled Janie's activity first, 'cause she was the person who asked first. Plus, it was Janie's idea.

Janie's activity had consisted of us each sitting down to write a "love letter" to our "beloved." I picked God to address, but every time I wrote the word "God," Janie crossed it out and wrote "Cameron." I started getting the feeling she'd had this activity planned. Janie's love letter was addressed to her *real* beloved—that guy Ian Burchill I mentioned—who's in our same grade.

Anyway, this is how it went: I started *my* letter with: "Dear God/ Guru, I'm so grateful to you for the blessings in my life..." Janie immediately snatched the pen from my hand, 'cause I wasn't quote "doing it right." She said "the beloved" couldn't *be* God or Guru. "And if you're talking to a *guy*," she went on, "you don't say you're 'grateful' for all of the 'blessings' he's freely bestowed unless he's giving it to you every day, and then more than once a day." She does this to shock me.

So, *I* say, "Show me where that's written down." And *Janie* says, "It's *my* activity. I don't *have* to write it down."

My letter continued, "I really want to know You 'cause it is said that when you know God, you can't help but love Him. So please let me know You and love You." Janie immediately cut all of the "You's," and put in "your penis." So *I* then declared I was done, which made Janie retort I was bad at it anyway, so we moved on to Janie's letter.

Janie started hers with: "Dear 'I'm-not-naming-names'." And I promptly wrote in "Ian Burchill." Next, she grabbed *my* letter, saying, "No use recreating the wheel," and then wrote, "I really want to *know* your penis, 'cause it is said that when I *know* your penis, I will *love* your penis" *et cetera*, which she seemed to think was just great, though, really, it's not a whole lot removed from what folks end up doing to fortune cookies when they tack on the words "between the sheets" to the ends. Like if your fortune says, "You will be very well-liked," you add "between the sheets." But still, Janie thought it was great. And just to keep the night from sinking *entirely* into the gutter, I snatched *her* letter away, and added, "Luv ya." Then I wrote, "P.S. At your next lacrosse game, I hope that you score the winning goal just for me." Ian Burchill plays lacrosse. Janie replied, "That's so *Disney*." So *I* said, "Well it's better being all kinds of *Disney*, than being 'Luscious Lascivious Laticia' like it seems like you are"—I was trying to think of a porn name there—and Janie replied, "That's so *lame*." Ian Burchill is sensitive ground.

So then we moved on to *my* activity—which is now. For mine, I tell her we're going to do yoga. Her reaction's not *totally* bad. Like all westerners—okay, most—she thinks yoga consists of mere poses you strike and then hold. But actually, "yoga" is Sanskrit and translates to "union." So yoga is actually *any* practice that brings about union with God, or that at least makes a stab at this state. So there's "*karma yoga*," which is striving for this union through action, by serving others while thinking of God. And there's "*jnana yoga*," which is striving for this union through wisdom, by employing discrimination. There's also "*bhakti yoga*," which is striving for this union through devotion, *et cetera*. I, myself, adhere to "*raja yoga*," which translates to "royal yoga," and which is the "royal pathway to God" in that it combines all the other forms, and is far more advanced. My kind involves meditation *and* wisdom *and* devotion. So even though I tell Janie we're going to be practicing "yoga"—we're really going to sit and meditate. *Ha!*

I show her the appropriate pose, which consists of sitting with your spine straight, eyes closed, and gaze lifted up to the forehead, to the point between the eyebrows, which is called "the Christ-consciousness center." Janie actually does what I say 'cause I think she is curious, though she grimaces all of the while. But before I can her teach the technique, she opens her eyes.

"*Why* exactly am I doing this again?"

"It will make you more attractive to *Ian*. Not to mention *God*," I put in.

"*How* so?"

"Well, it will make you more blissful inside, and that bliss will radiate outward and thus attract others. You'll be like a magnet," I say.

"Yeah?" she says doubtfully.

"Yeah."

And then, that is that. Except that is not really "that," 'cause right at that moment my cell phone rings—I never did turn the thing off like I dreamed, and wonder if he's looking for mayonnaise now. I'm tempted to simply not answer for it's almost eleven o'clock, but if I don't, I'll worry, so I answer.

The woman caller asks for me by name, and I say, "This is she," then she gives me her name, and it turns out she's a nurse from our very nearest hospital—Newton-Wellesley. She tells me my father is there, and then she gives *his* name, and then says, "Your father is fine. Only he's a little disoriented." And then she tells me that he fell, and that a neighbor found him, and that he was taken to the hospital by ambulance. And that they're keeping him there overnight for observation. And that I don't need to come right now, but could I please come get him tomorrow. That that's when she thinks he'll be released, in all likelihood. Tomorrow.

I get more information from the nurse, then hang up.

My father fell.

He's in the hospital.

He's "a little disoriented…"

This is bad! Really really bad! Really Really!

And here I was thinking such positive thoughts.

BIG HEAVEN

Chapter 14

My dad's in the hospital, so there goes my visit with Janie. There goes my spiritual retreat. There goes my well-planned-out *life*.

It's not nice to say, but I feel somewhat like he's doing this on purpose—sabotaging things. Like, God forbid, he should be left all alone. Like, it's an attention-getting thing. Unconscious, maybe, but I still want to sort of blame my father, even if it *is* subconscious.

When I think about it, all the times he's gotten into trouble were times when I wasn't around—that says *something*. There was the Hannaford Grocery accident when I was at a talk; there was his wandering that day into CJ's without reason or cause when I was with Janie; and now there's his fall when…well, you where I was. It's like he doesn't want me to ever grow up. Starting my own life. Leave home. It doesn't take a shrink to see *that*.

And frankly, I'm getting a little tired of it.

And, continuing on in this vein—which I've decided to do—let me also relay this: Though I'm not fully certain that I *can* blame my father for his fall—or to what extent I can blame him at all—I also believe I've done everything *I* possibly can to right things before I leave. I mean, what else *can* I do? I've taken his car keys away; I've bought him a cutting-edge pill box with a built-in alarm; I've even called him up on the phone and physically *waited* while he took all his pills. What else is there? *It's his turn*, I conclude. *His turn to make a real effort...*

So anyway, now, on a hot and muggy morning, having not slept at all the night before, I am headed to the hospital. Alone. Having no one that I can discuss all this with...I miss my mother so.

If my she were here, I could discuss it all with her. I don't want to discuss them with Janie, 'cause she would just get on my case—make it seem like I now have to babysit my father all the time, which I don't want to do. Janie's a bit of an alarmist to tell the truth. But my mother I could discuss such things with. She'd understand. No, it's not really a matter of discussion or understanding, it's more that she would step in and make it better—which she should. *She's* the one who married my father, after all—*she* picked *him*. My role in all this was just being born. She was betrothed. And while I know that it isn't really her fault either, a part of me resents her for leaving us. And a part of me resents God, too, if you want to know the truth, though I know that I shouldn't...

Basically, I resent my father, my mother, and God. It really isn't oodles of fun, resenting everyone, but that's how it is!

Anyway, when I first see my father in the hospital, he says, "*There* she is!" like this is a party, and I am the guest of honor and the last to arrive. I give him a smile—which is definitely *not* sincere— then ask how he is—he looks fine to my eyes, by the way. They said he was fine, and here he is sitting in a chair, fully dressed.

"Oh fine," he tells me. "Much ado about nothing, I'm afraid."

And *I* feel like saying, "No. It's *not* 'much ado about nothing' if it ruins my sleepover, makes me fret so I don't go on my retreat, and interrupts my entire *life-plan*." But I don't say this. I don't say a word.

Then *he* says, "How's Janie?" And I answer, "Fine"—the stupid word that *he* always uses—letting him hear how moronic it sounds.

Then we don't utter a word, though I see my father looking at my hair, which he dislikes—the way it always "hangs in my eyes"—so I say, "You're *not* going to mention my hair. Right?" My displeasure must show, for he mimes a "my-lips-are-sealed" move, by putting his fingers to his lips, then twisting them.

I say to him, "Good." I am not in any mood for my father. Before we can leave Newton-Wellesley, I've been informed by a nurse that the doctor has to give his okay. So now we are waiting for him.

I look almost anywhere else, as long as it's not my father. I look out his two big streaked windows, which show a large parking lot. I look at an old painting of geese. I look at the long metal tracks on the ceiling for the privacy curtains.

My father likely thinks it's a "teenager thing"—my bad mood. He believes there are loads of "teen moments" that go on, and that this is just one, I would bet, so I let him believe whatever he wants. I'm in no mood to clear all this up for him.

Finally, the doctor comes in. He's in his fifties, I'd say, with that "pattern" sort of baldness you see in men of that age, and with clear direct eyes that stare at you. That's the thing about doctors, I think: they have nothing to hide. They are in pure helping mode.

This one—Dr. Black—what a name for a *doctor*—first greets my father with a smile, then puts a hand out to me. He says he's the doctor in charge, and that he's seen my father three times since he arrived—twice last night and once this morning. He says that my father didn't hurt himself in the fall, but that he was acting pretty confused when they first brought him in, which can be normal in these cases, especially when seniors are hospitalized. "It's actually a form of delirium that tends to set in," he tells me, "but it's temporary. It's typically caused by a precipitous change in environment. Usually, when the patient gets home, things go back to normal pretty fast. In any case, Dad's much better today...Isn't that right, Mr. Proctor?"

"Fine," my father replies, like the two are old friends.

"Good. All right. Well I'm just going to perform an exam to see how you are."

He has my father remove his shoes, socks, and shirt, and sit on the bed. He tests his reflexes, listens to his heart, looks in his ears and his eyes. Then he says, "Now I'm just going to ask you some questions, Mr. Proctor, if that is all right. Rather routine. Can you tell me what season it is?"

"Right now?" my father demands.

"Yes. Right now."

My father looks out the streaked windows. "Spring," he declares, looking sure.

"Close. It's summer actually. Right in the middle, in fact." He jots a quick note on his clipboard.

"Well at least I'm only one off," says my father, smiling so the doctor can see.

The doctor smiles back.

Meanwhile, *I* am mortified. Of course it is *summer*. Who couldn't come up with *that*? It's ninety-degrees-plus outside. Dr. Black isn't fazed though.

"And can you tell me who the president is?" the doctor asks.

"That's easy. Obama. Barack Obama."

"Very good," says kind Dr. Black, making another brief note on his clipboard that only he can see.

"Now there's an election going on this year in our state. Martha Coakley is running. Can you tell me what job Coakley has?" He looks at my father.

"Her job?" my father repeats, clearly stalling.

"Yes. Right now. Or even the job she's running for," the doctor goes on. He waits, giving nothing away.

"Um…*politician*?" my father replies. "I mean, *that* surely says enough. Right?"

It's a joke, 'cause not only does it describe Coakley's job, it describes Coakley's character as in "the person's a real politician." My dad clearly meant it this way—as a lighthearted joke. Plus it lets him off the hook.

The doctor laughs.

I cringe.

Dr. Black is starting to be charmed by my father, I can tell. Good old dad.

Dr. Black puts his hands on his knees like it's time for brass tax, no longer using his clipboard. "Okay. Now can you tell me where you are right now. The name of *this* place," he says.

This should be a good one. I wait.

"The doctor building?" Dad says with a flash of teeth. I don't know if he says this 'cause he is nervous, or if he's trying to continue his joking routine or what, but I want to just disappear.

"Well that's right," the doctor replies with a smile of his own. "We *are* in a doctor-building. Do you know the *name* of the doctor-building?"

Hospital, I'm thinking. *Newton-Wellesley. Just say the common word "hospital." How hard a challenge is that?*

"The-place-where-they-have-nice-doctors?" my father suggests. "No wait. That's far too long for a name."

The doctor does no more than smile. "Almost done."

He goes through a series of hand-eye-coordination moves with Dad, where first he demos a move, and my father repeats it: Touch your finger to your nose, your shoulder, your back, the top of your head, *et cetera*. My father does quite well with these. At the end, the doctor gestures toward the chair, meaning Dad can leave the bed. Dad does the gesture as well, clearly mimicking the doctor. The doctor laughs. The only thing is—I'm not sure my father is joking, though Dr. Black thinks he is. And, joking or not, I'm thinking he's trying to make it *seem* like a joke. This in itself is worrisome.

Part of me thinks: Why don't you *stop* making jokes so we can get some good *drugs*? And part of me thinks: Keep making jokes so he won't know how bad you really are. Though I also think, *the doctor can't be totally fooled. My dad didn't even name the right season.*

Dr. Black asks my dad to get dressed, then nods for me to follow him out. We go to his office down the hall, take seats—he in the proverbial "doctor's chair," me in the seat right across. I wonder if he knows my age? This feels like it might an adult thing.

He starts in again about my father's delirium. How he's still exhibiting the tail end of this, and how it's relatively common in elders when they're hospitalized, especially when they suffer from dementia like Dad does, but how it's usually temporary.

Usually, I repeat in my mind.

Then the doctor goes on to explain how he thinks it'll clear when Dad gets home, and how it's cleared quite a lot already. How what we're seeing is not Dad's quote "baseline" end quote, adding, "Though your father's form of delirium is rather delightful. I must say."

124

Super, I think. *He's delightfully delirious.*

I nod at the doctor right, not knowing what to say or do.

He then tells me more about how noticeable my Dad's confusion was when they first brought him in. How, not only did he not know where he was, he started to talk about Martians somehow being in the room. Martians mucking up the furniture.

My jaw does a drop to my chest. *Martians?*

"I'm not saying this to alarm you, because, as you can see, he's much much better today, and, again, the behavior is typical. I just wanted you to be aware in case it happens again, in which event, you should call his physician right away, as it could mean more. But you haven't heard him say such things in the past, have you?"

"No." This at least is true. I haven't. Thanks to God…I mean, really, *Martians?*

He then starts reviewing Dad's meds, which he has listed on the chart in front of him, asking if he has been taking them.

I nod yes.

"Good. Because varying one's day-to-day meds, even a bit, can also produce strange behavior."

He *then* tells me how he's writing up orders for a nurse to come see us twice this week, with additional visits as necessary, and how Dad needs to see his primary-care physician as well.

"One of you will need to make the appointment," he tells me.

He writes the orders. He's about to hand them to me when he says, "Hopefully, this will clear itself up. We'll see what the nurse has to say. But even so, your father may gradually require more care. Speaking of which…" He pauses. "I understand it's just the two of you at home, but I was wondering if there was anyone else who could maybe help out? A family member perhaps who could lend you a hand? Maybe even move in for a time, perhaps till you're older?"

I swallow, though it's really a gulp—it's really a total panic attack. Then I mention my aunt—who exists—and lives only two towns away from where we live. This is false. And who is really involved in our lives. Also false.

This seems to soothe him, and he says, "Very good." Then he hands me the orders for the nurse, which I am to take to the receptionist out front, where they will presumably be fulfilled.

I take them out of his office and rip them up. I shouldn't have to say why, but in case you're unclear: It's that whole we-can't-let-folks-in notion. They might try and put my dad into a home—and me into odious foster care.

Bye-bye visiting-nurse orders…though I don't know what I will do instead. Dad's in the waiting room out front, patiently "waiting"—which is good. One of his socks he put on; the other appears to be hanging from the pocket of his pants. Oh, well. Chalk it up to the delirium.

Delirium, I think when I get home. *Martians…? Why was he talking about Martians?*—That isn't good.

And Dr. Black seemed to think the delirium could set in again, for example, if he ends up in a hospital. And what about the "usually" delirium "clears," but not always part?—I don't think I have to tell you whether that statement is good or not. It's not.

Once in my room, I Google "delirium," and discover the following from the Merck.com website:

Delirium is a sudden, fluctuating, and usually reversible disturbance of mental function. It is characterized by an inability to pay attention, disorientation, an inability to think clearly, and fluctuations in the level of alertness—that mean's "consciousness."

People with delirium…do not understand what is happening around them. They become disoriented. Sudden confusion about time and often about place may be an early sign of delirium. If delirium is severe, people may not know who they or other people are…

About 15 to 50% of older people experience delirium at some time during a hospital stay.

So. There it is: I can never permit my father to be hospitalized again. That should be easy. Why didn't I think of it before?

Later that day—as if his fall, his hospitalization, his talking about visiting *Martians* weren't enough—he can't find his glasses:

"Mo. Have you happened to come across my glasses anywhere?"

This is kind of question now causes me to cringe. And it's also, in its way, one of the most ironic jokes that ever there was, 'cause how can a person *find* his eyeglasses without them, so I start looking for them. My dad starts looking for them too, but in a really lame way, like in the same three places over and over: the end table next to his chair, the nightstand next to his bed, his bureau. I search those places as well, basically redoing what Dad just did, but then look in other places where a particular person in our household might leave them: inside the refrigerator; inside the dryer; under the steel kitchen sink…

At some point during this search, my dad yells out, "And Mo. Have you come across my wallet anywhere?"

This time I don't even bother to cringe. I just keep searching—all the same places I just looked, then new places, like shirt pockets, pants pockets, the dirty clothes hamper. Nothing. And all of the time I am looking in these places I think *my father could have lost these items anywhere*. Anywhere at all. During his fall. During his trip in the who-knows-which ambulance. Anytime during his hospital stay, but I'd rather not think about that, so I keep looking around the cramped house.

Finally, I call Newton-Wellesley, praying all the while. I don't even want to have to *think* about what it would mean if he *really* lost those two things. I get Admissions, who transfers me to the right nurse's station, where I explain what I'm looking for, and am put on hold, and then—you guessed—am disconnected!

I call again, track down the very same nurse, and then am put on hold again. When the nurse comes back, she tells me she checked the personal-items log the hospital keeps, and that no such items were listed for my father. She also did a spot-check of the room and came up empty. I ask if there's a hospital lost-and-found, and she says that there is, and that she'll connect me. Of course, I am disconnected again.

It takes few more calls to discover that lost-and-found's a dead-end, too, and when I ask for the name of the ambulance used, I get four. I want to cry.

I call them all. They, too, are dead-ends. Still, I leave our contact info. I don't even want to conjecture what all this might mean, but what it might mean is that I will probably need to replace my dad's glasses and wallet, which would mean tracking down the name of his optometrist to see if he or she would issue new eyeglasses, and if the prescription's too old to do this—which I'm betting it is—it would mean bringing Dad in for an appointment to have his eyes checked, then bringing him back when the glasses are ready to then have *them* checked, and I don't drive, and we don't have a car, and that only pertains to his *glasses*. Imagine the logistical nightmare of getting his wallet stuff replaced! Just to clue you in: There's his driver's license—

I think he'll need it as a proper ID, even if he never drives again—his social security card; his Bank of America credit card—I'll have to go to the bank with him and they'll require his ID—his other credit cards —I have no idea how many, or which ones, or if I'll even be allowed to make the replacement calls. If *he* has to call, I'll have to instruct him. Then there's his Harvard-Pilgrim card; his Medicare card and I'm sure there are more. More things I haven't even thought of. This is a disaster! My dad is a walking disaster.

He can't take care of himself, and now I will need to!

What this also is saying, of course, is that even if I *do* fix this stuff—and I frankly don't see how I ever can—it could happen again. He will stumble and fall and again be hospitalized and lose his glasses, wallet, key things.

What am I going to do?

What I do is, I go to my room, lie down on my bed, and pull the pillow over my head. Next, I start to cry, though I pinch myself to stop. I dig my nails into my palms and I don't stop. I feel so alone, so despairing, so afraid. *Why isn't my mother here?* I think. *I need my mother.*

"Mom," I utter aloud, which makes me cry more.

Where did she go? Why? Why now?

Why did she leave me?

I close my eyes and see her standing in the doorway with her silly knit slacks, a potholder over her hand. She smiles at me. But when I open my eyes, she's not there.

I cry and I cry, then I sniff and cry some more. Midway through, I turn on my fan so my father can't hear all my sobbing, then I cry much louder for a time. It's the only activity that fits: the only honest thing I can do.

"Mom," I cry one last time.

Then I think it: *Mommy! What am I going to do?*

I don't know how long I'm like this. My pillow gets pretty drenched, so I think it's some time. And then finally, it's weird, but I suddenly think about *God*. God is around, I recall. God exists. And my guru. I can't just forget about *them*. This gives me hope. Besides. I am the recipient of a prophecy, I've said. God couldn't want me to break it. Surely he wants me to go on.

And that's when I get this idea. It's a good one that might even work, so I get out of bed. I'll tell you about it—I promise—but first I think it's time I finally tell you about my prophecy.

Chapter 15

My prophecy took place when I was twelve. I'd been roller-blading with Janie along the Charles, and we were on our way home having reached the point where we customarily parted, and I was just saying my final good-bye to her. I turned my head around for one last shout when a car almost nailed me. It came speeding—and I mean *speeding*—around the corner. Of course, there *was* a corner, which means neither they nor I could see each other. Which means they were going too fast, since there was such a blind corner. This was on a side street off Moody—a street I had crossed a million times. I had just looked both ways before I'd turned and had just taken a step into the street when this car appeared. I felt it the exact same time I sensed it. This cyclone of air hit my face and I sensed the sheer jolt of its speed…

Granted, I wasn't looking exactly the second *before* I stepped into the street. And granted, you couldn't see or hear every single car from where I was, since it was a main street in a city, but in any case, I wasn't looking, and the driver clearly wasn't looking, either. He had a car full of friends, it turned out, and he was probably looking at them. Loud salsa music was pouring out of the car.

Anyway, I heard, then felt, then saw this for just a split-second and then I jumped back. Had I not, I would have been hit and would likely have been killed. The driver, at the same time, saw me and slammed on his brakes, and there was a screech, and his face was freaked-out, I recall. Our eyes met for an instant, and then he was gone.

I was so shaken up, I sat on the curb for a good fifteen minutes —okay, maybe more like five or ten, but it seemed like fifteen—my heart going wild in my chest and skipping some much-needed beats, then making up for the gaps by doing double-time, so that I thought I was having a heart attack—of course, it couldn't have been a heart attack; I mean, I was only twelve. So I sat there, stunned, while everything just kept on going on in slow motion, cars continuing down Moody Street; music coming out of said cars; people pulling into the bank behind me and going in.

Finally, when my heart had sufficiently slowed, I got up, and that's when this woman approached me. She asked if I was all right. I figure I must've looked funny—like my face was white as a ghost or something—a lot of time that had gone by since the incident, so I didn't believe she had witnessed the thing. If she had, she'd have spoken up sooner. Plus, right after the event, I had looked all around for reassurance—a person to even make *eye-contact* with—but there was no one. So all I could say was: "What do you mean?"

"You look like you've just had a fright," she replied.

"Yes," I returned. "Did you see it?"

"No. But I know about it."

This was odd.

The woman was in her late twenties, Hispanic, which was interesting, 'cause the driver of the car was also Hispanic, and what was *that* saying?—very attractive, with giant cat-like eyes that held your gaze. She was wearing loose gauzy yoga-like pants, a batik-printed shirt and sandals. She was noticeably slim. But returning to her eyes—for they were her most marked part—they actually shone. I know that sounds weird, even trite, but it's true. They did all of those things that you hear: glitter, sparkle, gleam.

Anyway, returning to what she had said about not seeing the scene yet knowing about it: I didn't even think to doubt her words, for I somehow knew to be silent And that's when she told me my prophecy. She told me I could have just died, but that I didn't, on purpose. That the whole thing was "planned in advance" to help make me open myself to what would come next, which was to say— her.

And then she told me, "The summer that you are sixteen, a momentous event will occur in your life that will require a decision on your part. Making the right decision will call for great courage, and it's important you rise to the occasion, for, in doing so, you'll fulfill your mission in life."

She smiled—big and wide—her eyes sparkled—and then she was done.

And what I did then was to nod, like I knew it was so. From then, I knew I was destined for greatness. It was the thinking of a twelve-year-old, of course—the thinking of all little kids—in fact, if she had proclaimed right then that I could fly to the moon, I would have believed that as well.

She turned to leave and I blurted out, "Wait!" as you would have, too, if you were me, for you'd have a million more questions to ask just like me. Even if you couldn't think of one at that moment, you'd *know* there'd be a million so you'd need her to wait.

She only turned and replied, "You have the answers here," and pointed to the center of her chest, and then walked off, whistling as she went. I didn't recognize the tune, though I knew it was nice.

But anyway, the reason I positively *know* what the momentous thing was that she mentioned in my prophecy, was when my mother died, I thought *that* was the "momentous" thing—I thought it *had* to be: it was pretty momentous—only that happened when it was spring—not summer, as predicted. And then, when the Center for Spiritual Union came to our town, when I first saw the flyer that advertised this, when I went to my first public talk—*then* it was summer, so that was the true, momentous thing. Finding my guru; finding his group; choosing to indeed be a nun…

That's how I know. And really, I did almost die.

And here's a cosmic aspect to all this: After I remember God and guru, and come to see that I can't just play dead, I get a call from the hospital. They've got Dad's wallet and glasses! I just have to go pick them up! How's *that* for cosmic?

Okay, and here's the idea I got after remembering God: The doctor inquired about a relative, and I, in turn, mentioned my aunt—who, like I said, is real—so now I start thinking, *Why not?* Why not place a call to my aunt and ask her up? It would ease my load, and I would feel better just having her here. An aunt, I reasoned, wouldn't leave me to foster care if something went wrong. At least I don't think she would. Not after she got to know me.

And either she'll say yes, is what I am thinking, *or else she'll say no. But even if she tells me no* now, *she could tell me yes* later—*the next time some key thing goes wrong in* her *life and* she *needs to escape*—which happens to people way more than you'd think.

It's worth a shot anyway.

And speaking of her life, I know this: She lives in Miami with her boyfriend—a guy she's not *really* that into, though she's been with him for years—and she works at some second-rate job, though I can't now think what. So if she's got this lame *job* she's not into, and this *boyfriend* she's not crazy about, either, and it's *July* in Miami right now—just contemplate *that*—why not take a road-trip up north to "The City to Watch?" Florida can be virtual hell in the dog days of summer, so it would be a good time to make my approach, I believe.

I make the call after deciding that I'm not going to tell her about my father just yet, 'cause that would be off-putting; and it's difficult asking for help; plus, she's my mother's sister, not my father's, so I'm simply going to invite her for a "visit."

Aunt Tony—that's short for Antonia—answers on the very first ring.

"Aunt Tony," I say. "It's your niece." There's noise in the background, so I add, "It's me. It's Mo."

"Mo," she says, like she's not all that sure who I am.

"Yes, me. How are you, Aunt Tony?" I ask.

"Oh, Mo…" she replies, trailing off. "I've been better." But that's where it ends.

"Gee," I respond. "That's too bad. I'm sorry to hear it." And I *do* sound sorry to the ear, though inside I am really thinking, *Jackpot!*

Aunt Tony just answers with, "Yeah." And I say, "Yeah." Then I ask her what's wrong, and she says, "What?" and I hear like all this noise once again but louder, like a TV is going nearby, and like there are several quite garrulous men in a nearby room, for I hear "hoo-ahs!" and claps and loud voices. Aunt Tony says, "*Quiet!* I'm on the *phone*! It's my *niece*!" Then she adds, "It's long *distance*!" like *that* really matters these days.

"Yeah," Aunt Tony goes on, "it's Phil—along with some other things." Then she tells me how Phil's not working right now, and how she's *also* not working right now, so there's no money coming in, and how, when there's no money coming in, it sure makes it easy to fight. And then she says—though I haven't had a chance to reply, "*Quiet!* I can't *hear!*" and then back to me: "Phil's got a bunch of the guys over to watch the game," and *then* she says, "Should I be *worried* if there are grown men in my house with bottle caps stuck to their foreheads?"

I smile, not only 'cause I'm thinking, *Mega jackpot!* but also 'cause I've seen Cameron do this. He licks the top of a Coke bottle cap, then sticks it on his forehead so it stays. It's kinda funny when he does it. And he does it without saying a word, which of course makes it funnier.

To Aunt Tony I simply say, "Well…"

"Hold on. Let me get these jerks to pipe down."

I hear only fragments, like "mess," and "volume," and "you're *kidding* me by saying that. Right?" Then I hear her name shouted, then something else I'm not able to catch, and then she comes back, saying, "Should I be *worried* if during the beer commercials with women in them, Phil starts *panting* at the women? I mean, I know he's only doing it for show. But *still*."

Luckily, she doesn't expect me to answer.

Finally I say to her, "Right. Well, listen. That sort of ties into my call. I was wondering if you want to come up? I mean, I know Miami's pretty hot this time of year, and my dad and I could use a little company, what with Mom gone and all, and, well, with you not working," I say, "and not getting on that well with Phil. You could make it a vacation! Stay just as long as you want." *Move in*, is what I am thinking. "It's nice in New England right now. You should really come up."

This is my nuts-and-bolts pitch and the best I can do, though at one point I do think to add how an "adult female presence" might be good, letting her think that I miss Mom, and that she could stand in as a surrogate of sorts, to ease my pain. I have no real illusions about this, but I figure if she thinks she'd be helping, she might be more likely to come, and she *would* be helping, just not in that particular way.

She says, "I'll think about it…" then she says, "No, you know what? I'll ask Phil. Hold on."

After a bang and a whistle, I hear her come back. "They actually asked me to make a *beer run* while they watch the game. They actually believe I'll *clean up* their big mess when they leave. Phil actually physically *goosed* me in front of his friends…Should I be *worried*?"

And I think, *Super-Mega-Jackpot!* and *I better clean out the spare room,* and I think, *Nunhood here I come!* but I say, "Well, you *could* worry. Or you could make a road-trip up here."

"I'm packing my bags," she replies.

Later I think: It's good that my aunt's coming up, 'cause, let's face it, I *really* can't take care of my father without help.

BIG HEAVEN

Chapter 16

Aunt Tony, as I said, is my mother's sisters—twelve years younger than my mother, which makes her forty-seven.

Aunt Tony has never been married, doesn't have kids, has trouble getting jobs—though no trouble accumulating boyfriends, or so I've been told—which is "not the ideal way for one to live one's life," to parrot my mother. Aunt Tony has lived in Tucson, San Diego, Lake Tahoe, and now Miami—all of your vacation spots. At most, we used to see her every three years—sometimes it stretched to every four. She showed for Mom's funeral, but only very briefly. Even my mom didn't talk to her much. As a result, I really don't know her that well, and I have no idea what my father thinks of her, but I'm about to find out for myself.

I approach the matter by talking to Aunt Tony, acknowledging how she is having spats with Phil, and doesn't have a job, and doesn't have much money coming in, so she should pay us a visit 'cause we could use a female presence in the house—in short, I play the Mother card—further acknowledging how we both had the thoughts—we did, but I helped put it there; I'm learning you have to be able to manipulate these things like this in life—and it was a very good idea, her making the trip.

My father says "Fine"—one of his all-time top-ten favorite words. So I answer, "Great," and he answers, "Fine."

Three days later, when Aunt Tony shows up, she is one hour and twenty minutes late according to Janie's stopwatch. I figure when you're driving from Miami up to Mass, being late by a little over an hour isn't all that bad.

Unfortunately, the announcement of Aunt Tony's arrival *is* bad— a shot from her sub-par exhaust pierces our ears.

Janie's thrilled. "*Somebody* seems to be here," is what she remarks. I look at my very best bud. She looks back.

We all go out—even my father. Aunt Tony is there in the driveway, extracting herself from her car—a beat-up Dodge Neon— wearing a jaw-dropping hat that is red, red, red.. It's straw, this red, red, red hat, and is boundlessly, lavishly brimmed.

Janie's more thrilled. I know that my friend wants to comment on the hat, so I elbow her hard in the ribs. "No commenting till you're *introduced*," I forewarn, though inside I am barely able to hold my smile…

I am very very very happy my aunt is here.

Everyone hugs—she even hugs Janie.

Janie stares at my aunt's hat will being tightly hugged.

Janie's even more thrilled.

Aunt Tony looks a little like my mom, though a skinnier version, maybe. She starts unloading her stuff and we offer to help, but Aunt Tony says, "No. No. It's good for me to finally move around. I've been sitting in that sardine-sized car far too long." She shakes her red hatted head at the car, then she says, "You girls just sit and have a visit"—as if I don't see *Janie* every second I'm alive; as if Aunt Tony herself isn't new—so of course, we help and she lets us. Before long, my father and Aunt Tony are in the family room, while Janie and I continue unloading…I am now, for a number of reasons, smiling broadly inwardly and outwardly:

First, most of my aunt's things aren't packed all that well. All right. Most of them aren't packed at all. They're loosely thrown in, like she left in a hurry.

I take her roller blades—roller blades??? Janie takes her laptop. I take her beach chair and umbrella. Janie takes her twelve-by-twelve TV. I take her boom box, made by Sony. Janie takes her Bose noise-canceling headphones—the large kind, which she hasn't, for some reason, updated yet. I take her yoga mat. Janie takes both of her pillows…

Of course—we each take several of these things at a time. I'm only spreading it out to make it dramatic for you.

Anyway, I take her lumbar-support cushion. Janie takes another big straw hat. Also red, red, red.

Most of it we carry to the guest room, but after awhile we just start dropping the stuff in the family room 'cause we're getting fatigued. I'm not sure the stuff will all *fit* in the guest room. My father just looks at it all, like he thought my aunt was coming for a day.

Aunt Tony says, "I'm sorry I have so much *stuff*; I didn't intend for you to work so hard. Of course, if I were *married* I wouldn't *have* so much stuff, because then what I'd have would be *joint* trappings, right? And I'd leave most of the joint stuff at home because my husband would need the stuff too, I presume—so I'd leave it. And then, too, I wouldn't be all that *attached* to my stuff because I'd *have* a real husband at home and I'd focus on *him*. But I'm not nice and happily married, am I? So instead I've got all this stuff to lug around, like my beach chair and CD player and food-processor…"

She looks lamely at the pile of her stuff, then continues. "Because I really wasn't sure you guys *had* all this stuff and I didn't want to just come out and *ask, s*o, sorry," adding, "you guys do have a juicer, right?"

Janie whispers, "Why wouldn't anyone want to get hitched to *her?*"

"Quiet," I mouth, giving ole Janie a frown while still smiling inwardly.

Next, my aunt looks at her watch and declares, "And I'm sorry I got here so *late*, but what happened was, I was on one of those roads around here—one-lane, you know, where you can't pass—and the guy in front of me, I *swear*, was going twenty just to bug me. I *swear* he was doing it for that. And he wouldn't let me pass, no matter what. I mean—I could have broken every last law in the book, and still he wouldn't," looking directly at Janie and me and finishing, "girls, don't ever break any laws."

We nod at my aunt. I think she likes having *two* of us here as it adds to her audience.

She looks out the picture window. Outside is our lawn, then a quiet suburban side street that runs straight in a line, then another lawn with woods behind the facing houses and cars in the driveways. Aunt Tony says, "Wow! We're really way out in the woods here, huh?"

That's one of her standard lines. Whenever she comes for a stay, she calls it "the woods." It isn't exactly Miami, I guess.

Janie says, "It's not '*the woods*'; it's 'The City to Watch', Aunt Tony."

I elbow Janie.

Aunt Tony ignores us. She's sweating at this point, though she really didn't do that much. She looks all around the cluttered room. "Why isn't the air conditioning on?"

We've never had air conditioning. She must be thinking of Miami again.

Janie says, "They don't have any."

"You don't have *air conditioning?* Well, that's just great! I'm in the woods, and it's a hundred degrees, and…"

Janie whispers, "I *think* we might have a complainer on our hands…*and* a blamer."

"Shhh," I try to say back, without making any noise. I am still somewhat smiling inside. My father, by contrast, looks confused that Aunt Tony's even here.

Finally, she says, "But listen to me just beating my gums and jabbering on. I should be checking on *you*. How are *you* all doing?"

She stares at all three of us at once. Then she comes over to me.

"And you, you sweet little thing. How are *you* doing, hon? You lost your *mother*—tch, tch."

It catches me so off guard, I don't know what to say.

Next, she goes up to my father and squeezes his hand. "And you. You lost your dear wife—tch, tch." At last, she points to herself, saying, "And me? I lost a very dear sister. What a real *shame*."

It's suddenly quiet in the room. No one breathes. Even the air outside the window is still. If we somehow actually *owned* an air-conditioner, it would momentarily quiet as well, I believe.

At last, Aunt Tony speaks up. "And look at me here now with you. I must look a fright after my trip, quite the fright." Then she says, "Who says that these days, you're thinking? It's a Masterpiece Theatre thing."

143

She removes her giant red red red hat—the one with the fancy brim. They must be a hit where she's from.

"You girls should think about getting yourselves a hat like this. They're great in the sun."

"They haven't caught on here just yet," Janie offers.

I elbow her before she says more.

"They will," my aunt replies.

"Good luck," says my old buddy Janie, though mostly under her breath.

I'm still internally smiling. Sort of.

Chapter 17

The first day, everything goes smoothly. My aunt spends most of her time placing her stuff throughout the house. She puts her food-processor/blender on the counter, along with her George Foreman grill, her wok—*we* have a wok, now we have two—her *Macrobiotic Healthful Living* recipe books, and cartons and jars of her food—garbanzo, soba, tea. *Our* food-processor/blender looks a little upset.

In the family room, she deposits her four weights—two each of five and eight pounds, her yoga mat—rolled-up, thanks to God, as a space-saver though it practically doesn't matter that the mat is rolled-up, as she puts it on top of her *step,* a two-foot-by-four-foot contraption that sticks out and could easily get in the way, our family room not being that big. In the bathroom, I find my aunt's flat-iron. There's also her hot-rollers—one seems to cancel the other, if you ask me, though I don't ask Aunt Tony; her L'Oreal Paris Excellence Cream, Triple-Protection, Ash-Blonde hair coloring; her fragrance-free Olay Regenerist Daily Regenerating Serum; her Olay Definity Anti-Aging Hydrating Cream *with* Essential Glucosamine Complex… you get the picture. Personally, I'd be a tad bit embarrassed to *have* so much anti-aging stuff, but maybe when *I'm* forty-seven-going-for-eighteen, I'll have a bunch of it, too. Next to all that is her eyelash-curler; a pair of tweezers; her Revlon Luxurious Lengths Mascara; six lipsticks—I should say six "ColorStay Soft & Smooth Lip Colors," all by Revlon, the shades incredibly similar after giving each a quick look —and a cover-up-stick-for-the-bags-that-show-under-the-eyes-when-you've-been-partying-all-hours-of-the-night—all right, it's *actually* called, I think, a "concealer," but you get the idea. And all right, too: Not *all* of this stuff is spread out for the masses to see. Some of it's stuffed in her makeup kit. But women *have* to check out each other's makeup kits. It's like this unwritten world-renowned rule. Plus, I have to admit: even though all her makeup takes up space—I like it. I'm glad that the bathroom's now just ours. That Dad will be using his own from now on.

So that's about it for Day One, except I do hear Aunt Tony call Phil on the phone three times. The first two times, she goes to the shady back deck to make the call. The third time I hear her say "Phil?" Then a pause, where he likely says, "Yeah?" And then she hangs up.

So that then is it for Day One.

It's a good first day's work, all-in-all.

I don't have to tell you—*I'm* thrilled.

So anyway, the next thing we know, it's Day Two. I sleep later than everyone else, and when I finally get up, I find Aunt Tony and my father in the kitchen, with bowls of what look to be gruel at each of our places, and a drink that is combination yellowy-orange and a pukey-hued-brown, and a big jar of wheat-germ in the center, for "extra flavor." My father is looking quizzically at the food—not eating. The juice, as I come to find out, is a carrot-soybean mix.

The moment I walk in the room, my father's expression lights up like I'm manna from heaven.

"Mo! Look who's here with us. It's the visiting nurse." He must have heard about a visiting nurse during his hospital-stay, 'cause no such quote "nurse" has dropped by, and no such nurse *will* soon drop by as I ripped up the orders for one, so he wouldn't have come by the inventive idea from that, though, admittedly, he may have come by it from the food that is sitting in front of him, which I'm not sure even a nurse would eat.

Aunt Tony looks at me.

I say, "No, Dad. No, no. It's Aunt Tony. You know Aunt Tony, Dad." This isn't going that well.

"Oh yes. Aunt Tony. Pleasure to see you again," my dad says, like she only arrived two minutes rather than two days ago. Then my father turns to me, and with *sotto voce* voice says, "Why didn't you tell me before I went out on a limb?" Then he turns back to my aunt. "So, Tony. To what do we owe this pleasure?"

Aunt Tony looks quizzically at me.

I say, "Oh. I asked Aunt Tony up to pay us a visit. I told you, Dad, about how it would nice for Aunt Tony to come stay for a while."

"Yes," my father says, "fine," nodding a bit to himself. Then he says, perhaps playing the mannerly host in our mannerly house, "I'm going to be watching the Patriots later today if you'd care to join me?"

This time, before Aunt Tony can look even more quizzical, I say, "Red Sox. Patriots. It's all the same," for it's still only mid-July, which means the Patriots haven't started playing just yet. I give Aunt Tony a smile.

My father says, "Yes. All the same. Except one is *football*."

He smiles too, like he's made a great joke at my expense. Then everyone smiles at once, to show all is fine. Well, my father and *I* smile. Aunt Tony really isn't smiling. Her mouth is intensely squinched up like she's doing higher math. I can see why men like her—why "accumulating boyfriends" isn't hard. She's pretty, my befuddled aunt, even *with* her wide mouth scrunched like that.

My father tries eating a small bite of the gruel. I take a sip of his "energy drink" to relieve him of it. "Mmm…Yum…Not bad."

My aunt gives me an even more quizzical look.

I give her a smile.

And that, at least for now, is how we leave it.

After breakfast, I survey the kitchen. There are dishes piled high in the sink, dishes on the Formica counter, dishes on the burners of the stove. The "gruel"—which is a barley-and-whole-grain-rice mix—took two pots, three measuring cups, and a spoon. The juice took a vegetable peeler, a cutting board, three knives, and a blender/food-processor, including three different *blades*. The whole presentation required some other odd stuff. Apparently, my aunt is mad about cooking, but not about cleaning up, so I decide to. This should be good for some brownie points, I think.

Afterwards, I pull Aunt Tony aside, so I can explain about Dad. She's got a kickboxing DVD queued-up in her player all ready to go, but she puts it on hold.

I say how Dad really was fine, but how he seemed to just plummet downhill when Mom died. I tell her how he was hospitalized only last week, and suffered "delirium" while there, and how we are still likely seeing the tail end of that. Then I tell her about his pills—how he has them, and how it's important he takes them, and how, when he doesn't, he might just exhibit a lapse, but how, in general, really, he's fine.

My aunt gives me a skeptical look, staring at me without moving her eyes. Then she says, "Thank you for telling me, Mo," and stares for even *longer* without moving her clear blue eyes as if to see what I'll do. And *then* she says: "Listen. This junk-mail just arrived the other day, or

148

maybe it *isn't* junk mail. It's an ad for one of those speed-dating gigs that they have called 'Singles on the Go'. I was wondering if you've heard of them, beause I was thinking of checking them out. When I'm free."

This could be helpful, I think. This would take her mind off of Dad, while at the same time helping her lay down roots. Dating is good.

"Yeah," I say. "I've heard of them. They're good. A lot of people… meet people that way," I say.

This is true. I don't go into what *kind* of "people" they meet. I don't know how perfect the unions are. I only say people can meet people, which is true.

This seems to bolster my aunt.

"Okay, good. Well I'm going to check it out. I did something like it in Miami in fact…" She stops right there, like she'd rather not rehash Miami. Then she says, "But really, these kinds of services tend to be a ripoff. I don't know why I bother. And when you *do* meet the guys, they sit like a lump on a log, and it's all up to you. Like it's the *woman* who's the utterly desperate one, when, really, *they're* laying out bucks, too. And all of the time that they're sitting like a lump on a log, they're checking out your *boobs.* I swear!" She makes a sour face. Then she says, "Oh well, what am I going to do? Roll over and die? No. What I'm *going* to do is get these here abs in shape, then I'm taking it to the streets, girlfriend. Watch out!"

I know it's hokey, but I like her calling me "girlfriend." Janie would be *thrilled* by it, but thrilled in the way she was thrilled with Aunt Tony's straw hat. Not "thrilled-thrilled" is what I am saying. Not literally, if you know what I mean.

She points the remote at her queued DVD, and presses it to get back to her kickboxing. My father is a far-away memory right now, I guess.

Anyway, in addition to doing the dishes after breakfast on Day Two, in the busy days that follow, I do other domestic chores.

For one thing, I still end up doing the grocery shopping like before, only now, I shop for the stuff Aunt Tony requires as well, 'cause, when you think about it, Dad and me are *two* people, while Aunt Tony is only one, and it's fairer for a person from the two-person group to step up. And so what if she's got "clear requests?" I can understand, considering the macrobiotic diet she's on—I think she went on it in Tucson, by the way, not Miami. In any case, what ends up happening is, I make a special trip to the Newtonville Whole Foods, and sometimes to Trader Joe's too, when, before I just went to the Hannaford right here in town and called it a day. But Aunt Tony has "definite needs," as I've mentioned, like shiso powder, green-brown lentils and kale.

Another household chore I've taken on is doing the dishes—every day, every meal—'cause Aunt Tony doesn't like to, plus she cooks, and, again, she is just one person, while my father and I are two, and how much does a single person use in the course of a day? A plate, a glass, a spoon…unless that person's diet is macrobiotic, in which case that person has to soak and then steam her brown rice every day—brown rice is sticky—and cook her gross kale every day, and siphon the juice from her kale so she can then drink it, and peel, core, and chop all her vegetables to put in the blender, and I'm not even telling you all of it.

And I vacuum, too. Well, I vacuum her small room 'cause I'm already vacuuming everywhere else and what's one more small room?

And I do the main bulk of her laundry while I'm doing our own.

In truth, she's ending up being lots of extra work for me, really. But what I am thinking is, it's the honeymoon period. It won't go on forever.

I'm planning to ask Aunt Tony for help, and I'm going to explain before very long in a very nice way. But for now, I want her to feel welcome. I mean, I *definitely* want her to stay. At least for a while.

After a week of Aunt Tony, I find that I've got stuff I have to do, so instead of meeting Janie as pre-planned, I call her to tell her I can't meet her.

"Why?" she says. "What's up?"

"Well, I've got some dishes I need to do, and some vacuuming. And I really need to run a few errands after that."

"*Dishes*?" my good bud remarks. "Since when do you *cook*?"

I should have seen that coming.

"Aunt Tony cooks," I reply, thinking this sounds majorly good—having a live-in who cooks.

"Well why doesn't she also do the dishes?" Janie asks.

"You know. One person cooks, one person washes," I say.

She waits. I can picture her face. Then she says, "And *vacuum*? Since when do you *vacuum*?"

"I just want the place looking nice. That's all."

"For Aunt Tony I presume."

"Yes."

"Well if *Aunt Tony* likes the place looking nice, why doesn't *Aunt Tony* vacuum?"

This doesn't deserve a reply, so I sit and I wait. Finally she says, "Okay. So there's dishes and vacuuming. I can't picture *those* things consuming your life."

"Well I have to pop over to Whole Foods later as well."

There's a pause. It's an expression of shock. "Whole Foods isn't even in *town*. You don't just 'pop over'," Janie states.

"I know."

"You don't even have your license yet, you know."

"I know that."

"You guys don't even have a *car*, unless you include Aunt Tony's old heap, which I wouldn't. You'll have to take the smelly bus," Janie states.

"I know."

"So you're going to take a bus, schlep all the way out to Whole Foods, and then what? Jam all the stuff in your *backpack* to *carry* it back?"

"That's right."

There's another pause. I can picture her face. "All for Aunt Tony, of course?"

"Yes."

"Well?"

"Well what?"

"Well why are we doing all this for good old *Aunt Tony?*"

"Oh. She's on this macrobiotic kick, you know, and she's always running out of things…"

"That's not what I mean. She could do *something*," says Janie.

"Oh. Well. She would, but she had to go meet this new guy. For this dating service she joined." I know what Janie's going to say next, so I don't give her a chance to speak. "But I look at it this way: she's putting down roots, which is what I want. And you know my aunt. If something's more than a block or so away, like Whole Foods, she says we're 'in the woods' which I'd rather not hear. Plus, I want her to *like* it in Waltham."

I don't really have to explain these things to Janie, but I do anyway.

Janie says, "I thought your aunt came up here to *help*. Not so you could help *her*."

"It's the honeymoon period still," is what I say back. "You can't forget *that*." There's a smile slightly showing on my face that Janie can't see.

"Well I sure hope Aunt Tony is worth it," she says, obviously not "getting" the honeymoon period.

"She is," I retort, though inside I'm thinking, *I am, too*.

At some point, Janie got wind of the fact—all right: I told her—that Aunt Tony's been complaining about the lack of good services nearby, the lack of "real stores" in our town—by that, I think she means Saks—the absence of day spas within walking distance, so we give my aunt a tour of "The City to Watch." We figure she should know her way around, especially if she's going to be staying for any length of time—I *hope* she is. We travel to downtown on foot, 'cause A) we don't have a car, and B) we don't drive—or have I got that that reversed?—and C) it's what teenagers typically do when they need to get around—riding bikes would be *gauche*. We could of course pile into Aunt Tony's car—the beat-up Dodge Neon, I mentioned—but Janie and I *like* walking. Besides, Janie wants to see her wear her hat.

She wears her hat.

At first, all goes well. When we get to downtown, Janie says, "There's McDonald's, there's the Exxon, there's Joseph's II Family Dining." We haven't unearthed Joseph's I as of yet. "And there's Watch City Petro—it's actually called that. There's the 'Parking-in-Rear/For-Lease' building…"

I cut in and say, "There's the Wendy's where *Janie* works," and give my buddy a shove—which is really an elbow, though shove sounds better.

"Open till two AM. 'It's good to be nocturnal'," Janie says, quoting a banner in the window that shows a raccoon ogling a chicken-fillet. "'Do what tastes right'," she adds, again quoting Madison Ave.

So far so good.

"There's the 'CVS-slash-pharmacy'. It's open twenty-four hours," Janie says. "There's Tony D's Convenience Shop complete with Keeno, snack bar, sandwiches. The Marlboro's are special price: four-seventy-six. And there's The Mad Raven. It's a bar. There's Joe Sent Me, another bar. There's Bullets Bar & Grille, another bar…you should really try and pop into those; they'd like your red hat. Then there's Dunkin Donuts…" Janie says. I figure we're going to stop there, 'cause once you have found Dunkin Donuts, why go on?

But we don't. Instead, we turn left. And that's when the day starts to turn, too.

"There's Immanuel Cleaners. That's where Mo's dad likes his dry cleaning done. And there's the Hannaford Grocery where he gets all his food. He doesn't go in for that nature stuff. And there's Maria's Home Cooking where he likes to get lunch…tomorrow you can bring him down."

Janie waits.

Aunt Tony just gives her a look, then she says, "Don't tell me: 'Mo's dad' is a code for *you*. As in: you want me to bring both of *you* there for lunch."

"No," Janie says. "Mo's dad. And there's Waltham's very own Blockbuster where you can rent him his movies."

I'm positively horrified. Leave it to Janie. I want Aunt Tony to *like* it up here. We haven't yet sat for our one-on-one chat, so I *have* to speak up.

I say, "I think what Janie means is, like, you know, on the days that I work. If it's just you and Dad in the house and you want to get out. See a few of the sights in 'The City to Watch'."

I'm trying to keep it light. I smile.

"Yeah, right," Janie says. "Sure. Or *maybe*, whenever Mo's father actually *needs* anything, *you* could go get it. You know where everything is now," she states.

I glare at Janie.

She glares back, then returns to my aunt. "None of it's far, as you can now see. Waltham's not *only* 'The City to Watch,' it's 'The City That Has Tons of Stuff All Packed into a Small Area'. You're now a witness to this."

She gives Aunt Tony a smile, though she shows only lips.

Aunt Tony starts to fiddle with her hat, as if a great wind has come up. Janie, I think, makes her nervous.

Anyway, little by little, my aunt starts noticing things about my dad. Of course, she's bound to.

One morning, she told me how, when they were hanging in the family room together, he mentioned his parents. Something about how his parents were coming to stay, so they'd have to clean out the spare room to get the place ready for them (the spare room's the room where Aunt Tony is staying).

"It was like he thought his parents were alive," she remarked. Then: "Didn't they *die* a long time ago, or do I have that wrong?" And I had to tell her, no, she didn't have that wrong. I then went back to his pills—about how he has them, and how they help him with memory—perfectly normal, I added, given his age—and how, if he forgets to take them, he gets confused, but how, really, in general, he was fine. I had been helping with his pills—handing them to him when I was home, and calling him when I was not. Sometimes it went well and sometimes it didn't. And sometimes *I* forgot to call him. Sometimes I was really pretty lax…but, oh, well. I didn't go on with the rest, which was that if *she* could help out here and there—like help Dad take his pills—that would be good. And if she could drive him where he needed to go, or just to get him out of the house, that would be even better. And, if she could do her own *grocery shopping…*

Of course, I didn't say all that 'cause it's too soon. The honeymoon period is what I was still thinking.

But anyway, after I mentioned his pills, she let it all go and remarked, "You know, it felt a little passive-aggressive in a way—that thing about cleaning out my room—like he wasn't too happy to have me here," to which I replied, "Oh, no! He's thrilled. I'm sure." My aunt gave a skeptical look, so I tacked on, "Really. He's incredibly easy to get along with. But you can see that for yourself."

This at least was true.

He is the one who cleans his plate; he always says things like, "Fine," and "Swell," and "The pleasure is really all mine," and "Nuts" instead of a swear word like balls, or shit, or F something, so as to never ever offend. He was brought up in the fifties, as I mentioned. In *Maine,* don't forget.

However, regarding what Aunt Tony had said, I *had* noticed that whenever she entered a room, my dad did *not* say: "*There* she is!" the way he did when it was me, nor did his eyes light up. They turned a metal-gray and clouded-over. In fact, I was getting the feeling myself that Dad wasn't thrilled she was around. She does take an awful lot of energy, my aunt.

Anyway. Leaving that behind for a moment, and moving on: Another time, Aunt Tony told me that she found the peanut butter stuffed in the freezer, the ice cream stashed in the fridge, and the root beer jammed in where the peanut butter goes, and I said to her, "Yeah. I know. He does that." Then I said, "To be perfectly honest with you, I do it, too. You know, you're in a rush, and you shove the mayo where the granola bars go. Maybe you've done that as well?"

I wasn't sure how this would play, and held my breath.

And *then* Aunt Tony said, "And you know he left the stove on."

It was like she was saving this one—like this was the bomb she'd let drop.

I thought: *Oh no*! I thought: *This is it*! I thought: *We're sunk*!

Aunt Tony just stared, so I didn't know what I to do or say, and did nothing at all like a deer caught in her headlights.

After a full solid minute of staring, she went on, "But he said he was coming right back to heat up some soup when I asked him, so that's why the burner was on."

I nodded, and added, "Right," but Aunt Tony continued to stare, like she knew *something* was up. Actually, you'd think it would be pretty clear by now…

So then I start to worry. Not only do I worry about the stove being on—was Dad *really* going back to make some soup, or was he simply just covering up and had really forgotten? I also worry about Aunt Tony just *being* with Dad—what more he might do and try to conceal that she might finally see. In fact, I end up worrying *so* much about what Aunt Tony will think, that I don't even worry about *Dad*. But here's the thing: Aunt Tony is key to my plans for helping take care of my father, so in worrying about what *she* thinks, I really am worrying about Dad, right? At least, that's the way I choose to look at these things.

In any case, over the next two weeks, my aunt stops being a spy, and instead becomes Helen of Troy. The Mata Hari. Cleopatra. Any famous flirt or *femme fatale*. She's met someone through "Singles on the Go," which makes me glad. It means she is laying down roots, which I like. The only thing is—she is hardly ever at home. Between her pilates class at Yoga Plus, and her *teaching* a kickboxing class there, and her now seeing this "single" who is surely "on the go," and whose first name is Dan. Pro: Less time at home to see if the stove is on. Con: Less time at home to see if the stove is on.

Chapter 18

Still, even though my aunt's really busy, one day, as she's going out and I'm coming in, she says, "We have to make time to have a chat—me and you," which makes me worry that when we *do* "have a chat," she's going to complain about my father, inquire about his condition, and ask if it's the reason I invited her up.

Some of the reasons for this thinking are as follows:

First, he still doesn't seem all that sure she's really moved in.

Next, he still doesn't know who she is all the time.

Finally, he still thinks his *parents* might move in, which would necessitate my aunt moving out.

Of course, this doesn't go on all the time. Sometimes he's quite lucid. Sometimes he knows all too well that Aunt Tony's moved in, and that she isn't moving out all that soon, that both her and her "singular diet" are here to stay.

In any case, we do indeed "have a chat." It happens one day right after lunch when both of us are, oddly enough, home, she having just returned from a spin class, me from a run—okay, it was a walk to Good-for-U Health Food Emporium on Moody Street where I picked up some spices, namely, ume, plum vinegar, barley, miso and sage for my aunt. On seeing me walk through the door, however, all of her good barley-miso intentions fade away, and new ones take their place.

"Why don't we whip up some brownies and have a nice talk? I feel like a girl-talk today."

"Okay!" I instantly reply, nodding my assent. At the mention of "brownies" and especially "girl-talk," all my fears about her bringing up my father instantly leave, and other expectations take their place.

I'll be honest with you. I've been looking for signs from my aunt of her being the "nurturing type," 'cause if I want her to take care of my father, it would be good if she was and, I'll be honest with you yet again, I haven't seen too many signs of this. A brownie slash girl talk endeavor, however, seems nurturing. It makes me think about my mother, almost as if Aunt Tony *is* my mother, except my mother never baked, though she was always there in the kitchen when I got home. The kitchen was always so warm, though not from baking, more from those fragrant roast chickens she made that I told you about—I will *never* forget those roast chickens. The minute they were done, but before they were "served officially," I'd pick at their skins, relishing their grease, eating right over the pan, and my mother never denied me this treat—me picking her roast chickens skin-bare. In fact, she encouraged me. After all: I was her only child and those chickens were roasted for me, pretty much, as I recall. I'd pick and pick and pick, expressing my pleasure with "yums," and this made her glad. So my "okay!" just now to my aunt might be perceived as a tad enthusiastic, certainly more than the circumstance warrants, as perhaps I associate her brownies with those fabulous birds. I guess I miss my mom…but that's all right. Mustn't forget the etymology of the word "enthusiastic:" It comes from the Greek *entheos* meaning "having God within," and, as I've said before: having God within is a pretty good state. Besides. I wouldn't mind a lengthy chat with a female adult…

Aunt Tony opens the print-smudged refrigerator door. "Hmm. Problem: We're out of eggs. Oh well. We can substitute oil, and that will taste fine." She rummages about in the cabinets—the high ones and low ones below the stove and above the microwave, and next to the stainless-steel sink. Then she says, "Second problem: It looks like we don't have oil *or* brownie mix…I thought *everyone* always had oil and brownie mix." She smiles at her own little joke, then says, "Well it's better for our waistlines this way. Right?"

"Right!" I agree with just the smallest edge of disappointment in my voice.

"Okay. Well let's just sit right here and have a chat. I'll make tea."

"Okay!" I say and sit.

She makes us tea by filling two cups with water, sticking them in the microwave to heat them, then plopping into each a rounded Chanakara vanilla honeybees tea bag. "It's known for its liver-cleansing traits. Also for its kidney-cleansing traits. Third Chakra," she says with a smile.

"Okay!" I say.

Her hands ring her mug. "This is nice."

I smile, thinking about ten—okay, a hundred—ways how to make it nicer, thinking ahead of what I can *add* to this talk, though it hasn't officially started yet. I sip my tea and tell her it's good. Then, just to be funny, I add, "I feel my liver cleansing as we speak."

She laughs—which is good—though with my mother I never felt the need to make jokes, but that's all right: 'Different strokes for different folks', right?

She says, "So I want to tell you about my guy. I already told my friend Sue in Miami, but now I want to tell you." Then: "I guess I just want to tell everyone!"

I lift my eyebrows some, like I'm waiting for something real good, really juicy, like we two are "girlfriends" and she can dish freely with me.

She raises *her* eyebrows too, like the sex is real good. Then she says, "Okay. Well. Let's see…He's fifty-one. I'm forty-seven, to be honest, but I tell people forty or forty-one, depending on my *mood.*" She winks. "But he looks really young," she goes on," and he's got all his hair. And he's not even a little bit overweight. Well—not much. Those things are key, by the way, when a guy gets into his fifties, Mo. Mark my words. Though a hairline that's slightly receding is not all *that* bad."

I nod like to say, when *I'm* forty-seven (i.e. "forty-one"), *I* won't mind a receding hairline either.

"So he's handsome…and fun," she goes on. "He's got the best sense of humor in the world. You can't underestimate that in a man. And the best part is…drum roll, please…he seems to really *like* me. You can't underestimate *that* in a potential beau, either."

I nod like I understand, and I really think I do. I watched the first-ever *Bachelorette* on Netflix, and in it, right at the end, Trista had to choose between two guys, and she chose the bachelor I would have chosen. The one who was ga-ga for her. The one who wrote her love poetry. She *didn't* choose the other guy; the one who said that they could "work on their relationship…maybe": turn it into something "sort of special…perhaps." *Good choice, Trista,* I thought. *Way to nail it.* So I know what Aunt Tony is saying right here.

She then shyly brings up his job, telling me Dan is a bartender at a really nice inn—"Free drinks!" she says with a wink—but how he really only does that "between jobs," 'cause what he *really* wants to do is start his own business on the web, and how, if you're looking to start your own business, you should do it on the web. "Am I right?" she asks with a squint.

"Right!"

Dan's idea, she tells me next, is to take traditional slogans, develop a new twist on them, then put them on T-shirts and mugs. Stuff like that. She gives the example that *he* gives the most, which is the slogan, "There's no place like OM," which would pander to meditators and such. "Good. Huh?" she asks.

I nod, thinking it *is* pretty good.

"Now, he didn't *come up* with that one—it's just an example—but he did, on his own, think up this: 'I did not have sex with that woman. But I'm working on it.' And, '*I* didn't inhale, either.' Those are cuts on Clinton's lines, in case you didn't recognize them. Good. Huh?" she repeats.

I nod again, though I'm pretty much thinking I've heard both of those before.

My aunt sighs. She takes a long sip of her tea, then looks around our small kitchen as if seeing it for the very first time. As if we *might* just be at a tropical outdoor café, and she's only appreciating it now after conquering jet lag. "Gee this is nice."

I nod and she sighs. Then she sighs some more, like she wishes Dan were with us right now—here at this "outdoor café in romantic Cancun," or rather like she wishes he was with her *alone*, and not in a public setting either, more like in a private cabana with the flap zipped-up tightly—sigh; sigh. She looks out at nothing but air as far as I can see. Then, starting to come to, she says, "Oh. And in the meantime—until he gets his business going—he might move back in with his mother."

She waits, slyly checking me out, so I no more than nod. Then she tells me she knows how it sounds—a man of fifty-one, moving back in with his mother—but "that's just how narrow minds think." How the way you need to look at it is this: His mom's got the room, and Dan's got this crummy apartment even a rat wouldn't like, and if he's there he can keep his mom company so it's really win-win. At least until his web business takes off, and then who knows? Maybe they could build a whole compound of houses. "Who knows?" my aunt gamely restates.

"Who knows?" I repeat.

Part of me *does* believe this, but another part is thinking about that conversation we had on the phone, roughly a month ago, where my aunt was complaining about her no-account then-boyfriend Phil, prefacing all of her questions with: "Should I be *worried*...?" like "Should I be *worried* if there are grown men in my house with bottle caps stuck to their foreheads?" "Should I be *worried* if Phil tries to *goose* me in front of his friends?" And now I think we could preface what she says about Dan the very same way: "Should I be *worried* if my bartender boyfriend's going to live with his *mother*?" But like I said—only part of my being thinks this. The other part believes the "Who knows?" part. Besides. My aunt is basically beaming at me between sighs, so I, like a "girlfriend," beam back.

All right. Yes. True. I haven't made my move to "Level B," where I tell my aunt exactly what I expect from her. Where I try to, at long last, come clean with my aunt, but I want her entrenched before I try. I want her to like it here. To be unable to contemplate *not* living here. To have too many ties, so that whatever "here" might next present, she will deal with it gladly. Or, if not entirely "gladly," still, she will deal.

So that is my plan.

"Level A" for the moment, "Level B" for the future.

Chapter 19

In any case, there isn't endless open time to think about it, 'cause the very next day Janie calls me. She tells me we're meeting by the river today, and that she's not taking no for an answer. I fully acquiesce 'cause it is Janie, 'cause she said that she's not taking "no," and 'cause I've had it with vacuuming.

She gives me the details, which is nothing very new: two-ish; our bench; bring chips. Then she tells me Cameron's coming. And *then* she tells me to wear my hair down—not in its summertime braid—as she and Cameron have a bet as to how I look best, and need to see me with my hair down.

This is a little bit strange.

I shrug before saying okay.

And then it's weird: When I get to the river, Cameron is very much there, on the bench, but there's no Janie. This is weird, 'cause Cameron either comes with Janie, or comes after Janie is there, as if it's an after-thought only on his part. As if he "happened" to be in the area, saw me and Janie on the bench, and decided to join us. But now Cameron's present without Janie.

This is scary weird.

"Hey," he says when I arrive.

I utter, "Hey." It's just what you say to a boy—you would never say the ultra-nerdy "hi."

Then we just sit, pretty much—Cameron leaning forward on his knees, me being sure to do the opposite, which means leaning back. It's like we are posed—"Strangers on a Riverside Bench one nice day"—and then there is nothing. Silence. Crickets. Cars. And it pretty much stinks, I decide, for here I now am with a boy—a boy who is *Cameron*—and there's nothing to say. And you can't count on boys to converse. Everybody breathing knows that. Or at least—not most boys, and Cameron fits into this "most boys" group, which means all it's up to me...

This stinks. Really. I mean it. By way of starting, I say, "What's up?" This is cool. I am trying to be "cool."

And Cameron says, "Not much. How 'bout with you?"—which again totally stinks.

"Not much." Then, "Well, you know my aunt is up."

"Oh yeah, I heard. How's that going?"

"Oh, good. Good...Everything's swell," I add on. I say it with sarcasm—nobody ever says "swell". Janie would be proud. Though I don't want to be sarcastic-sarcastic. Only cool-sarcastic. And only in front of cool Cameron.

We sit.

Another reason being alone with Cameron stinks is that I can't stare at his neck. It would be way too obvious. With only two of us here on the bench, anything either of us does is open season. Look all you want, but *do not* look all you want 'cause it'd be way too obvious. But if Janie were here, she could create a diversion, and *then* I could look. But Janie isn't right here, which means neck, you are definitely out.

I'm thinking all this, so not talking, which means it is quiet—as I said, boys don't talk—till Cameron finally says, "So what have you guys been up to—you and your aunt?"

I'm surprised that he talked—quite pleased. I say, "Janie gave her a tour of 'The City to Watch'. *That* was good." I give another wry smile.

Cameron says, "I'm sure," and I say, "Oh, yeah. She's got this red hat, you know? And Janie told her she should visit like all of these bars, so people could *see* her red hat, 'cause they'd love it."

Cameron just shakes his sweet head with a smirk of his own. I love his wry smirk—I love *him*—which makes me think that I shouldn't be alone with him here. Which makes me wonder just what we are doing by the river alone. Which, of course, makes me think about Janie.

"Where is she?" I wonder aloud.

"Your aunt?" he facetiously says, 'cause he knows I'm not referring to my aunt.

"No. Janie."

Some geese paddle by.

"Maybe she's in bars with your aunt."

I give him a look.

He looks back. I love his eyes: they're a perfect green. Then he says, "Maybe she isn't coming."

Something in the way that it's said—the matter-of-fact way—makes me think he might be in on this. It makes me think he might know that I like him, courtesy of Janie.

I pray to the universe not. But maybe.

Some ducks paddle by.

I say, not knowing what *else* I can say, "You think she stood us up?"

"Maybe," he replies, and then he says, looking right into my eyes, "but why would she do that?" And so he knows. Damn that Janie —not really—she has no right. She's obviously only doing this to discourage me from being a nun, using Cameron as her "weapon" though what she believes will take place on a public park bench, I don't know. "The City to Watch" *must* have spectators watching. But then I think: If Cameron was in on it, too, that means he likes me as well or he wouldn't have come. So now both of our secrets are out. I want to wring Janie's neck.

Still, I'm not admitting to anything. I'm putting it back on Janie. With what sounds like a trembling voice I say, "Well if she *is* trying to set us up, it was brilliant of her to do it on a public park bench. What did she think would happen?"

"You never know," Cameron says. So now it is even more clear: He definitely likes me. He leans in just a little to prove it.

My hands are shaking. They literally are. That's why she told me to wear my hair down...to think I was fooled they were going to have a vote.

Cameron says, "So do you have any theories on this?" and looks at me with those eyes.

It's ridiculous. It's Cameron...It's *Cameron*...If there was anyone I wouldn't be a nun for, it would be him.

But I am going to become a nun.

He leans in more.

Those are his eyes, his lips. That brand new body of his. I say, "You know she's only doing this 'cause she doesn't want me being a nun, right?"

And he says, "Are you a nun yet?"

"No."

"Then I guess I can kiss you. Janie says that you need the experience," he adds.

"Oh. So you're doing this just to please Janie?"

"I'm complicit, too," he answers.

It's one of those "melt-you" lines. Totally utterly "melt-you."

I try to think about God.

Cameron leans in. He puts his arm around me. It rests on the back of my neck, touches my shoulder.

He's warm. He's wearing short sleeves, so I can feel the warm touch of his skin. I'm always cold, but he's warm. I close my eyes, not thinking too much about God, for, it is true that I'm *not* a nun yet. I feel his lips, and then that is it. Cameron is kissing me. Magic. I can't believe how it feels. It's wet, soft, warm. It's all of those things that you hear. It's absolute heaven. And then he uses his tongue, and that's heaven, too. He wraps his other arm around me; I wrap mine around him. I use my tongue, too—it's only my second French kiss! It's stunning. I want to rip off my clothes right here on this public park bench and…I mean, it's Cameron!

At one point, he says, "If you want me to stop, say 'stop'."

He's toying with me. He knows I don't want him to *stop*. It's like offering an addict more drugs, I would guess, though, *Not fair!* is what I think next. *God certainly has a lot to compete with!*

Later, I tell myself it was a meaningless momentary lapse.

I refocus.

These things happen.

Why, even the saints have troubles, and I'm no saint—surprise! Saint Anthony, to name only one, was tempted by many different people in his life, people who tried to get him to stray from his deepest belief—that isolation was the truest form of worship. Ammonaria, one of his sister's friends, tempted him with sensuality. The Queen of Sheba tempted him with riches. And Hilarian, a former student of his, tempted him by morphing into Science. Imagine that! And of course there were Jesus' temptations, and those of Saint Joseph. And the Buddha was tempted by dancing girls, right before attaining liberation under his tree...

Damn that Janie.

Later I think: It's sort of too bad that you can't be a nun and still have a boyfriend, and, you know, still get married and have sex, but there's a reason why you can't, and I'm fully "down" with this reason. It's that whole you-can't-cross-a-lake-in-two-boats thing. If you try to cross a lake in two boats—with one foot in one, and one in the other—you're not going to get very far. That whole you-have-to-make-a-choice idea. You can't serve both God and mammon. What all of this *really* is saying, however, is simply that if you want God—if nothing else will do—you have to devote your whole life to Him. You have to forget boys. Put God first.

Here is a story I heard about this: One day, a man came across the most beautiful woman he'd ever seen, and, on seeing her, he became instantly enthralled, and started vowing his undying love, and asking if she would be his for all time. The woman replied, "I'll consider it. But first, you must go see my sister, who lives just down the lane, and who is even more beautiful than I."

On hearing this, the man immediately took off to find the sister; but on finding her, he discovered an ugly hag, so he rushed right back, saying, "You lied to me. Your sister is not more beautiful than you." And the woman replied, "You lied, too. You swore your undying love, and then you took off." This is how God feels when we choose His gifts, His world, His *maya*, over Him.

We must not be the man who rushes off.

So, clearly, I cannot pursue things with Cameron. I have to resist. It's like when you want that second helping of dessert, though you know you must not, and you know if you *do* take the plunge, you'll gain like a hundred-zillion pounds. It's just like that. You could also compare it to walking past a really cute house in your town—not Cameron's—just when it's starting to get dark, and lights are coming on, so you can see the inside really clearly, and someone you know—not Cameron—is visible there in the window, maybe watching TV, and you want to just stare for all time. But you don't.

Resisting temptation is like that.

I can see now why they cloister folks.

BIG HEAVEN

Chapter 20

Time passes, and still Aunt Tony's not helping, so I decide to make my move. I've given it plenty of thought, and if Aunt Tony's going to be all cozy with me, all "let's-dish-about-Dan," all buddy-buddy-over-tea, then I can be cozy with her and lay it on the line for her. But first, I decide to throw a dinner party for her and her beau, as a kind of grand gesture. I figure I *have to* perform a grand gesture, 'cause asking my aunt to take over when I leave is quite grand—I'm talking this summer flying back to L.A. with the monks and nuns. The least I can do is throw a dinner party for her.

As for the invitees, in addition to Aunt Tony, the boyfriend, Dad, Janie—the usual suspects—I'm even going to mention it to Cameron, to show that I'm not enamored of him. To show this to Janie, to Cameron, and yes, to show this to myself, but especially to show it to Janie so she'll drop all her match-making stuff.

We work it so that Janie will furnish the wine. We could just have Aunt Tony buy—she *is* the requisite age, after all, which here is a ripe twenty-one—but the dinner party's *for* her, so I really don't want her to do anything, plus Janie really *wants* to do it. Ian Burchill has a brother it turns out, who occasionally buys, and Janie wants a reason to talk to Ian.

I offer Janie money for the wine, but she tells me "no sweat," it's on her. "Whatever money I spend on the wine, won't be *near* the price of admission this thing will be worth."

I try to believe that that's good.

But really, Janie is great, 'cause she's using money from Wendy's for the wine, and let me tell you this straight-from-the-hip: they don't pay a whole lot of money at Wendy's.

I, for my part, will use my Embassy-Cinema money to cover the food—which isn't a big wad of cash either, let me say—though I'm not about to *cook*. Instead, I find this Asian place that doesn't use MSG, and that can cook "macrobiotically," and that supposedly never uses animal products—who knows, really—and I pass the idea by my aunt, who tells me it's great; she *loves* the idea of a dinner party, and I arrange for the food to be delivered.

When it's time for the dinner, Aunt Tony and I are downright giddy. It's almost like what I imagine college would be like—getting ready on a Saturday night to go to a frat party—which I won't ever get to do—or what it would be like getting ready to go visit Cameron at *his* college on a Saturday night—which I also won't ever get to do. Still, I can picture these things in my mind in our giddy state.

Aunt Tony and I get dressed before we put our makeup on, so we don't mess up our makeup with our clothes. I wear XO jeans, sandals, and a shirt I recently bought that's a little bit sheer—it makes me look boss, I believe, and *I'm not a nun yet*. Aunt Tony wears espadrille shoes, and a gauzy lime-green pantsuit that stretches and clings—the top clings so much it puts in overtime. Then it's time for makeup.

Aunt Tony lets me borrow Luxurious Lengths Ebony Mascara for the eyelashes, Dreamy Dusk ColorStay Lip Color for my lips, and

Lancome Perfect-Stay eye-shadow for over my eyes. I don't need to use any blush, she reports, 'cause I literally "glow"…

This is really fun.

Half-an-hour later, Janie arrives with Cameron in tow. She hands me the wine—two giant bottles with tops that screw off—saying, "This way no one will feel guilty if they want a second glass." Once this interaction is done, she looks me over.

"New shirt?" she asks with a squint.

"Yup."

"Aunt's makeup?" she knowingly states.

"Yup."

"Good," she pronounces. Next she looks Aunt Tony over. "Lovely as ever," she says, "though I don't see your hat," then, to my father, "Always a pleasure, Mr. P," though she doesn't, I notice, look *him* over.

My father is sitting in the family room in his chair, and Cameron joins him. He looks *really* good, I discern, with that neck and his curly brown hair, so I quickly look away.

I carry the wine to the kitchen, wondering whether to chill it or not—it's rosé after all—when a car slows in front of our driveway, and eventually stops.

"It's *him*!" says my aunt in a half-whisper. Even if it *is* him, he can't hear. He's outside. This means my aunt is excited, of course.

Janie quickly goes to the window, stretching her neck. "A *Peugeot?!*" she exclaims with surprise. "I thought you said he was poor?" Actually, whatever it is Aunt Tony "said," it wasn't to Janie, it was to me, then *I* spilled to Janie, so who knows what I originally said?

Aunt Tony corrects, "Well, it isn't *his* money; it's his family's. The question is whether he can get at it or not."

"Point taken," Janie replies. "Though I didn't expect a *Peugeot*."

She continues to stare.

We stare at Janie.

I think she is interested in Dan, 'cause her father took off when she was three, so all grown men of a particular age tend to interest her, especially the ones she doesn't know.

"Khakis," she says, going on. "*That* I expected...pretty good-looking," she duly admits, not exactly revealing whether she truly expected that or not. "And look. He brought me *flowers*!" she exclaims.

"Quit it," I say with a shove.

On hearing the "flowers" detail, Aunt Tony stands by the door, smoothing her top. Janie, just to be funny, inches in front of her. I stand, too, as I am the hostess for this thing. Then Cameron stands up to be polite. Then my father stands—he, out of all of us, *gets* politeness—which is how it comes to pass we all are standing when Dan saunters in.

Dan is...how can I put this...boyish. He's got to be fifty-one at the least, yet he's got long sun-bleached hair in his eyes, and baby-face apple-shaped cheeks, and a cute upturned nose. He looks like a surfer dude who never gave it up, though his looks are a little bit ruined, I must say, like he spent too much time in the sun, as well as the bar-room. Like he took his good looks and just ran and had a good time with them. The fact he "comes from money" makes good sense if you can picture his look.

In any case, Dan's not the slightest bit intimidated by our greeting line. He takes each of our hands in turn, starting with Janie, and assuming that *she* is the niece, says, "*Enchanté*" while kissing her hand.

"I'm just the friend," she replies, under-impressed with the man, I can tell.

"Surely not *just*," Dan retorts, giving my best friend a wink. To me he says, "And you are surely not 'just' the reputed niece." He kisses Aunt Tony on the cheek, pumps Cameron's hand pretty hard, and when he gets to my father, he says, "Ed. It's a pleasure." And my father, not to be outdone in the charm department, seeing as how he wrote the book, after all, says, "The pleasure is really all mine."

We all take our spots around the table, which is already set. Janie starts things off by pouring the wine. "Adults can have as much as they want. Teenagers only a taste."

Our "taste" fills the whole glass.

I go around scooping food onto everyone's plates from the cardboard containers. People start drinking the wine—at least, the "teenagers" do—yet before I know it, the real pros, Aunt Tony and Dan, have finished theirs, so Janie offers them more. "Aunt Tony, may I just top you off?" Her "top-off" is another full glass. "It would be my pleasure, Dan," she says, blatantly modeling his earlier talk.

She wants to get them drunk.

Everyone eats the food; everyone loves and compliments it. Cameron chows his down so fast, it looks like he never was served.

I make my announcement about how there's no MSG in the meal —feeling a little like a girl scout as I do—which makes Aunt Tony say, "And let's thank the heavens for *that*. MSG really does a number on me. And when you combine it with *alcohol*…well forget it!" she says, drinking more.

Janie smirks.

"There are *lots* of things you shouldn't mix with alcohol," Dan says, his eyebrows both raising at once. "In fact, I remember…well, it was in college. Years and years and *years* ago. Let's just say we had *too much* 'MSG' at one time."

My aunt laughs.

They drink some more.

Then, before I know it, they both start talking about their college days like they were last week. And, to be more specific, they start reminiscing about their college days "*on* MSG," if you can believe it. I can't. There are minors present at the table.

It turns out—and I knew this already—that Aunt Tony and Dan went to the same college, though Dan was a few years ahead of my aunt, so they never actually met there. This was at UMass, in Amherst. The story goes that Dan—who "comes from money" as I said—first went to Princeton, then "left" that institution midway through—i.e. he was kicked out—and went to UMass.

"That's the only reason rich folks *go* to that college," my aunt said. "Why would they otherwise? I knew a lot of such screw-ups out there."

Anyway, they're close to being done with their second big goblet of wine—courtesy of Janie—when they start with these stories of UMass in which they had too much accursed "MSG" and did wild and crazy things.

They start with the college-kid typical: throwing up at inappropriate times; being pulled over for unspecified moving violations while "on MSG"; having campus security barge into dorms due to "MSG floor parties." Every time they say "MSG," they give each other a look and practically burst. For instance. Dan says: "One time, I remember—and this took place Halloween night, when *anything* went at ZooMass like people jumping off of *buildings*," he says, "me and my buddies dressed up like the characters from *A Clockwork Orange*. You remember: British bowler hats; eyelashes done with mascara; suspenders hooked over white shirts—you kids might *not* remember—anyway, we decided—we somehow just got it into our heads—that we were supposed to direct traffic on University Ave. Directing traffic came to be our *raison d'être*. So there the four of us were, out in the middle of the street on a very dark night with our hands lifted proudly to stop people, or to wave them left or whatever." He laughs. "We ate *a lot* of Chinese food that night. And it didn't take long for the police to show up, let me tell you. In fact, that night, we had free lodgings, courtesy of Amherst."

He means, of course, they spent the night in jail.

"Must have been some MSG," Janie says. Not that I blame her.

"Yeah. *Great* MSD…LSG…" Cameron adds.

This is a take-off on LSD, in case you didn't recognize it—though I bet that you did. Cameron doesn't mince words—or not very much. Not that I blame him, either. Still. I give them each a pretty stern look so they won't wreck the night.

They look back.

Janie fills everybody's wine glasses—teenagers', too, at this point. *Why not?* we're all thinking. My aunt then says, "*I* remember, *I* used to ride on guys' cars—I mean *on* the guys' cars: on the hoods—holding nothing but two flimsy windshield-wiper blades, which isn't smart. The guys would only tool around campus—going thirty at most —but still. You shouldn't ride around on hoods of cars. No matter *how much* MSG you've had."

She says this like we really might not know. Janie takes a long drink. My father just continues to eat—he's a slow eater. He's also quiet in social situations, enjoying them in his own way, which means often he's often oblivious to what's being said—he always thinks the best of people.

Then: "Kids. Don't try this at home!" Dan tacks on.

Everyone laughs.

"How 'bout us trying it at college when we're Chinese Food junkies?" Janie asks.

The adults, including my father, ignore this remark.

"Why do you think they call it dope?" Cameron says. "Oh sorry. That's a reference to actual dope. Not MSG."

The adults ignore this cut-down as well, but I don't. I stare at Cameron. I stare and stare and stare…maybe it's the wine?

Dan has cleaned off his plate, so Janie gets him more. Cameron gives Janie a puppy-dog look, so he gets more, too. My father, on seeing all of this, clears the last bite off *his* plate, then gives *me* a puppy-dog look, probably noting just how well it worked for Cameron. I turn the look on my aunt. Maybe it's the wine but I think: *Aunt Tony can help out.* It's why I invited her to our house, after all and this could be excellent training. Plus, *I* went and planned the whole dinner party.

I say, "Aunt Tony will get you more. Right, Aunt Tony?"

"Right," she swiftly agrees, getting right up.

"Why that would be fine," my dad says.

She finishes off three containers—in getting him more.

Next, I notice his water glass is empty as well. My dad's taking meds, so I'd rather my dad drink water than cheap wine.

"Dad. Would you care for more water?"

"Why yes," he says. "How kind."

I look at Aunt Tony again, not even having to speak, and she does it. She gets up, gets the pitcher, pours for my father, then leaves the porcelain pitcher on the table.

This, I think, is good…I drink more wine.

Dan—oblivious to all of the schooling that has just taken place—says: "Do you remember elevator surfing at UMass?"

Cameron holds his head in his hands.

"How could I forget?" my aunt says. "*I* never did it, thanks to God, but I certainly heard about it."

"Nasty," Dan remarks, grimly shaking his head. Then he turns to us "kids." "What you do is, you get up on *top* of an elevator—usually by getting it to stop between floors, so you can climb on—and then, while two different elevators are moving, you hop from top to top." After a moment, he tacks on for dramatic effect, "People have *died* doing that."

"'Nasty'," Janie wryly repeats, 'cause she can't hold it in.

Cameron says, "This is your brain. This is your brain on MSG." It's a take-off, of course, on that commercial: "This is your brain: this is your brain on drugs," though nobody listens to him. Well, I do. I listen. I stare…it must be the wine.

Cameron looks back with these eyes that say: This is par for the course. It's exactly what one expects from older people. Then he looks right back with these eyes that say: I want you.

I look, then I look right away. I really can't look at Cameron.

My father seems clueless to it all—our drinking, the drug talk, the looks me and Cameron exchange. He's just enjoying the party.

Aunt Tony then brings the conversation back. "Well *I* never really ever did it," she says.

"I never really did it, either," Dan remarks.

I wonder what all of these "reallys" mean? They act like they each deserve medals for never "*really*" elevator surfing. They're like kids trying to top one another—get the best laugh.

Dan says, "I remember…"

"No, me!" Aunt Tony cuts in, giving him a nudge.

"No, me."

And Aunt Tony says, "Ladies first."

And Dan says, "But *I* am the guest."

And Aunt Tony says, "Oh, all right. But *then* me."

They're laughing.

Janie and Cameron exchange looks. Then they both give *me* looks.

I look back.

Dan tells another quaint story—nothing you really need to know —and Cameron holds his head in his hands again.

Janie says, "My! Look at the time!" Then: "Well this *has* been an enlightening night."

And Cameron says, "Yeah. Remind me to never go to college."

Nobody's listening to Cameron—except me.

Finally, I think about my father, suddenly wanting to include him somehow, since he hasn't really contributed much, and I say, "So what about *you*, Dad? What's the wildest thing *you* ever did while at college?"

"Well let's see…let me think…good question. I know! One time, a couple fraternity brothers and I went to a sorority to serenade a girl I happened to like."

"*Really*?" I say. "What'd you sing?"

"We did the Buck Ram song, *Only You*, that was performed by The Platters." He sings it for us—almost the entire song, about how only the beloved can make the things of this world seem right—and then he looks at me.

It's beautiful, I think. Corny and dated as hell, of course, but beautiful. They threw away the mold when they fashioned my father. It's really amazing.

Janie and Cameron like it, too.

Aunt Tony and Dan clap.

Imagine, I think, *standing outside in the cold, straining your head toward a window, singing your heart out to a girl you happen to like. Only You...* I'm totally proud of my father, blushingly so, though maybe it's the wine, and say, "So how did it go? Did she *like* it?"

"Well. We never officially went out, if that's what you mean." He laughs.

"How many people went to sing?" Cameron asks him.

"I could only get a couple of other guys, so including me, there were three."

"See? That was the trouble. You need at least four-part harmony when singing to a girl, then she would have followed you to the grave."

Cameron's being funny—his usual wry self—but I also get the sense he's being wistful, like his hidden inner dreamer's coming out—though, again, maybe that's just me and the wine thinking.

Cameron and I look at each other.

Janie says, "Is *that* how beguilement works? *I* thought it took MSG," and then we are back. Dream-time over, reality setting in again.

Aunt Tony suddenly offers to do the dishes.

I think: *This is really great,* but then, when she goes to get up, she actually staggers a bit like she's going to trip, so Janie and I do the washing, which, I guess, is fine. I mean, Aunt Tony means well. Plus she's happy with how the dinner party went, which means that *I* am happy.

Chapter 21

The day after, I see in retrospect that not only was the dinner party "interesting," that so was Dan. Let me in earnest say this: You have to walk a mile in somebody's shoes before you really know them. You need to see each one of their lives, know what the bulk of their karma is—*then* you can judge. But then, *I* don't have to date him. My *aunt's* dating him, and she seems to like him pretty well—maybe she's into his neck?

In any case, she seems happy and things are going strong. Since before and after the dinner, my aunt and Dan have now gone bowling, dancing, out to dinner twice and have had many enjoyable "sleepovers" from what I can tell, though never one here. I know about these, 'cause Aunt Tony isn't at home when I finally go to bed, nor is she home in the morning when I finally get up—and this at eleven. She hums on those days when she gets back, and this word gushes out of her mouth that she never used before. The new word is "hoot"—she really does say this—as in, "You're a hoot, Mo. A regular hoot." The day after the sleepovers, everyone's a "regular hoot" per my aunt.

The guy must be awesome in bed I think.

They next day, Janie comes over. I've made a jug of pink lemonade for the occasion—pink's necessary on a hot, sunny, partly-humid day, and we're all sitting out on the deck, we being Janie, my father, myself and sort of Aunt Tony. I say "sort of" regarding Aunt Tony 'cause she's in and out of the house, fetching different outfits for the show. She's giving us a "fashion show"—more on the hows and whys later.

Janie's wearing a wrap-around Jamaican-style skirt—short—and a nothing-to-it black bikini top. She's also got her Jeff Gordon sunglasses on—wrap-around, impenetrable, black—and every time she comments on something, she flips the dark sunglasses down to expose her eyes. It's her way of adding punch to what she says—very large definite periods, and sometimes exclamation marks—you will soon see for yourself.

My father, for his part, is wearing his Gilligan hat—of *Gilligan's Island* fame. I'm making him wear it 'cause he fries in the sun. Also bermudas that show his white legs and dark Gold-toe socks.

I am wearing my "Disney" clothes, which are gym shorts—so not all *that* bad—my Red Sox World-Series-Champion T-shirt, and my New Balance sneakers. The reason my clothes *are* "Disney," is 'cause any Tom, Dick or Harry could wear them, and they don't show my breasts. That's if you were to ask Janie, that is. At least, this is my *assumption* of what Janie would say, based on knowing her for seven-plus years, but still, if you *did* query Janie, she might say some men actually *like* "Disney"—in fact I am betting she would.

Last but not least, at the moment Aunt Tony is wearing her workout gear: turbo-kickboxing pants, chartreuse headband and a snuggly-fitting micro-fabric shirt that appropriately "breathes," though it doesn't much matter *what* she's wearing, 'cause Aunt Tony is "trying on" clothes for our group by holding different outfits to her front, and saying "Ta-da!" so what she is wearing quote "under" the clothes, is secondary.

Anyway, the occasion for the big show is that my aunt's going off on Dan's yacht and is figuring out what to wear. Or trying.

"What does one *wear* on a yacht?" my aunt says, as if the magnitude's clearly beyond her somehow.

"Never trust a yachtsman," Janie says, flipping her Jeff Gordon sunglasses down and back up.

I look at Janie, of course. She looks back, though now through the sunglasses. Then she says, "What's he *doing* with such a pricey boy-toy anyway? And if he's *got* a Puegeot and a yacht, then why's he planning to move back in with his *mother*?" Then: "Sorry. Blame Mo. Mo told me."

I say, "It's his *family's* money—his *family's* yacht. It's hard for him to get at right now." Then I tack on a mumbled "Sorry" too.

"*Never* trust a yachtsman who has *money*, Aunt Tony." Janie repeats flipping the glasses down and back up.

Janie's taken to calling my aunt "Aunt Tony" in case you didn't notice. Aunt Tony likes it, I think. She's told me that Janie's a "hoot." Call it girl love.

"You're a hoot," my aunt tells her now, as if reading my mind, then, "I can't believe I'm going on a yacht! Whoo-hoo! Now what to wear?! When I first go to board, should I wear this, do you think, or this?" She holds up two outfits in turn.

"How many people will *be* on this yacht?" Janie asks, though she already knows, and I bet is just asking to lead the conversation somewhere.

"Just me and Dan," my aunt says.

"And will you stay *docked* for this entire affair, or will there be 'yachting' going on?"

"I think we're going yachting."

"Well. Then you want to wear just as little as you can." This time, she flips her dark sunglasses down like that's that. Fashion show over.

I give her a look.

She looks back.

Aunt Tony says, "What an incredible hoot!" and *then* says, "but I want to see and be seen. At the yacht club for and by Dan. Now *this* outfit's smart and classy. But this one is smart with a come-hither sort of look. Both sexy *and* smart."

One outfit—the smart one—is a knit set, but one of those thick, expensive, country-club knits that tend not to show any faults, and by "faults" I mean flab. Not that Aunt Tony *has* flab, but if she did, it wouldn't show. That's Saks-Fifth-Avenue knit. The top is a cream and peach stripe, and the pants are light cream. She has a lovely cream jacket, as well, and a darker peach scarf to top it off. I, myself, can't wear cream pants—they'd be brown before you could say "cream"— but oh well…this outfit *is* very "smart."

The other is also pastel: a low-necklined, sheer, lime-green top and a flirty lime skirt edged with ruffles. She also has matching high heels—different than the ones for the knit set. I, myself, can't wear high heels as they totally numb up my toes and turn my arches purple —but oh well. In any case. I am pondering, pondering, pondering… which to wear, which to wear? It seems quite important, somehow.

I am starting to lean toward the knit, as I'm picturing boarding taking place in the day, while I see the low neckline more as your nighttime attire, but then I must wonder if the knit is too "ooh-la-la," which makes me say "Hmm" a few times. "Hmm…hmm…hmm" and makes *Janie* blurt out, "Men don't *like* to see sexy and smart. Right, Mr. P.? So what you should do is *be* sexy at night, without a sole thought in your head, and then, the next morning, over the *Times*, and those French Gauloises cigarettes, and some fancy British scones scored from Whole foods, make sure that you *do* appear smart, so he'll know he can't push you around. So the knit set over coffee, Aunt Tony. And the lime set for when you board. But what *I* want to see is what you're planning to wear in between, when you're fully 'unmoored,' and it's just you and old Dan in the Captain's Cabin. French-Maid sort of getup, perhaps? Lion-tamer? Naughty little school-girl number?"

I throw my "bud" Janie a look, nodding toward Dad.

Janie says, "Sorry for that, Mr. P.," looking contrite.

"No apologies required," is what my dad says, smiling like he very much *likes* such talk.

Aunt Tony only gives a laugh. "You don't have to worry. *That* I've got covered." She winks, then: "Ooh, I am so excited! I just wonder if something is missing; if there's something I need? What else might a sailor gal wear?"

Janie says, "If I were you, Aunt Tony, I'd bring the Gauloises, the *Times*, the British scones, those articles of clothing we discussed, a martini shaker—hopefully *Dan* will remember the mixings—a Morse Code kit for typing out your SOS and a thoroughly-tested escape route." Then she adds, "*Never* trust a yachtsman with martini mixings," and flips her dark sunglasses down.

Aunt Tony now gazes at me. "She doesn't like men? Is that it?"

"Only well-muscled lacrosse players," I say.

Janie looks at me; I look back.

And that's about all that I have, for then my dad says, "Did somebody mention martinis?" and everyone laughs.

So my dad's having fun with all this.

So Aunt Tony is psyched.

So everything's going just great.

The day after my aunt gets back from her yacht trip—late—she sleeps in even later than me, so it's creeping toward noon when she gets up—I find her at the table in the kitchen, without any food at her place. No wheat germ, no gruel, no tea. This is strange. She's sort of just…what's the expression…sitting.

I go over. She's got this vague look in her eyes, which I guess is to say Dan screwed her brains out—not that I *really* know what that means, of course, and not that I should be using such talk—but her lips are parted and wet, and her eyes are all dewy and vague, and she's staring at positively nothing as far as I can tell. Maybe she's staring at a spot on the wallpaper that shouldn't be there, like an old piece of whipped squash from Thanksgiving? Like a minuscule piece of pixie dust? In any case, besides her placid gazing, she's doing nothing. Nothing at all. If she were a cat, she'd be dozing in front of a fireplace, sporadically purring, sporadically licking herself. Suddenly, I kind of wouldn't mind knowing what it is like to have your "brains screwed out," so I sit down across from my aunt.

"Hi," I start.

"Hi." She looks at me, then away, like she's not even sure who I am. Like I could be another spot of whipped squash or more of that pixie dust.

"Have a nice time on your trip?"

"Oh. Mo," she says, now looking. "It really was out of this world."

"Oh good. Good. I want to hear."

"Mmm," she dreamily says, returning to the speck of whipped squash or pixie dust. To get her to focus I say, "Why don't I make some tea?"

This look comes over her face like she'll never need to eat or drink again. This everyone-alive-should-have-their-brains-F-ed-out look. At least, I imagine the look to be this.

I make the tea.

When I set it before her, she lets out an "Mmm…"

"Well then," I say to the air. Luckily that's all I'm required to say, 'cause in addition to being all dreamy, my aunt is a talker. Plus, I think the tea revives her some.

"Oh, Mo," she utters again, vaguely taking a sip. Then she tells me how romantic the whole weekend was. How at night, they docked at this marina, but really far out, throwing the anchor over. How they sat out up on the deck, under the stars, drinking margaritas, and how there was just a small moon in the sky. Just a slight slip. Not one of those full moons you see—all bloated and puffy and full of itself. How this was far better, 'cause it seemed to convey the promise of something. She tells me about the flag softly hitting the mast—that nautical *ding* sound you hear. Then she tells me how the best part wasn't the moon, or the dinging, or the sex—though all of that was good, she tells me, great even—it was the things that Dan *said* to her after the sex.

She looks at me, sizing me up, then says, "What the hell. You're a grown woman, right?"

We're about to get to the good part, I think.

She starts out—bam—telling me how men get all vulnerable right after sex. "For women it's different," she says. "Women can pen entire symphonies right after sex, but men feel used-up. Spent. In fact,

I once read in *Cosmo* that men ejaculate at the speed of twenty-eight miles an hour, if you can imagine. That's *gotta* do a number on you." She lets out a laugh. "Plus, men have to wait before doing it again. Women don't," she confides.

She starts getting dreamy again—likely *writing* her symphony—so I clear my throat.

She looks at me.

"Anyway, after the sex," she goes on, "he started by telling me how good I was for him—all 'healthy' and stuff, as he said—into right eating and exercise. I don't know how 'healthy' we were being, Mo. We'd just finished three margaritas, but oh well. Then he said he liked my abs. He said he needed more of such stuff in his life: the eating and exercise, I mean, not the abs."

She laughs.

"So anyway. After he told me how good I was for him, he started to open up—to tell me things. He started to talk about Princeton: why he got kicked out of Princeton and ended up at UMass. I knew he got kicked out of Princeton. Apparently, there was this party one night in his suite, and the cops showed up because of the noise, and, as Dan put it, the cops were *not* invited in, and they *needed* to be invited in, or else they couldn't *go* in. But they went in regardless. It was a 'private party' Dan explained.

"The next thing anyone knew, events escalated. There was an altercation, and one thing led to another, and Dan *swore* that the cop shoved him first, but regardless, he was arrested for assaulting an officer, and while he was conveniently handcuffed, the cops beat him. They beat him up pretty darn bad. The whole incident was eventually cleared from his record, yet Princeton was a thing of the past."

Aunt Tony pauses, going all starry-eyed again, so I scrape my chair.

She looks at me vaguely.

"So anyway, I thought that was it. That he confided in me about Princeton and that would be it. Not bad for a single night away, I decided.

"But that wasn't it. Get *this: Then* he told me—and this is pay dirt; not that I revel in misfortune, but just get *this: Then* he tells me how he's always had trouble with authority—especially when the authority's unjust, which most of it is—and how this goes back to his childhood when his stepfather wailed on him. It only happened a couple of times—then he got too big or something—but his stepfather totally lost it a few times and beat him up. Beat him pretty bad. The guy had been drinking, of course, and some other things were going on as well, but it had a really major effect on Dan. He hasn't been the same since, and it's taken him *years* to see this—years and years of pricey therapy—and he decided to *share* it with me. Imagine. So that's why he wants to go into business for himself because he doesn't want to work for anyone. And get this. *Then* he told me—and I remember this part word-for-word, sap that I am—he told me, 'But that's in the past. Now is the time for the future.' And he looked at me then, as if maybe, just maybe, the moon rose and set by my word, and he really hoped it did. He really really hoped so," she tells me.

She starts going moony-eyed again, but then snaps back. "If a man ever tells you about his childhood, Mo, *especially* things about his father, pay attention because everything follows from that. So pay attention." And then she drifts off again.

I start to drift on my own. I wonder how things are between Cameron and *his* father? I don't really know much about his father. All

I *really* know is that he still *has* a real live father in the house—not a stepfather. I suppose I could ask Janie, but then if I *did* ask Janie, I'd have to give her a reason why, and she's not all that easily fooled as you probably know, and I could never ever tell her the *real* reason, which means if I want to ever know I would have to ask Cameron. Or better, I'd have to wait till he turns all "vulnerable" and tells me on his own, which only then serves to make *me* go all the more dreamy. Dreaminess, I guess, is contagious. So then I start thinking more about Cameron. I think about his neck, and his lips, and his dick—these aren't "nun-like" thoughts. I think about how Cameron might be after sex. Whether he would tell me about his father. Whether he would tell me he loved me. Mush like that.

Ah, love.

My aunt, when I finally focus back on her, looks pathetic, I think, with her lips all parted and wet, and her eyes all fogged-up. I wonder if I look like her. She gives a look back as if saying there's no other way to be. We sit at the table like this for the next ten minutes communally dreaming.

Part of me wants to tell Aunt Tony about Cameron, like she did with me about Dan—describe what his lips felt like, and about his incredible eyes, and about his incredible neck. To confess just how much I really want him, and to maybe even ask questions about sex, like, is it *really* all that folks say? All that the love songs proclaim? From the way Aunt Tony is looking, I'd say that it is. I just want to utter the words…I guess I just want girl talk.

Aunt Tony's the first to come back, for there's more to her story it seems.

"And then," she says, "right at the end, Dan took his finger, and ever so lightly, he moved it down over my lips, then my chin, then my neck…then down, down, down, down. He said he was tracing his future on me." She beams at this prospect, my aunt, and I beam right back. *You* might find all of it silly, but we two don't. Trust me.

My aunt sighs.

I sigh.

Ah, love.

Oh, and in case you're a *man* reading this, I'll clue you in to something. To a woman, having a man confide in you is like the pot of gold at the end of the rainbow—better even than hitting the lottery. It's what all women everywhere seek and strive to achieve. It is Tara to them.

This is just FYI.

Anyway, returning, just for a moment, to my prophecy, and to how it relates to the Cameron-dilemma, for it does: My spirit guide warned me I'd be faced with a decision, and that making the right decision would take certain courage, and before, while I knew that being a nun meant renouncing the world—alcohol, drugs, sex, *et cetera,* even how one structures one's time—I didn't believe it would take *that* much courage, 'cause I loved the way I felt in meditation. I loved the sheer state of transcendence I achieved. There was really nothing like it in the world. Not beer, not nature, not laughter, not sex —okay, I didn't really know about sex—but still, I would have opined "not anything." But now that I'm thinking about Cameron, I can see where the courage comes in.

I've got courage, but it's too bad that it takes so much of it.

BIG HEAVEN

Chapter 22

Okay. Here's the thing: He asks me out. Before he did, I had decided I wasn't going to think of him in that way, and definitely *definitely* not date him, but then, when he asked me, when he engaged in the *actual asking*, when it was him there in person before my eyes, with those lips, and that hair, and that neck, those eyes you could literally fall into and never escape—well I couldn't say *no*.

He asked me on our riverside bench, a time I was waiting to meet Janie for our diurnal chat, but Cameron showed first. Again, I believe it was planned by those two, but what am I supposed to do? Never meet Janie? It's really a little unfair, 'cause there are two separate beings called "them" and only one of me. But, okay, moving on, we were sitting there on our wood bench after doing our "heys," and it was summer, as I know you know, and I don't have to tell you what *summer's* like. Summer's *amazing.* And he was wearing his Arcade Fire T-shirt, so you could see his tan arms—I don't have to tell you what *arms* are like—and you could see his thick beautiful neck, and there was moisture at the base of his neck, which must have been sweat…enough said!

Anyway, we were sitting there, and he put those incredible eyes on me, then he asked me. What was I supposed to reply? A version of "no?" I mean, *that* would never happen, so "yes" tumbled out of my mouth as in: "Yes, I will go to the movies with you," though I didn't have to say all those words. I only had to answer yes—he said all of the movie part—and all the while, I was thinking: *I'm not alone.* Others have been tempted and, yes, eventually succumbed. Heck, even the saints had their troubles, as I know I've said, and I'm no saint. Buddha had his dancing girls; Jesus had his forty days and nights. All right, true, those two didn't succumb. But I bet you some other saints did—I'm going to Google it when I get some time—but in any case, it's true. And I said yes.

After that, we settled on a date and a time, then we talked just a little bit more before Cameron took off, though I don't know what we said. All I remember is this roar going on in my ears, and my fingertips pulsing with blood, and a dryness in my mouth—and that I didn't want Cameron to know. That's all I really remember.

It was a little exciting, and, yes, that's too bad.

Anyway, this is what I do: I blame my aunt. I blame her dreaminess, her longing, her lust, as if it's contagious. And I blame handsome Cameron as well, what with that neck and those eyes. And I definitely strongly blame Janie for setting us up. So it's not in any way or shape my fault. That is what I decide, though, of course, there are a couple different ways of actually looking at it. One is that it's simply not my fault, but how far is *that* going to get me? I mean, it's really God's fault. He's the Prime Mover who made us the way we are.

Another way of looking at it is if I'm *really* going to give myself to God—which I'm *really* going to do—then I need to proceed with zero reservations, and in order to do *that*, I need to know what it is I'm giving up, so I can give it up with zero reservations. How can one choose God over every other thing, if one knows not what those other things *are*? So, in a way, I am doing this for God, so I can find out what those other things are, and then reject them, and *then* go to God.

God is actually going to thank me one day.

I think.

At least, this is another way of looking at it.

So, here's what happens. We go to the movies. In fact, we go to the Embassy Cinema, where I work, 'cause I get a discount there—why not?

Cameron insists that *I* pick the movie, 'cause I am the one "in the field" as he says, but I don't *want* to pick the movie, 'cause I might pick a film he doesn't like—I'm pretty darn sure that I *would* make this gaffe—and with this thought in mind, I'd then probably pick a movie he *would* like, but that I wouldn't. The sexes very rarely agree on movies, and you can take that to the bank. So what I end up doing is—you're going to choke on your soup bone at this—I let *Janie* pick the movie, 'cause she has a lot more experience with such. I know. It's like rewarding her for her underhanded tricks. But, really, so what? And she picks *The Hundred-Foot Journey*, which turns out to be a really good movie we both really like.

I'm not going to tell all—I want to skip ahead to what's really good—but I will say this: We split a buttered popcorn during the movie. Cameron put his arm around me once. I felt nervous off and on through the two-hour film, but still somehow followed the story-line...it's really is a good movie.

Afterwards—remember, I'm zeroing in on the "good part" here—we hung around the lobby for a time. He talked. Then we went outside and walked to his cool beater car, an '82 Mustang. He talked some more. *Then* we stood beside his beater car, in the open-air cinema parking lot. I probably don't have to spell it out for you: He talked even more. For someone who is not your basic talker, he talked up a storm, and I'm not even sure what he said. It was very hard to focus. I was looking at his eyes and you-know-where...No, not there! At his *neck!*

Finally, it got to the point where I wanted him to kiss me, 'cause how am I supposed to choose God if I've never been kissed? Well, hardly ever. So I suggest we go for a drive to encourage a kiss. In fact, I think I even suggested it in the middle of a sentence, but when was I *supposed* to suggest it? The handsome boy kept talking and talking.

We got in his car. He took me to Woerd Avenue, to a parking lot recently put in for launching of boats. The new lot, and the new ramp, and the new, recycled-wood dock are all brand new parts of the River Walk, of course. He parked so we faced the Charles River. We were the only two people there.

I thought it was cool, going there, 'cause Woerd Avenue is pronounced "word," which by itself, all alone, means "truth," "amen," "lay it on me, brother"—at least when you hear it from rappers, it does —so I thought it was cool. We were parked, all alone, on Woerd Avenue, and still he was talking.

Most of the time that he talked, he didn't really look at me—he looked at the river, or into the middle distance somewhere, or out at the buildings across the dark river—though once in a while he did look, to see if I was catching his drift I suppose, which I wasn't. Still, I nodded to say that I was. Really, how was I *supposed* to listen? Love goes deeper. It takes place on an entirely other plane. Listening's only for show is what I believe. In fact, the minute a person starts to talk, it gives you a get-out-of-jail card that allows you to stare, especially when they aren't looking back.

Finally—somebody had to make a move, I mean, how long could he keep *talking*—and, luckily, I saw this stray eyelash on his cheek, so I went to get it off while he talked. In other words, I *touched* him. I had this really weird notion that I could show him the eyelash on my finger, let him blow if off and make a wish—but that's pretty dumb. That's more like what a boy's supposed to do to a girl, or rather, more like what a girl often *wishes* a boy would do—not what happens in real life—yet *I* ended up doing it, 'cause I had to do *something*.

I couldn't believe I was making the move, yet desperate times call for really desperate measures. Right?

After I touched him I said, "You had an eyelash there" to explain my rash move. And then I examined my finger and saw it was a whisker, not an eyelash. So then I announced my mistake, feeling like a fool, mentioning it was a whisker.

"It's been known to happen," he said back, the tiniest hint of a smirk on his face.

I smiled. This was wild, I thought. A *whisker*…

It was all or nothing now that I had touched his cheek, so I touched it again. "Well anyway," I said, languorously lifting my face, closing my eyes.

"What are you doing?" He looked amused by the whole wretched ordeal.

"I'm waiting for you to kiss me," I finally announced.

This was straightforward and clear. Cameron would like *this*.

"I thought you were going to be a nun. I'm actually respecting you by *not* kissing you, 'cause I thought you were going to be a nun."

He's teasing me, I thought. Testing me. Wanting me to admit just how much I really liked him *before* he would kiss me, so I chose to tease him right back.

"You're right," I said, "I am. But I'm going to need *something* to remember when I'm cloistered away. *Something* to remember all of those long lonely nights in my room, week after week, month after month…you get the picture." I smiled at this.

"We'd better make it memorable then," Cameron said, and he kissed me.

It was great.

It was a little like last time, yet totally new. This time it was incredibly hot. He kissed me this time in a way that made me eat right out of his hand—there's no other way to describe it. He kissed—but not *too* much, not *too* powerfully—just about powerfully enough, then he backed off, waiting, almost resting you might say, then he started again, so that I wanted it, and wanted it bad. He went in, then backed off, then went in…it was like he was a veritable master at this!

His hands were around my waist at that point, and I slipped them under my shirt so we could touch skin-to-skin. I moved one of his hands to one of my breasts, undoing the bra so it snapped open. I was a little embarrassed about my breasts, 'cause they're not super huge by today's standards, but it didn't seem like Cameron minded. In fact, I'd say they were a hit.

And then—this was quite brazen, I admit, but since I'm indeed going to become a nun, I *had* to be brazen—I felt him, but just through his pants. It was amazing. It was this hard, unknowable lump that I wanted to know. It was an incredible turn-on.

A few minutes later, he unzipped his pants, took his penis out of his fly, and I felt it for real. He didn't pressure me; it was just there—out in the open air—and I did.

It was astounding. Great. It was everything you hear—all silky-smooth on the outside, all ramrod-hard on the in. It felt pretty big, I decided, though I don't know what "big" really is, though his felt big. It was my very first "hard dick," as Janie would say—I can't wait to tell her! I was so horned-out, I wanted it inside where I ached. All these sparks were flying around, like on the TV show *Batman.* Kazowie! Kabam! Pow!

I wonder if it's always like that with a boy, though I think not, 'cause I'm not attracted to every boy the way I am to Cameron, so it would follow that attraction either causes the spark or makes it bigger. Either way—it couldn't be like this with every boy. Only him.

When we finally decided to call it quits, or rather, when *he* finally decided to call it quits 'cause he's a gentleman, and, in these cases, it's up to the guy to decide to call it quits if they really want to *be* a gentleman—he sat a little straighter in his seat and zipped up his fly while I re-hooked my bra and pulled my shirt back down.

Cameron said, "Memorable?"—referring to all of those nights I'd be cloistered away.

And I, in a gush, told him, "Yes."

It's funny. Getting him to talk about his father never even entered my mind.

The next few days, I try really hard not to think about Cameron. I think about God instead. I re-read all the pamphlets and journal articles about how romantic love just doesn't last—the T-shirt study, for instance, about how people tend to choose lifelong mates, based on the smell of sweaty T-shirts. Ugh. I read about the lives of the saints and the temptations that *they* had to face.

Yet that doesn't mean that when the song *Chasing Cars* comes on the radio, I don't sing along. Nor does it mean I don't cry at the end of *Casablanca*. Nor does it mean I don't think about walking by his house at different hours of the night, hearing that song from *My Fair*

Lady playing over in my head, the one about having to be on the street where your love lives, no matter how much people stop and stare at you.

Thinking about such a cornball song is really nothing like me. That's really more like my father. Love is screwing with my head, is what I think. Go figure.

And though I do really try to resist, I also do this: I have my hair highlighted. I buy a push-up bra. I buy lacy lilac panties that go *with* the push-up bra—however. I don't shop at Victoria's Secret for these things; I shop at The Limited to make it more chaste. I also buy a lipstick at the mall, though it doesn't even count as an actual "lipstick" being it's a Revlon ColorStay Soft & Smooth Lip Color, the shade of Wild Honey.

All this makes me feel bad, 'cause I am going to become a nun. Then I remember to blame Aunt Tony…I have a feeling she's not a good influence on me, and, frankly, I'm not sure how I feel about that right now.

Anyway, later that week, my aunt revives. She becomes less dreamy, less lethargic, less spaced-out, yet she's still clearly in love. And 'cause she's still in love, everything's going just great. In fact, a very strange thing comes about: Not only do my father and Aunt Tony really start hitting it off, my aunt starts doing things for him—even to the point of chauffeuring him places. All this, without a solitary word on my part about it needing to be done. It's like, now that she's in love, she's stepping up to the plate, seeing the need that's around her. It's like love itself is occasioning miracles. I've heard that can happen.

So far, and all on her own, she took Dad for lunch at Maria's Home Cooking, then took him for a haircut at Davio's Barber Shop, which is only a couple of doors down from Maria's. Another day, she actually went to Whole Foods all on her own, and brought Dad. He moseyed from station to station, went the report, sampling the food, and breaking into song as he did. Not only that, but he actually conjured up songs that went with the food. Like when he sampled the feta-cheese pizza, he sang *That's Amore*, by Harry Warren and Jack Brooks, about the moon hitting your eye "like a big pizza pie." At the bakery station, he sang the traditional, *Hot Cross Buns*—depositing raspberry rugula into his mouth. And when he sampled their Darjeeling tea—surely you see this coming—he sang, *Tea for Two*, by Vincent Youmans and Irving Caesar.

People loved him. Customers and workers joined in. Nobody minded at all—him eating the food.

My aunt proudly called him "a hoot," but that's 'cause she's in love. I think it's her state's having an effect on my dad. I mean, he's happy, too. Love is most definitely contagious.

In fact, one day, just as I enter the house, I hear my dad say, "No, officer. I didn't even see the Indians."

It's a joke. One of his faves. The first joke he ever really told me in fact—at least, the first that I *remember* he told. A real cornball joke, though it has its own charm, like everything else linked to Dad. This one goes—okay, it *is* a bit racist, but it's not *my* joke, don't forget, and don't forget, too, he told me it ages ago, before political correctness took hold, and *he* heard it even longer ago than *that*—not that that's an excuse exactly—so here's how it goes:

A lady was driving the wrong way down a one-way street. An officer pulls the gal over. When he approaches he says, "Hey, lady. Didn't you see that arrow?" And she says the line about the Indians…

My aunt laughs. "You're a hoot, Ed! A regular hoot!" she declares.

They're sitting in the kitchen, with big bowls of green cabbage soup in their spots, and my father (though he *hates* cabbage soup), has polished the whole of his off, thus keeping his record untarnished in the clannish clean-plate-club.

And Aunt Tony's duly following his lead. She says, "I have one! I have one! Dan told me this. You'll *love* it. Three presidents—Bush, Clinton and Ford—were all in this row boat…"

They look up as they hear me come in. I give a quick wave then walk on, pretending I'm going to my bedroom for something—I'm not —but I want them to have time together to forge their own special bond. I go to my room, leaving my door slightly open. I hear my aunt —happy, loud—then her laugh—she must have just finished telling her joke—and my father's low laugh mixing in. Next, I hear my father, then more raucous laughter shaking the house, then my father loudly breaking into song to top the day off.

The rest is your virtual "cake," as it were.

Chapter 23

And then, just as quickly as things brightened a couple of weeks ago, things begin to sour.

The first sign that something is wrong—and this about a week after the yachting trip—is my aunt going all around the house, banging things. In the kitchen, she bangs the maple cabinets. When she goes to her bedroom, she bangs her bedroom door. Once *in* her bedroom, she bangs all the drawers in her bureau. I'm sure she bangs the refrigerator and freezer doors too, but they don't produce that much noise.

I think, *Uh-oh*.

At one point, my father says, "*That's* really unpleasant. What's with all the unpleasantness?"

I tell him it's nothing and give him a look as if to say, don't worry. Then I say, "It'll probably just take a little time—whatever it is."

My father replies, "Well let's hope it doesn't take *too* much time." My father doesn't much *like* unpleasantness.

At first I decide to just stay out of her way, in hopes it will blow over. In case it's a lover's spat—which from all that Janie's told me and I've read, I'm certain it is—and, before long, the banging does indeed cease, but it's replaced by a permanent scowl on her face. She scowls at everyone. Me, my father, Janie—even the employees at Whole Foods. The scowl is "unpleasant-looking." In fact, one day my father blurts out, "When will the home-health-aid be leaving?" which of course makes my aunt scowl more. Finally she directs the scowl at me. I shake my head like to say, "It's his pills...never fear...we'll work it out," in a head-shake. Luckily, Aunt Tony's too mired down in her own world to call me to task. Still, though I was patiently waiting for it to blow over, I think, *I should step in—offer her a shoulder to cry on.* I mean, I need Aunt Tony to *like* it here, so one day I offer up this: "Anything I can do, Aunt Tony?"

She scowls, then demands, "What do you know about flight attendants?"

I think, *Uh-oh,* and reply, "No more than anyone else."

And *she* says, "Well I thought *I* knew flight attendants, as much as the next person, but it turns out I *don't* know flight attendants. I don't know flight attendants at all!"

I think, *Uh-oh.*

And then she says, "And do you know *why* I don't know flight attendants?"

"No."

"Because, apparently, Dan met one on a plane almost a year ago, and has kept in touch with this gal ever since, and has decided to bring it all up with me *now*."

I wait before I say, "Oh."

And then she says, "And do you know *why* he decided to bring it up?"

"No."

"Because he's planning to fly out to see her, and he thought that he should 'inform' me of this."

All I can do is to nod, though the nod is more like a shake that says, "That no-good-son-of-a-blank."

My aunt picks up on my shake-nod, then says, "He is *so* off my list. *So* off," adding after a hurt pause, "The jerk!"

I nod again, and this time the nod is a nod.

Then she walks off, shaking her own outraged head like now that she's told me, she has to process the whole thing anew. Like she can't believe what he did.

My poor aunt.

That no-good-son-of-a-blank.

Hours later, I see her again and she says, "You know what it is? It's 'cause he confided in me. That's why. Men can't *stand* having you know anything about them, because then they believe they look weak, the jerks. So now he's got some flight attendant…she better hope he doesn't open his mouth."

She walks off, angrily shaking her head.

Ah, love, I can't help think.

Anyway, later still, I talk to Janie about all of this, and she comes up with a plan even though Janie's never been convinced, and still isn't, that my aunt is going to work out in our household—be in any way a *help* to my father—still, she decides we should actively rally the troops and go on a hat-shopping spree with my aunt to cheer her up, thinking if anything's going to do the trick, a new hat will. Janie goes for a show of solidarity, saying, "We're with you on this hat-thing, Aunt Tony! Definitely bring on the hats!" which means we will have to *buy* one, too. Janie never likes to see a man get the better of a woman.

We go to Macy's—"The Magic of Macy's"—which Janie thinks is way too mainstream, though I've always liked their parades. Still, Macy's is our only solid option at this point, so there we go.

We go, in fact, to the Burlington Mall, where a Macy's store is. Aunt Tony drives. Janie sits up front, 'cause she is "big-boned" and 'cause she is Janie.

We're both a little concerned, to be honest, 'cause it's already well into August, and straw hats are what stores stock in March, maybe April, so there's a good chance they'll be all sold out, yet, when we get to the hat-and-glove section, which is on the main floor—there they are! Surprise!

"Who would've guessed that *these* wouldn't sell," Janie says, but so only I can hear.

We march right over to the display rack. Aunt Tony seems thrilled—but we all know, not really, that really she's quite down in the dumps. She immediately goes for the red hats—go figure. She puts this red hat on her head, that looks very much the same as her other red hats, and says, "Have you girls ever heard of the Red Hat Society? It's all of these women who gather for functions wearing blazing-red hats. That's how you know they belong—the red hats. Their motto is, 'All my life, I've done for you. Now it's my turn to do for me.' Their 'main responsibility,' per their website, is 'to have fun'." She pauses, then says, "When they say 'I've done for you,' they clearly mean children and *men,* don't you think?"

"They're the same thing," Janie whispers, then says aloud, "All men are pigs."

She takes the red hat *off* Aunt Tony, saying, "You already own pimpy red. Navy your color, Aunt Tony. It's navy for you." She takes a navy hat off of the rack, plops it on my aunt, then says, "There. You're a prettier, better Jackie O."

Unfortunately, Janie's got a *peach chapeau* picked out for me. When she plops it on me, I say, "You've *got* to be kidding. I look like I'm going to see the *Easter Bunny*."

"Or like you're going to Walt *Disney* World." She thinks she's pretty funny, that Janie.

I, meanwhile, pick out an *orange* number for Janie—really just a darker shade of peach—and plop *that* one on her and say, "Oh, that will *never* do. It clashes something awful with the blue." I'm referring to the blue streaks in her hair. Okay, they're really turquoise.

"What can I say?" Janie says. "It's so hard to be original."

"Yet you seem to muster on through. Day after day."

"You girls are hoots," my aunt says, yet she doesn't say "hoot" like she used to—with the same piercing get-up-and-go she once did.

It's sad.

In any case, the "hoot" comment brings Janie back—back to Aunt Tony and her troubles, and away from the hideous hats. "All men are pigs," she repeats, like she has the caustic line memorized, and there's no way of getting around it at all. Then she says, "Ever wonder *why* the female praying mantis bites off the head of her mate when they're finished with sex? There's a reason. Ever wonder *why* all the ants in a colony work for the queen? Again, a reason." Then: "Ever wonder *why* all wars are waged by men?"

Janie takes the navy hat off of my aunt, like we're going to ring it through, wrap it up, but instead says, "It's all just a lesson, Aunt Tony. Never have sex till you're married. *Always* hold out for a ring."

Aunt Tony says, "Weren't *you* the one insisting I wear a *French maid* outfit when I went yachting?"

"Well. We've sure learned a life lesson there. Haven't we?" Janie's become pretty sour on men, 'cause Ian Burchill has been giving her the snub…plus, remember, her father left her.

Still. Everyone's acting like men are the number-one problem: Everyone's wrapped-up in male-bashing, while I don't feel that's our way out, as I think men are fine. Maybe that's *my* problem?

In any case, 'cause we are being "good sports," I take home the peach hat, Janie takes home the orange hat—dark peach really—and Aunt Tony takes home the navy. We should start our very own mixed hat society and excommunicate the word "red."

My aunt tries to pull herself together. She really tries. She buys a new cookbook. She even makes a new recipe out of said cookbook; she even wears her new navy hat as she drives to the gym. But, still, I can feel something more needs to be done, 'cause Aunt Tony's sighing a lot now. She's left off the banging and scowling in favor of this.

After a few hours, I conclude sighing's worse.

Janie and I discuss the situation, and Janie declares that a hat doesn't fully compensate for a man—*especially* a man with a yacht on his hands—so we do more to cater to Aunt Tony. One day we take her for a facial. The next day we get her a massage. The third day we take her for a pedicure. Okay, we don't actually take her for a pedicure, we do it ourselves in Janie's room—me doing the cuticle-pushing-back, Janie doing the rewarding massaging and painting—and when we're done my aunt says, "It's too bad you two don't have dicks." I guess we did a good job. In any case, it turns out we're not home a lot.

On the fourth day—the day we're taking her shoe shopping—I'm just on my way out the door when Dad says, "Is my little girl going out *again*?"

"I'm just meeting Janie and Aunt Tony to cheer Aunt Tony up, 'cause she had that really bad break-up with Dan just last week."

"*Aunt Tony*?" my dad says. "I thought you gals just went out?" He's of course referring to Day One and Day Two and Day Three.

"She needs extra cheering-up it seems."

"I'm not sure I see the appeal," my dad says, though more to himself. Then he says, "Gee, that's too bad." And *then* he says, "Well next time, when you're not in a rush, I could take you to lunch…my treat," he puts in. This is another joke, 'cause he pays for everything anyway. "Or, you could do me the honor of giving me the pleasure of your *company*," he adds.

"Sounds good, Dad. I will. Only now, I have to go," I say, feeling just a little bit bad. As I'm closing the door, he says, "I wonder where Aunt Tony lives?"

Anyway, after all of the catering we do, Aunt Tony does seem better, which is to say that we don't really see her that much. She's out at the gym, I surmise, or out being picky at Whole Foods, or out simply showing off her toes—who knows? Maybe she's out closing bars? All I *do* know is that the kitchen stays spotless for days on end, 'cause she isn't around to destroy it on the hour, and I end up having to vacuum less. Janie thinks Aunt Tony is out doing "rebound-type stuff," like eating huge sundaes and such, which, "as long as no *men* are involved" Janie says is all right.

Ian Burchill *still* isn't talking to Janie. Janie's decided that at this age it's all about cliques, and that Ian is basing his infantile decisions on who is in the right clique. Janie's obviously not. Yet she thinks if they met somewhere else—in Paris, say, in ten years—they'd be madly in love. That they are "made for each other" as they say. Of course, that doesn't make her think he's any less of a jerk *now* for not liking her. As for giving actual credence to cliques…ah, love.

But, returning to my aunt: It turns out the male gender *is* involved. Or at least, Dan is involved. Or perhaps I should say my aunt has recommenced contact with Dan.

The way I find out is like this: Aunt Tony's cell phone's on the fritz, which is fortunate for me it turns out, 'cause Dan, in responding to Aunt Tony's advances, leaves lengthy detailed messages on our home machine, which I then get to listen to. I'm careful to, after I listen, hit "save" so it seems I never listened at all.

In one of them, Dan says: "We've been over this, Tony, and I'm sorry you happen to feel this way, but I don't see what more can be done, considering the circumstances."

In another, he says: "Tony. You said you've been driving by my house at all different hours of the day, waiting to catch me with 'her.' I find this unacceptable. If you keep all this stalker stuff up, I'll be forced to alert the police, which I don't want to do. You must cease and desist"—he really does say this—then he continues, "We had a good time, but it's over. We each need to move on. And, by the way: 'she' is not around right now, so you're not about to 'catch me with her.' But there might be another new 'she' in the future. That's up to me. I wish you well, but I don't expect to hear from you again."

Wow, I think. *Yikes. Zowie.* Humans sure can be complicated.

Both times, after I listen to the messages, I go to the mirror and practice my "poker face," in case Aunt Tony ever *asks* if I listened to them. "No," I say, shaking my head, watching my lips form a pout, which is what is called a "tell" in poker and to be avoided at all costs, so I try again. "No." I'm going to have to work on my lips. Actually— all of my face kind of gives it away, 'cause my eyes go all doe-like and wide, and my eyebrows lift up, and my forehead lifts a little bit, too, like to show I'm "sincere." I even try without the "no," with just a little shake of the head—but this is far worse, 'cause every last inch of my face freezes up. Let's hope she doesn't ever ask me.

It turns out she *doesn't*, and instead becomes madder than ever. This makes me figure that the "stalking" of Dan was what she was up to for her "rebound-type stuff," 'cause now that she's "ceased-and-desisted," she's around our cramped house a lot more and she's back to her banging.

My father's more put-off than ever, which isn't good.

"Oooh," he lets out when she bangs. "Can't you *do* something, Mo?"

I shake my head and shrug, wondering if I'm using my poker-face looks by mistake. "It's temporary, Dad," I reply. "Only temporary." Shake, shrug, shake.

He gives back a sour look, exhibiting utter disdain.

It's something we'll have to ride out, I think.

It was better when she was a stalker, I think.

Still, the anger isn't entirely Aunt Tony's fault, for one day, she nabs me in the hall and pulls me into her room. My dad's at his usual post, calmly watching TV.

"Mo. You have to *do* something about your father." Her eyes are ablaze.

"Why?" I ask. "What's up?" There's a lump in my throat.

"Well he came in my room and took my *clothes*. He went through my bureau, my closet. He took the clothes and dumped them on the floor! On the *floor*!" she repeats. "It's impermissible!"

I gulp.

"They were all in a heap when I found them. And there's more: He took all the food I'd just bought, and stuffed it in the flower boxes out on the stoop—those empty half-rotting-out flower boxes. *Outside!* He's basically dumping all my stuff! When I confronted him, he said, 'Was that yours...? I didn't know...Gee...' Bull-crap I say. I mean, I know he gets confused sometimes, that I grant you. But there's a difference between confused and aggressive, and this was aggressive, trust me. He doesn't want me here anymore and he's made *that* more than clear."

She waits for *me* to reply, but I'm tongue-tied. I'm shocked that my father really *did* all those things—this is my *father* we're talking about—but then I think, *maybe he really hates the banging.* Maybe, as a person gets older, they just can't put up with as much and they get all persnickety. I mean, It is my father's house.

And then my aunt says, "I think there's really something wrong with him, Mo. Have you talked to Elder Services? Maybe we should call Elder Services. Maybe we should see what the options are for him."

"No, no, no," I say. This would be bad. *Really* bad. We can't get Elder Services involved. Or Social Services. Or anyone!

While my aunt waits for me to say something more, a slew of excuses come to mind—his not liking the banging; the pill one; how, when somebody new first moves in, everyone has to adjust—but none of these I know are what she wants to hear, so I tell her I'll talk to him.

"I will," I confirm. "Soon." And she simply answers, "Okay." And that then is that.

However, I don't speak to my father right away, 'cause I'm already late for work. My shift goes from three-to-eleven, so when I get home, my father's in bed, and then, the next day, Aunt Tony beats me to the needed-father-talking. I'm just on my way to the bathroom when I hear a loud shout, then "Ed!", then, "What's my makeup doing here?!"

I think, *Uh-oh,* and duck into the bathroom to take a quick look.

It's true. My aunt's makeup *isn't* all sprawled on the counter in one jumbled mess. It isn't anywhere at all.

I hear, "You can't keep taking my stuff! You simply can't *do* that! This is *my* stuff! So, why is my makeup in the trash?"

"Well it's a nice organized spot," my father replies.

And my aunt says, "No. It's *not* a nice organized spot. It's the *trash!* If you no longer want me here, just say it!"

There's a very long pause, then I hear, "Well. It is a trifle bit crowded. Not to offend."

Every last inch of my body constricts.

"Ed. Your parents are *dead.* No one's moving in. Your wife is *dead.* I'm your wife's sister. I am your sister-in-law."

"Well, I wouldn't put bets down on *that.*"

I close the door and run the bathroom fan, not desiring to hear any more, though what I do hear are angry storming footsteps in the hallway.

I'll have to have that talk with him soon. *Real* soon!

BIG HEAVEN

Chapter 24

I wait till my aunt leaves the house and I simmer down, then I decide to make lunch for my father—have our little discussion over food. He likes it when I wait on him.

I make Campbell's chicken noodle soup as a break from the barley. This is 100% sodium, 100% processed, 100% fat—you can see the golden fat globules floating around. It's comfort food. It's yummy. I also pour him a big fat tumbler of root beer loaded with ice—his favorite, as you just might recall.

We start the discussion with small talk. "Mmm," he says as he eats. "I didn't know you could cook!"

This is a joke I believe, though I'm not fully sure. I think to myself, *It's a joke. It's a joke. Relax.*

To add to the small talk I say, "It *is* really yummy."

He nods as he slurps from his spoon. He's not a big talker when he's eating.

Today he is wearing tan Dockers, old boat shoes, and a short-sleeved, blue polo shirt that brings out his eyes. His eyes are watery-sweet. Also, his face is all soft and unlined 'cause he is pudgy as I've said which makes him look young, overall…It's not easy to accuse a face like that.

I think about how to ease my way in. I consider bringing up movies—he likes movies and I do get my check from a cinema, after all—specifically *The Hundred-Foot Journey*, but then I realize he hasn't seen that one, so then I think of telling him about the Death Cab for Cutie show that Janie and I attended last week at the Agganis Arena. I purposely didn't mention it earlier 'cause it doesn't add much to my story, though it *was* fun. But I don't bring the rock show up either, 'cause my father doesn't go out to rock shows, 'cause he's not the appropriate age and he hasn't anybody to go with, and he doesn't drive—I'm thinking now that he might just feel bad about the driving if I bring up the show. So *then* I think of asking what he's planning to do with the rest of his day, but he doesn't do much...

"Want some more soup?" is what I ask.

"Mmm," he says with a nod.

I get it, and then I just start. Small talk can only take you so far. "So," I say. "Dad, I heard there's been some trouble regarding Aunt Tony."

"Oh?" my father replies, looking up from his soup.

I nod, though mainly just to tell myself to keep going. So then I say, "I mean—I've heard *you've* been having some trouble regarding Aunt Tony."

He looks at me like to say: "Just spill, Maureen. I really don't relish this game-playing." He hates it when I treat him like a child, and I can't blame him, so *then* I say, "Well, I heard there's been trouble with her food...and her clothing...and with a bunch of her make-up," I bravely put out.

"Oh?" my father replies. Some soup has dripped onto his chin, so I sign for him to wipe it. He's not exactly making this easy for me.

"Well I heard—and this from Aunt Tony, of course—I don't really think she would lie—at least I don't *think*..." I'm equivocating again, and I know he hates that, so just blurt it all out: "She said that you went in her room, took a bunch of her clothes, and then dumped them—I mean, you dumped them like right on the *floor*." I wish we were not having this talk.

He looks at me.

Nothing.

"And then there's the matter of her food," I put in. "And her makeup," I tactfully add.

Nothing.

So then I put in, just to help him out, "I know she's been difficult, Dad, what with her banging. I do understand that, Dad."

At the mention of the banging, he returns his attention to his soup. So *then* I say, "So do you remember actually doing that, Dad? With the clothes?" It's direct, it has to be asked.

"Of course," he says to me now as if saying, What? Do you think I'm a moron? He's using his "father tone"—never good—and he doesn't add anything *on* to the "of course." He doesn't, for example, say *why* he would pilfer her clothes, then dump them in a heap on the floor, and I didn't ask him outright. I mean, you'd think it'd be a thing he'd volunteer.

But since he doesn't, I just say, "Right. 'Cause actually, Dad, she's staying here now—in the guest room. And she's going to be staying for quite a long time. Maybe forever even. And we can't be moving her clothes around on her, you know? Well, not *on* her, but…" I realize I'm using a "we." Not good.

"I know that, Maureen," my dad says irritably, like he's losing his cool.

I can't blame him, but I say, "Good. 'Cause it wouldn't be good if it happened again. So tell me that you're not going to actually do it again. Okay?"

"Of course," is what he replies. He is using his that's-quite-enough-Maureen voice, which I, to be honest, know well, so that's that. Plus, he's *agreeing*, which is good, though his agreeing isn't giving me the satisfaction I'd like…still…and then still…so *then* I say something I wish I didn't have to, since I am the child, not the adult, and I can tell that he's not in the mood, and he is a Gemini, as I have said, so he's got these two sides and so could turn on me in an instant, "Do you know *why* you went and did it, Dad?"

This is precarious ground, but I feel it needs to be asked.

He looks at me as if checking to see if I really expect an answer.

I, in my own way, look back, as if saying, yes, I do.

So then he says, "No," like it's a perfectly valid reply, and though it is *not* the reply I am looking for, it will have to make do for now. I'm not going to push anymore.

We go back to our soup—spooning, slurping, dripping. My father appears to be enjoying his a lot. After what seems a long time, he finally looks up. "I'll say this for you, Mo," he puts forth. "You're a much better cook than your aunt," and smiles at me sweetly, working his old father charm, while I smile back. What else is there really to do?

Later I think, *It's hard to have a full-blown conversation with someone who basically primarily agrees with you.* Those kinds of talks are pretty short when you pay them any mind. The U.N. should try them. Their members would be home in time for dinner. Maybe even lunch. And though I suppose I should be glad it went so well— deep down, I know it went *too* well. That's too bad.

And speaking of things both going well and then again not—Cameron hasn't called. Not since our *The Hundred-Foot Journey* date.

The reason that's *not* going well is the age-old obvious reason that everything *is* going well but I'm not sure I want him to call, or rather, I'm not sure it's good to want this, since I am going to become a nun, seeing as how it's my prophecy and all. Yet I also really want him to call, which pretty much stinks, way deep down—all this wanting, yet knowing you shouldn't, yet wanting it still. Probably, I never should have kissed him, but I did…It's all just incredibly confusing like that.

And then I start to wonder, as well, whether Cameron might indeed be like Dan, and just doesn't think like us girls. Maybe he doesn't believe it's important to call. Maybe he doesn't even really care.

In any case, I decide I need a break: A break from Cameron, a break from Aunt Tony, a break from my father, so I instead set my mind upon God.

I'll be honest. When everything was going so swimmingly peachy there, I kind of forgot about God. Well, I didn't *forget* about Him; I just didn't think about Him as incredibly much—not as much as I should have. Also, I missed a couple of the group's monastic talks. But now, with things *not* going swimmingly well, I find myself thinking about God once again. There aren't any atheists in foxholes, right? Not that I'm proud to admit this—that God mainly enters my mind when life isn't going well—but God's *maya* is so very tempting, you get caught up. So that's actually a compliment to God, right? Like, well done, God (hey, I know. I'm brown-nosing here).

In any case, I see what now has to be done: I have to go to a spiritual talk, talk to a monastic while there, and get the old ball rolling—something I was intending to do on the spiritual retreat. It suddenly occurs to me that this whole thing—everything that's recently gone wrong—might actually be God's test to see if I am committed to Him, and once He sees I am, He'll make it so things fall in place so I *can* be a nun. In fact, that's likely part of my problem. I haven't left things up to God, so now I will.

In the ballroom, I sit in the very front row as a way to atone for my sins—not that I didn't sit up in the front row before, it's just that now I am doing it with *intention* behind it.

It feels really good to be back—like being back home. The whole room is filled with spiritual vibes—I don't know how else to really describe it—somehow elevating your everyday consciousness. Our guru's picture is there on the altar at the front of the room, so I bow to the picture. He's smiling at me—like he always is.

Brahmachari Paul is again the introducer for the night. He's as adorable as ever, with his sweet Midwestern ways—and body, and face which I'm suddenly more aware of.

People clap when he reaches the stage.

He says, "Good evening. It's so nice to see you all here. The talk for tonight is entitled, 'Developing the Appropriate Attitude for Loving God,' and just to ensure that *we* all have the appropriate attitude for hearing the *talk*, I have the following story for you."

People laugh. Already. *Before* they even hear the story, they laugh at the very *idea* of laughing. Me, too.

"There once was a man," Brahmachari Paul says, "who always was late to everything. One week, he was scheduled to go see his dentist, and the day before his appointment, he telephoned the dentist's office to see if he could be late. The receptionist replied, 'That will be fine. We'll just have to skip your anesthesia.' The man, it turned out, was on time."

People laugh. It's a really good story.

"That just goes to show," Brother goes on, "what adopting the right attitude can do. To tell you more about cultivating the right attitude, it is my extreme pleasure to introduce Sister Satsita."

People gasp, and then clap, and then clap some more…

People apparently *like* Sister.

Sister is pretty, young—still in her thirties, I'd guess—yet fully ordained per her ocher robe color. That's to say she's not a "nun-in-training." She's arrived. She wears her hair pulled back in a bun, and has a cute, ski-jump nose and blue eyes. I can see 'cause I'm in the front row.

She says, "Good evening," and again, people clap. Then she looks out at the crowd, smiling at people she knows, acknowledging faces—it's the feminine touch—the brothers never do this, from what I have seen.

"It's so nice to be here," Sister says, "and to see so many of whom I have spoken with before, as well as so many new faces. Welcome to all.

"Tonight's talk, as Brahmachari Paul so delightfully introduced, is on 'Developing the Appropriate Attitude for Loving God,' but the question that first must be asked is: *Why* should we love God?"

She waits.

"We should love God 'cause we are a part of Him. God, it turns out, is the only true thing in the world, and we are a part of this truth. There is not one thing we could do in all of this world, were it not for Him.

"Let me also say this: God *wants* our love. It is said that God has everything He could ever possibly want—everything in all of creation—but the one thing He doesn't possess is our love. He did this on purpose, it is said—He gave every single one of us free will—so we could choose what to do with our love. God is not about to take our love from us; we must give it freely. That is how God chose to set the universe up. God wants us to decide that we love the Giver of the gifts, more than the gifts themselves.

"The very highest law," Sister goes on, "is to love God. That's why Jesus said, 'But seek ye first his kingdom and his righteousness, and all these things shall be added unto you.' And our guru has said that you can follow all of the rules—a million fast rules—but if you don't love God, you have nothing. Conversely, if you love God, with *all* of your heart and your mind, you don't need any rules."

She pauses here for effect. It's a good place to pause, I believe, for it's a really big statement…

She smiles.

"Okay. So loving God is important, but how do we get there? It is said that to know God is to love God, so the more we experience Him, the more we'll want Him, the more nothing in creation will do—nothing on this earth—but we need to *want* to know God. We have to put in the effort. And to do this, we need the right attitude. Attitude, in everything, is critical.

"Brahmachari Paul already told you a story about this—a good one, I have to admit, that I *won't* try to top."

People laugh.

"But to try and bring the point home, I'll tell you one more—he doesn't get *all* of the laughs. You see, there was a woman," Sister says, "who was staying in a very nice hotel, but who was going crazy because of piano-playing next door. Finally, she'd had quite enough, so she called the front desk. 'The guest next door is playing the piano!' she cried. 'He does nothing *but* wildly play the piano. You must tell him to stop!' And the manager replied, 'Oh! But I can't do *that!* That is the famous Stravinsky who is practicing for a concert to be given tonight. He *must* play', and the woman replied, 'Oh! *Stravinsky!* Well that is quite different!' She then called up everyone she knew and told them to rush right over, so they could listen to the marvelous Stravinsky. Which just goes to show that it's all in our attitude."

Sister concludes, "May all of you, approach your unceasing search for God as being far better than listening to Stravinsky."

She bows with humility and grace, and then is gone.

Afterwards, both Sister Satsita and Brahmachari Paul are present in the foyer to greet people. This is really good, 'cause I need to at last go up to one of them, and, as I said, get the proverbial ball rolling. I'm thinking of approaching Brahmachari Paul 'cause he's not a monk yet —not fully—which means his standards might not be as high and I might just pass. Ha. Plus, he's the really funny one. With luck, I could even schedule an interview for later in the week, 'cause my plan, as I've told you, is to be accepted into their postulant program *before* they go back to L.A. and hopefully even fly *with* them when they go, and thus fulfill my prophecy. So I don't have a whole lot of time. They're leaving in three or four *weeks!*

I mean, what I *don't* want is to fly to L.A. blind, only to be later sent home 'cause of some problem I couldn't foresee—some requirement I still need to meet or a lack of devotion perceived on my part—some deficit that a *monastic* might see, that I couldn't, determining, say, how I might mix in a tight-knit community like that of an ashram, or how I might deal with authority figures—whatever—

anything that could then render me less-than-ideal and allow them to reject me out of hand. I can't have that kind of thing hitting me smack in the face. I want confirmation, as I've said. Reassurance...

The thing is, I remind myself now about the age requirement for being a nun—eighteen—which makes me think I should put the meeting off till I'm more gussied up, like decked out in heels, for example, and have put on a little more makeup, since then I look older...

I am thinking I should pretty much look a little older for this, really. I imagine our conversation playing out like this:

Me (going up to Brahmachari Paul): "I just want to tell you— you're really funny."

Brahmachari Paul: "You should see when I make jokes."

Me, smiling, then me telling him what I intend, then asking if there's any advice he can give.

He tells me the minimum age is eighteen.

I say to him, "Right"—not acting surprised, as if I *am* eighteen.

Then he tells me how they like you to finish up whatever you're engaged in. So if you happen to be in school, for instance, they like you to finish with that.

"Right," I tell him again, as if I am finished with that.

And then he tells me how they like you to be adaptable, so you can live in a close-knit community like that of an ashram, and how they like you to deal with authority well. In other words, all of that other stuff I already said he might say.

All right. I'll be honest with you. I know that he *does* say this stuff, 'cause I eavesdropped on another woman discussing this same kind of thing with him, and this is the stuff he told her.

Lastly, he comes to say this—and this is a part I *do* imagine 'cause I didn't just chance overhear it—by chance, deliberately, what's the difference at this point: "It's not always easy. The training is rigorous. But if it was easy, everyone would want to be a nun."

I imagine him saying it like it's a joke—a real cut-up they tell in those close-knit monastic circles—so I laugh.

By now, it's like we've already had the conversation.

I glance over at Brother before I leave, and note once again how adorable he is.

It's too bad he is a monk, I think.

BIG HEAVEN

Chapter 25

When I return home from the spiritual talk, Dad's dozing soundly in his chair with South Park on TV. I don't think he was actually *watching* South Park; I think he was watching Dr. Phil, which is on right before South Park. In any case, I turn the TV off, which of course only wakes my father up. So then I turn it on.

"Hi," I say.

"Oh," he says. "Mo."

I notice his glass is on the table again—naked, meaning without any coaster—which further means that it's left a white ring on the veneer. He's been taught that he's supposed to use a coaster. My mother's rules. I start to clean up, when I notice a strong smell of poo in the house. I think: *Oh no.* I do a big sniff to see if I'm actually registering things right.

"What's that smell?" I ask.

"I don't know," my father replies. "I was wondering myself."

He looks pretty clueless regarding it all. I sniff again.

It can't be coming from him as it's not all that local. So then I start tracking it down, which doesn't really take very long. It's a very small house.

It's coming from his bathroom—from every imaginable spot in his bathroom: from the toilet seat, inside the toilet, on the floor around the toilet, even from the wall directly next to the toilet-paper holder. There's even a little brownish discoloration on the faucet handle. The total smell is overpowering.

I leave the bathroom, walk down the dim, narrow hall till I'm back with my father and say, "Dad. There's poo all over your bathroom. Did you have some sort of an accident?"

I don't know *why* I say this, except it's something you tend to say without thinking when you encounter this kind of situation, right? Like solidly stating the facts so you can plot out your course.

My father says, "No…I don't *think* so." This isn't good.

So then I say, "But, Dad. It's all over your bathroom. It's in *your* bathroom. Nobody else uses your bathroom. It *must* have been you."

He says, "I don't *think* so. But it's hard to remember from time-to-time. You know?" This definitely isn't good. *Not good, not good, not good!* Why can't he simply acknowledge it, so then we can move on? *Why can't he simply be normal,* I think? And suddenly, I feel so alone, like I'll have to make all the decisions, all by myself. I can't count on my father. I won't ever be able to *really* count on anyone again. But I think to ask, "Are you all right?" Please don't tell me you're sick, is what I pray. I'm not set up for "sick."

"Yes," he tells me. "Fine."

I should have known. I should have known my father would be "fine." With him, it's always "fine."

And, suddenly, I'm mad at my father—so spitting mad I could scream! Even though it is clear it was out of his control, and even though he likely wasn't feeling that hot at the time, and even though it might be related to food poisoning—I'm still mad! Screaming and spitting mad, really. I feel zero empathy for my poor father, and this, it turns out, makes me madder. It's strange how such processes work.

You end up mad at yourself for being so mad, and that's the worst mad that there is. Still, I take my anger and put it on him. I've pretty much had it!

I kick the wall before I leave the room and hear a picture frame shake. Maybe several shake. I go to clean things up. I have to do it before Aunt Tony gets home—wherever *she* is. I'd prefer she didn't know about this.

Mad as I am—I'm *really* pissed—I decide to approach it logically and efficiently, so I gather supplies before I go in. Luckily, my mother keeps rubber gloves beneath the kitchen sink—I guess I should say, "kept," however, I do say "luckily," 'cause rubber gloves are a thing I would *never* think to buy. Never ever. Never in a million years. Regardless, I get the rubber gloves, then I go into the main bathroom where the cleaning supplies are kept, and I get Comet, a toilet brush, a sponge—even a bottle of Scrubbing-Bubbles, and then I venture into Dad's bathroom.

And so I clean.

I do what has to be done.

A few times, 'cause I'm feeling so sorry for myself, I plug up my nose with my fingers, or shut both my eyes, or dramatically scrunch up my face, but most of the time, I just do the job.

It's harder to clean than I thought. It's all caked on and dried up, so that I have to scrub really really really long and hard, and rinse out the sponge way more, too, which turns the water, well, just nasty. You don't need to know all the details. It's truly disgusting. It's an aspect of being alive, yet it's totally gross.

It breaks down like this: The toilet seat's not *too* hard to clean, and, for the toilet, I use the plastic scrub brush, which isn't that bad, but the floor is way harder, 'cause the poo is in the grout between the tiles, and grout is a *misery* to clean. And then there's the wall, which is nothing but paint, but turns out to be hardest of all. I *really* use elbow grease there, which ends up making a bigger, rounder, browner mess. Not smaller.

As I'm cleaning, I think how some people do this for a living—change bed pans and stuff—really *do* this, I mean—but how I've always known it wasn't for me. Anything to do with bodily fluids is not for me. Some people are cut out for some things, and some aren't, and it's nothing that you should feel bad about. It's just a fact. I could never stick a needle in an arm, for example. So the fact I'm disgusted by Dad's poo is nothing that I should feel badly about. But at the same time, I think, *I can't let my life become this. Is this what my life's going to be?* and I start to cry.

When I'm done crying —it doesn't end that instant; it takes a while—I put the cleaning supplies away without saying a word to my father, then I seek shelter in my room.

I feel like hiding. I feel like crawling in under the covers and never coming out. Drilling a hole in the floor and dropping in.

I don't even look at my guru.

I lay numbly on my bed.

It's summer, so I shouldn't get under the covers, but I do, and as I get under, I think, *Why is this happening to me? This shouldn't be happening! I'm too young!* And this starts me crying again. I can't see living my life like this. I cry and cry.

I cry for what must be an hour—till my throat is raw and red and my eye sockets ache—then I start to get angry again. I decide to get out of bed: Take action. I'm going to check my father's pills, which is always a barrel of fun for me.

I'll be honest with you: I haven't been checking them. I've been too wrapped up with Aunt Tony, I guess…and with Cameron…and Janie…with every other person *except* my father 'cause—and here I'll be honest again—it's not that much fun being fixed on him, especially when it comes to stuff like him taking his pills.

I'm expecting to find them a disaster and they are. There are supposed to be two pills in each of the morning slots and three in the night slots, as I've mentioned. What I find is six pills in one slot, and no pills at all in some others, and four of the same kind in another random slot, *et cetera*…It's a mess, to put it mildly.

It infuriates me no end. I think, *I shouldn't be in this alone.* And then I think, *I'm not. My father is in this, as well. It's his mess.*

I decide to have a talk with him. Wake him up. Shake him out of his fugue somehow. I have to make him realize just how serious this whole matter is, and how much his actions affect me, and how much he is *ruining my life!* It's time I had it out with him.

I bring the pillbox into the family room as State's Exhibit A. I say, "Dad. You haven't been taking your pills like you're supposed to, huh?"

There is nothing mitigating in my voice. In fact, it is stone hard.

And he returns, "Well I would *hope* I have."

And *I* feel like saying, I would sure "hope" you have too, but it *isn't the case!* Instead, I say, "Well it turns out you haven't. The pill box is an absolute *mess*. How do you think it got like that?"

It's a rhetorical question, of course. I don't expect him to shout out "*Mea culpa!*" and he doesn't. When he *does* decide to answer, he says—in his own rock hard voice, "*You* must have filled it like that."

I'm infuriated. I say, "I *wouldn't* fill it like that, Dad. *Why* would I fill it like that? It's all wrong! It's supposed to be *two pills* in the *morning, three* at *night.* We've gone over this and over this. In the morning: white and pink. In the evening: white, yellow and pink. See? Two, then three: two, then three. And instead, what do we find? We find two days *totally* empty! And those *aren't* two days in the past, they're days in the *future!* They're supposed to be *full!* And then we find that some compartments have *six* pills. They're supposed to have *two.* Or *three.* What in the world's going on?!"

He says, "Oh. You're going to be talking in *that* tone, are you?"

"My *'tone',"* I say, "is secondary. *This* is important. No. This is *crucial.* You *have* to do what I say. It's *crucial* you take your pills!"

"Who died and made you boss?" He shows me a fighting-mad face. This *infuriates* me.

I lose it. I totally do. Something just pops.

I say, "I *am* the boss, Dad, though I don't want to be, and yet I *am,* 'cause *you* sure are not! You're the *parent,* though no one would know." Then I say, "Do you know the things you've done *wrong*?! Let's count. One: You've crashed the car. Two: You don't take your pills. Three: You wandered into CJ's one time—God knows why—and I had to get you. I leave you, for even a *minute* alone by yourself, and you fall and are hospitalized. I can't even leave for *one night!* And what else? Oh yeah. You leave the stove on. You think your *parents* are alive. You take Aunt Tony's stuff and trash it. And now you're incontinent, and you don't have the foggiest *clue!* How's *that* for a list?!"

I feel my nails dig into my palms 'cause it's awful what I'm saying—truly bad—but I just can't help it. All hope of having a *future* is at stake!

I say, "If you don't wake up and get it together, *you're* going to end up in a home, and *I'm* going to end up in foster care. Is that what you want? To see your own daughter in *foster care?* I feel like you're doing this on purpose to…to upset me! And also to upset Aunt Tony!"

"*Aunt Tony?!*" he says angrily. "Aunt Tony's been…"

"I don't *care!* I don't want to *hear* about Aunt Tony! Do you even know why she's here? It's to help take care of *you* 'cause *you're* not able and *I'm* not going to. I can't. I didn't sign up for that. I'm not the person who *married* you. I have my life to live, and you, you're *ruining my life!*"

He looks at me with eyes like I am his Judas, like he can't believe his own ears, and then he just walks out on me. Just like that. Or rather not "just like that." It takes *doing* on his part. First, he gets out of his chair—pushing on the armrests like it's hard. Then he shuffle-steps to the door. And *then* he walks out. He isn't wearing shoes. He goes out in his socks. Men's dress socks. Gold toe. I know them well 'cause I wash them! He slams the door as he makes his way out, like that is his "statement."

I think, *Good.* I think, *Now he will finally wake up—watch what he does.* I think: *I've pussyfooted around far too long—somebody had to wake him up.* I think, *I'm going to have to go get him.*

BIG HEAVEN

Chapter 26

Later, I feel pretty bad about what happened between my father and me. No one should be yelled at. Not even tyrants or dictators. Yelling accomplishes nothing and only contributes to violence, and two wrongs don't make a right. In fact, people maybe become tyrants or dictators 'cause people *have* at times yelled at them.

So even though I don't believe in yelling—and I don't—and even though I feel especially bad that I yelled at my father—and especially bad about the things that I said—I don't have any regrets about the overall message. My dad needs to improve his behavior and, of everybody living on this earth, it's up to *me* to have to teach him this. That's just the way it's worked out. *C'est la vie*.

Still later—and continuing on with the "lesson-teaching theme"—I think this: *I'm not going to keep on doing everything for him*. If he wants someone to make lunch, or butter his bread, or pour his Barrel-Head root beer for him over ice—tough. He'd better learn to do it himself, 'cause that's going to be our new theme, and learning that is going to be our new agenda.

Anyway, what I decide is to be cordial to my father, but that's it. I still do the grocery shopping, so there's food in the house if he wants it; I still do his laundry at least once a week; I still pay the bills, and have *him* wobbly-Hancock the checks—I never told you that part, but

I do—but there it stops. He is a man on his own is how I approach it; though, he quickly one up's me. Even though I play it cool when I see him, *he* plays it cooler, so that *I* start to look like Suzy-Sunshine in comparison.

"Hi," I let out when we meet—the usual greeting, though cooler.

My father just sits there and looks at me.

It's interesting, 'cause he doesn't look down or away—he just looks, and in the long look, he lets me know all the things I've done wrong, and how he hasn't *forgotten* any of them, and he might not *ever* forget. At least, not until an apology is offered, and an Oscar-worthy apology at that. And even *then* it might take a little time, is what his looks tell me—Geminis, I'm guessing, holds grudges. But in any case, I don't apologize, I just say, "Hi," then I tell him where I'm going, and what time I'll likely be back, as if he is still a "responsible parent." And where he used to answer: "Fine. Have a nice time"—now he no more than just looks at me.

So relations between us are even cooler than I wanted and, it's funny, for now that my father is angry, he doesn't seem nearly as clueless. It's as if the anger has sharpened his wit somehow. In a way it's really too bad that, along with everything else he forgets, he can't also forget our fight, but that in a nutshell is irony, right?

And as for Aunt Tony, she goes from one craving attention, to one who is quietly wary all the time, like she's got a side bet on our feud, except she isn't incredibly wealthy, so it can't be a *big* bet. That kind of interest.

And the only other thing I can report about Aunt Tony is that she's been calling her ex-boyfriend, Phil—the one in Miami; it's as if the two are conspiring on something—maybe rekindling their romance. I really don't know. All I *do* know is that I'm not going to count on my aunt anymore to help out. I am counting once again on my father.

In any case, and on top of like *everything* else, later that day Cameron calls. He leaves a message for me on my cell, asking if I want to get together, and to call.

I found out from Janie—too late—that Cameron didn't call me before, in other words, for *ten* friggin' days after our date, 'cause he and his folks went to Quebec on summer vacation—like *this* is the excuse of the year. Cameron didn't even tell *Janie* about his planned trip. Janie had to first find out from me he hadn't called, then call Cameron, and *then* hear it. *Then* she told me. *He*, of course, couldn't tell *me*. Janie—who's all ga-ga about her friends dating—tells me it's no major deal, and that Cameron really likes me. Really, she assures. But I think it's just like a boy to forget the rest of his life 'cause he's "on vacation." Likely, it never even dawned on him to call, 'cause he knew he couldn't see me while away, so why bother? And now that he's back, and he *can* see me, he calls. There's a certain basic logic there, of course, but it's missing *so much!*

Just like a boy, is what I think. *Just like a typical boy.*

I don't call back. In a roundabout, mystical way, I blame Cameron for a lot of the trouble I'm having, which is a roundabout way of saying I blame myself. It's like I'm being punished somehow. It's like 'cause I kissed Cameron, lusted after him, even bought a new bra set for him, the rest of the trouble is happening with my father and aunt. It's like God is letting me know that's not for me. Cameron, sex, lust—not for me. That being a nun *is* for me, and that I have to go back to God.

I don't call Cameron back, even when he leaves two more messages, which kind of eats away at my nerves. I mean, I'm tempted. Really tempted. I want to call him, but I don't.

A day after Message Three, Janie calls me. This, of course, I could have predicted with both my eyes shut. "Hey," she says, "what's up?" And then, before I can *tell* her what's up, she says, "Listen, I was talking to Cameron, and *he's* kind of wondering what's up, you know? I mean, I know you guys went out and had a fabulous time, and now what? Nothing? You're not returning his calls? What in the world's up with *that?*"

And I'm thinking, *Yeah. And Cameron didn't call for ten days either. What in the world's up with that?* but I don't say all of that. I just say, "News travels fast, or so it seems"—which admittedly is a non-answer.

"Yeah…so…what's up?"

"Nothing."

"C'mon."

"I really don't want to get into it now. You know?"

"No, I don't. Tell Janie."

There's a pause, during which I am not "telling Janie," so Janie says, "C'mon. Tell Janie. What's up? Janie doesn't judge."

"Janie judges," is what I reply—hey, she *does!*

"Only 'cause *you* screw things up"—see what I mean?

So then I say, "Janie gives advice."

And Janie says, "Janie *has* to give Mo advice. Someone's got to. Mo keeps screwing up." Then: "So tell me. What is it?"

I'm not going to tell her *too* much, but if I don't give her something she'll hound me—plus, well, I *have* to tell *someone*—so I say, "Oh, it's just that my dad's been like moving my aunt's stuff when she isn't around, saying folks are moving in, you know? Like he doesn't really want her here."

"What folks?"

"Just…folks."

"And there *are* no such folks coming. Right?"

"Right."

"Is he taking his pills?" Janie asks.

"Sometimes. I mean—as far as I know." This isn't true. "I mean —I fill up the box like every day." This is practically true…sort of…I really don't want to get into it with Janie.

"Well, you know. Even if the pill slots *are* empty on any given day, there are still lots of tricks he could pull. He could hide the things under his tongue, then flush them down the toilet later. He could stockpile them under his mattress for when he wants to pull the plug. He could feed them to your dog—you don't have a dog, don't you? I mean, you didn't just go out and *buy* a dog, right?"

This is Janie's "funny" side. She *knows* we didn't just buy a dog. I scrunch up my face. Janie can't see my scrunched face, but I bet she can sense it.

"Maybe you *should* buy a dog," Janie says. "A dog would help keep your dad company. Your *aunt* certainly isn't doing the trick."

This is not the kind of advice I particularly need. I say this to Janie.

"How 'bout a hamster?" she says.

I don't respond.

"I know. You and Cameron can get married, and have a whole frigging busload of kids, and then your *kids* can take care of your dad."

I wait if she's going to be like *this*.

"Sorry. It's just that none of my suggestions are any dumber than thinking your aunt would ever work out. And while we're on that subject: You've likely been giving too much attention to her, and not enough attention to him. That's maybe part of the problem."

"Well if it makes you feel any better, I've *had* it with her. *And* him."

There's a pause, then Janie says, "*Oy veh*," though she isn't Jewish. Then she says, "Tell Janie. C'mon. Spill."

I tell her. Or rather, I tell her some of the things—I can't tell her *everything*). I tell her about the banging. The scowling. Dad trashing Aunt Tony's stuff. Then I tell her how Dad made a really big mess—I don't tell her what kind—and how we had a big fight, and how now I'm simply not talking to him…not really…not much…

"That is just childish, Mo. He's your *father*," is what Janie says, like father is some mystical word.

"Well I wish he would act it," I say.

This time, it's Janie who doesn't utter a word, like she's hoping I will "hear myself." Then she says, "Listen. I haven't said too much up till now, 'cause I could tell you didn't want to talk about it, and that you probably wouldn't listen if I did, and I wasn't that sure how bad things had gotten myself, but your dad's got an illness, Mo. You know that as well as me. He can only do what he can do. The pills might help, but…"

"He could sure do a heck of a lot better; I tell you that."

"Could he?" she asks.

"Yes. Yes, he could. I mean—you don't live with him, Janie, so you can't see. He does this stuff on *purpose*. He's acting out. I can tell. I mean, take the pill box, right? It's an absolute mess! I mean—it's even more of a mess than it would be if he was *really* wacked out, like back when he had delirium in the hospital. He's just doing it to try and get attention, like some spoiled little kid."

"I don't think so," Janie answers, sounding awfully sure of herself.

I say, "He's got to take things seriously, Janie; he's got to at the very least *try*. I'm sick of trying." Then I add, "Sometimes I think all he's *really* trying to do is wreck my life."

"Listen to yourself," she finally says. Then she says, "Maybe *you* need to stop your avoiding."

"What's that supposed to mean?"

"Well, he's your responsibility. You can't keep sticking your head in the sand."

"*Responsibility?!*" I shout. "I'm *sixteen!*"

We wait.

Janie does better with silences than me. Janie *loves* silences; she lives for the things. Finally, she says, "Okay, fine. You're sixteen. But he's your *father* and you're his *daughter*…What would God or your guru say?"

I'm not even going to entertain such a subject with Janie. I say, "Leave my faith out of it."

"Okay. But good luck being a nun with an attitude like that. And with your father the way that he is," she willfully adds.

I think about telling Janie again how my being a monastic was prophesied back when I was twelve, right after my near-death experience. How it was prophesied for when I was *sixteen*, which is right now…but why give her the opportunity to come back at me with *more* mean words?

We end on a rather sour note. Actually, we both hang up.

It's too bad.

And lastly, there's this: Almost immediately after my reassuring phone call with Janie, Cameron calls, which again I could have predicted with both my eyes shut. The moment I see the caller ID, I let trusty voice-mail pick up.

"Hey. It's me. I thought I might catch you. I talked to Janie, and she said you've got all this stuff going on with your dad which has you pretty tied-up. I'm…sorry to hear about that. If you want to talk about it at all—give me a call. Though if you're too busy right now, I understand. Okay. Bye."

Leave it to Janie to go blab to him the minute she's off the phone, like she's the town crier. Still, it was a sweet call. A sweet message. Sweet. And it *is* the fourth time that he's called…I almost give in, but then I think, I have other things to think about. And he didn't call me before for a whopping ten days. Yeah, I have other things to think about.

Chapter 27

For three days after our fight, my dad eats nothing but corn chips based on the crumbs that I find in the used bowls on the table and empty bags in the trash. I don't any proof of any other food around—not even dried crusts of bread. Not that I'm bothering to notice his diet. I'm not. Not that I in any way *want* to notice.

Still, one night, right before I leave for a monastic talk—a key one for which I have plans—I decide to again make him soup 'cause he honestly loves it, and 'cause it is easy—I mean, all you do is open a can—and 'cause he says I'm a very good cook when I do. All right. He *usually* offers up this, though he hasn't recently and there's a good chance he won't tonight, 'cause of our feud. Yet my gesture might be looked at as a peace-offering, which would be good. Not that I'm listening to any of the things Janie said—I'm not. It's just that I feel a little bit bad for my father.

I make him his favorite: Campbell's chicken noodle soup. I leave it out on the table along with Ritz crackers, his other American favorite, and Barrel-Head root beer over ice. It's not the healthiest dinner in the world, but what can I do?

I tell my dad I made soup, and that it's waiting right now on the table so he should probably get up. I'm not going to actually eat with him 'cause I'm going to a talk, but it is a start.

My father doesn't move from his armchair. He sits like a lump, looking angrily at me. So then I tell him where I'm going, and how I won't be back until late so he shouldn't wait up, which is a dig, really, 'cause he never waits up, so this is a dig on his parenting skills. And then, 'cause he *still* isn't moving from his chair—just sitting angrily—I say, "You better get a move on so your soup doesn't freeze" which admittedly isn't nice. Then I add, "You can't just eat *Fritos* all day"— another quite obvious dig 'cause he's making me mad.

I don't get a "Fine," out of him, or a "Why, how incredibly sweet!" or even a "My *favorite*! How did you know?"—which would be one of his lame jokes—I'm starting to miss them. I just get a look of anger and expectancy at the very same time—expectant of an apology from me, I figure, but I don't give in. I turn my back and leave, thinking about how pathetic he is, wondering what my *mother* ever saw in him.

It's not a benevolent thought, and I wish I didn't have it, really. I just want to become a *nun.* That's all I want. I don't want to have unkind thoughts.

And speaking of my mom, I definitely definitely definitely miss her, but I'm not going to talk about that.

Anyway, that night, I hobble to Main Street to hop on the bus to Harvard Square (I'm wearing heels and makeup and a skirt—I never wear skirts), and the heels make it hard to walk fast, or, at all really, but I've done it so I'll look more "grown up" for when I speak to a monastic tonight—which I definitely plan to do.

I find, as I hobble along, that I'm still fuming at my father. His snubbing me over the soup just makes me all the more glad I'm moving on. Glad that I have God; my guru; plans to be a nun; plans for a meaningful future…there's even a spring to my step as I think such liberating thoughts…which is really the way it should be, right?

The ballroom inside the hotel is totally crowded—almost two times as crowded as usual, which is strange. When I mention this fact to a man standing next to me, I'm told it's the monastics' last talk. That's why so many are here. That they're heading back home to L.A. tomorrow…

I can't believe I didn't know. How very strange. I guess I had thought they were staying through August—that would make three solid months if they stayed right through the end of August—but it must have been an assumption on my part. I must somehow have gotten it wrong. I haven't consulted the schedule in a really long time, what with everything else, and it's now the middle of August, and they're going…

How very strange.

Brahmachari Paul comes up to the stage. Of everyone who has spoken thus far, I wish that Brahmachari Paul more than anyone else could stay, and he's not even a full monk—I wish, of course, they *all* could stay, but especially Brahmachari Paul. When he gets to the podium, he bows to the picture of our guru, then he bows to us.

People clap.

Brahmachari Paul smiles.

People clap more. His last talk. *This is really sad,* I think.

He is wearing his cool ocher shirt and khaki pants—he doesn't yet merit a robe. He's got that Midwestern good-looking face which is just like a prize. It's like he shouldn't even be on our planet, he looks so good.

He announces the topic for tonight's final talk which is, "Our Trials and Their Purpose." This is indeed apropos when I considers my current life. It's like God and guru once again have a message for me personally. This is good.

Brother says, "So. Trials, huh? What can we say about those? Anyone here ever have any?"

Everyone laughs.

"Our trials," Brother goes on, "can truly seem hard—even depressing at times—but like everything in God's world, they have a purpose. To try and shed light on this purpose, I'll tell you a story:

There once was a man who decided to climb one of the highest peaks in the Himalayas because he heard that a sage lived there. It took this man many many days to reach the summit, and he had to endure extreme hardships all along the way, including mind-numbing temperatures, altitude sickness, exhaustion. At last, he arrived at the summit, and he went to the wise man's cave and sat at his feet. 'Tell me,' he implored, 'for I have traveled very long and very far to be in your presence, how you came by your wisdom.' The wise man replied: 'Good judgment comes from experience.' He paused and then added, 'And experience often comes from *bad* judgment'."

Everyone laughs. Brahmachari Paul smiles sweetly. He has these magnificent corn-fed teeth to top off his good looks.

"I bet we all appreciate *that*. Our trials give us experience which, if processed in the right way, can give us the judgment to help us have *better* experiences. To tell you more, it is my great pleasure to introduce the speaker for tonight's final talk, Brother Satnarada."

It's at that point that I stop focusing, or at least focusing well. I do catch some bits here and there—how our trials exist mainly to bring us closer to God; how only God will satisfy us, *et cetera,* but I don't take the full lecture in 'cause I'm too shaken up. I hear mostly noise the next hour—a droning voice, a whooshing and roaring in my ears like they're plugged up with water. I only come back to the present when the droning voice stops.

There's quiet now. No one in the ballroom even breathes. Brother puts his hands on the lectern, looks at us, and finally says, "Well as most of you know, this is our last public talk. We're packing our things and leaving tomorrow. I just want to say what a pleasure it's been getting to know you, and ministering to you through God's grace. May God bless you and be with you all."

He bows to the picture of our guru, then he leaves the stage.

People clap briskly then stand and offer an exuberant ovation. It's the first time everyone has, but I keep thinking, *It's sad.*

The clapping goes on a long time—for far longer than Brother's in the room. There's a quality to it that states We know it's the very last time—the very last talk. You all—all of you—were great. We love you. Come back!

It's sad 'cause I'm not sure anyone has any idea what they're actually in for now. How they'll now have to fend for themselves, without the monastics around—no more monastics to give weekly talks, lead them in guided meditations, and inspire them through chanting. They'll still have our guru, of course—the guru is *always* present, one can't ever overlook *that*—but they're not going to have the great blessings bestowed by the monastics, or the meditations that go really deep, 'cause a Brother is there, though I will as I'm still planning to join them. But still, I can't help think, *Endings are hard. Especially ones where folks lose something. Those are like the saddest of all.*

I leave after I bow to my guru. I know: I got all gussied-up— heels, makeup, a skirt that goes down below my knees—and I didn't even talk to a monastic. I didn't even try to go up to one 'cause really, it's just way too sad when you stop and think about it.

BIG HEAVEN

I'm no longer prepared.
It's just too sad.

Chapter 28

The next day, I got to work at one o'clock. At work, I keep my cell phone silenced in my bag, and my bag underneath the refreshment counter, though I check it about every hour—just idly, just, I don't know, because—and four hours into my shift, there's a message waiting for me from home. That isn't good and I think, *Uh-oh.*

It's Aunt Tony. "Mo. Your father left the house like hours ago and isn't back. He's never been away for this long: It's been literally *hours*…Can you come home? I'm worried. Call me."

She did indeed sound pretty worried, like worried *sick*, which then serves to make *me* worry more. Partly I'm worried for me—which is admittedly selfish—and partly I'm worried for him—which is definitely not—and think, *This stinks. It positively does.* I wish this were not happening now.

I tell my boss, Marie, there's a problem at home, and she lets me go without a thought. There are always too many of us anyway.

On my way home I try and stay calm by thinking of the places he could be. *He could be at CJ's,* I think, idly perusing the paper, but CJ would have called, I bet. *He could be at Maria's Home Cooking,* happily *eating* Maria's home cooking, *or at Hannaford's, "browsing" the food like he does. Maybe he's going from one of these spots to the next, and the next, and the next...* Any of these sound good if you don't consider the total amount of time that has lapsed.

As I'm walking, I call Aunt Tony back and tell her where I am. She says she's *so* glad I'm on my way home, and she's located a picture of Dad to give to the police—who she hasn't yet called as she wanted to talk with me first—and she's jotting down info on him like hair color, height, weight, *et cetera,* but that she'll probably also need his date of birth and social security number. Also, she'll need to list any medical conditions adding, "besides, of course, the obvious." Her voice is stretched tight as a drum. She sounds like a wreck.

It's all somehow moving too fast.

I say, "I know where he likes to go. Let me check a few places on my way home. You just wait there for his return." Then I tell her how we don't want to call the police just yet, though I don't tell her why. I just say that.

My aunt only wails, "I'm not very good at this stuff!" And I feel like saying, "No kidding," although I refrain, and answer instead, "Don't worry. I'm on it."

I decide to check the downtown places first, and save CJ's for last, since CJ's is right by our house.

At Maria's, I push through the stenciled glass door. Maria herself is there, with her husband, and only two quiet tables of customers since it's still early. I ask—as coolly as I can—if she's seen my father today. "No," she says. "Why? Is he *missing*?"

This is what really stinks 'cause now everywhere I go, all of the downtown business owners are going to know my father is missing. Soon everyone in town will know there's something amiss, and as a result, they're going to be doggedly watching us from now on.

I say, "He's probably just out for a walk since the day turned out so nice," and bravely add, "Thanks, Maria. Please don't worry."

She—with her loose gray chignon and stout frame—looks worried. And this is only my very first stop.

I pretty much repeat this conversation in Davio's Barber Shop, and Immanuel Cleaners, and even in Hannaford's grocery, where I know a couple of the check-out folks, and they know us. "The City to Watch," as I've said, is really a pretty small town despite its cool name…

Nothing turns up.

And then, I find myself outside CJ's store. I think how I have to be extra circumspect now, extra cautious, 'cause CJ's is where Dad ended up the last time he chose to take off, so there's already been a clear strike on that front.

What I do is, I walk in totally "casual-like"—okay, not really—and I say, "Hi," and CJ says, "Hi." Then I say, "Gee, it was nice out today," 'cause it's now swiftly moving toward six, so the "day" part is over almost, and CJ says, "Yeah. Except I was in here the whole day so I don't really know." And I answer, "Yeah. Right. I hear you." And that's about all that we have to say, so then I say, "Listen. I haven't been home as of yet—I just this minute left work—but Dad was going to pick something up if he got the chance. Some…um…shampoo. So I was wondering if he ever made it in…? To pick it up…? 'Cause if he didn't, I'll get it myself, I was thinking."

Pretty darn smooth when I say it here, though it sounded worse when it exited my mouth if you can believe it, 'cause all of my hesitations filled the store. I mean, hesitations are so much bigger in actual life.

CJ says, "He hasn't been in."

"Huh," is what I reply super casual-like—not really—then I think: *Even if he had been in, what would that really have told me?* That he was spotted three hours ago and has been missing ever since, my harried brain replies. It really wouldn't serve to tell me *anything*. I've done nothing but waste CJ and my time from the minute I stepped in the door.

"Everything all right?" CJ says, and I say, "Yeah, fine. I'm just going to get that shampoo." So now I must *buy* a shampoo that is priced almost twice what it's worth 'cause I said that I would.

CJ squints as he gives me my change, as if he is looking for something. Then he says, "Well you take care. Give a yell if you need anything."

"Will do," is what I reply, though even my simple "will do" doesn't sounds elusive. And then I am on my way home, thinking only of hospitals. How maybe my dad is in one. How maybe he fell, and was taken by an ambulance to a hospital, and didn't have his wallet on him, and how now *I'll* have to track him down, and what all of *that* will mean...

What it *would* mean is it would be on his record. Another hospitalization. Another strange fall. Social Services would have to visit our house and who *knows* what would happen then?. And, worse, maybe he's seriously hurt. I should contemplate *that*. Maybe he's been hit by a car? Maybe a train's run him down? *Anything* bad could have happened—anything at all. I mean, maybe he's calling my name at exactly this instant? Maybe he is breathing his last breath...

Maybe I never should have yelled at him.

When I get home, Aunt Tony's yakking on her cell phone, though not in any "official" capacity. She's talking to Phil, I discern—using him to try and settle her nerves. Our house line stays open. She hangs up shortly after I appear.

"It's now been six *hours*," she says, her face pained. "He's never been missing this long, Mo. Do you think it's your fight? Do you think he took off 'cause he's mad?"

They're good questions, and, of course, I have already thought of them myself. Maybe he's staying away just 'cause he's mad? But where could he *be* all this time?

I give her a shrug.

"I got all this together for the police," she says.

The police.

I look. On the table is a photograph of me, my mom, my dad, at my Middle School graduation. Me in a white cap and gown. A parent at each side. My poor mother's smile is so large it could crack her in half. Next to the photo is a paper with stats about Dad with the dreaded word "Alzheimer's" crowning the list of medical problems.

"What did CJ have to say?" my aunt asks. She looks like she's waiting to be electrocuted.

"Nobody's seen him," I answer.

"We have to alert the police, Mo."

She's frantic.

I tell her I'm going to look for his wallet. If it's missing, it would on him, so people can identify him. Then I tell her I'm going to call a couple hospitals, 'cause that's how it happened before…sort of. I don't give her any more details, like about his prior hospitalization during which he believed he saw Martians—'cause she really doesn't need to hear all that right now.

She says, "I'm really no good at this"—her voice sounds all out-of-whack—and I want to answer, "No kidding," but I don't. Then she says, "Shouldn't the *police* do that, Mo? Call the hospitals? Shouldn't *they* be out looking *right now*?"

"Try and stay calm," I advise, like *this* is the key. I am trying to put off the police. The police are really the *last* step.

"I'm really no good at this," she tensely repeats, whatever good that does.

I think: *Maybe Dad left us a note. Maybe he left some kind of evidence to say where he is.* Maybe I'm grasping at straws. Still, I kick off my search. If I know he took his wallet, I'll sound that much better informed if I have to make calls.

I search.

I start in his room. I'm frantic, so I'm not really searching that well. I start out by searching the visible places in the room like his bureau-top, his nightstand, his bathroom, then I search the not-so-visible places, like inside the dresser drawers and all his pockets. I even search his medicine cabinet and hamper, but don't come across any wallet. This could be good or it could be bad.

As I'm searching, my aunt pops her head in every two seconds to suggest the police. "He's not in his right mind. He shouldn't *be* out alone. What's he doing out all by himself for all of this time?!"

We make a deal: We'll wait until seven, then call the police.

It is six-forty-two.

I say, as I'm looking around, "You didn't find a note by any chance, did you?" And even as the words leave my mouth, I hear how sophomoric they sound—how totally dumb. My aunt shakes her head. And then she is back on the phone, using her cell so our home line stays open.

I, for my part, go to the window to see if he's there. This is bad.

At one point, I say a prayer to God, asking that He bring Dad home safe, and soon, and that there be "no harm done" as I put it. Then I think to say: "Or please just let what is best happen"—which is very very brave, overall, but which is also quite smart 'cause whether you believe God exists or not, He always knows best. It's part of the true definition of "God." I really believe that, though I don't always act like I do. I don't always turn matters over the way that I should. In fact, there are loads of things I *don't* turn over, 'cause I want to maintain some "control," or so that goes, though that's rarely the best. But now, I do turn the fate of Dad over to God.

My aunt does some really fast pacing all over the house.

And then, at ten-of-seven—almost six hours after Dad left, and eight minutes after my prayer—a car pulls in front of our driveway. The sound is unmistakable 'cause I've been listening for it for so long, so I *definitely* know a car's pulling up at our house.

I return to the window. It's not the police, thanks to God, or an ambulance—more thanks to God—or any kind of emergency conveyance at all. It's a dark-colored four-door sedan, with a passenger who is my father. Oh, my God! This is good! Oh, my God!

I run to the door to meet the occupants of the dark car. I tell my aunt to wait inside, 'cause I'm thinking I'll be doing some fast-talking to the driver, and I don't want her changing whatever story I might tell, though, of course, I don't actually *tell* my aunt that. I just give a giant thumbs-up on my way out the door.

The driver is in her fifties, which is good, since it means she, too, likely has older parents who require her care, and so can relate. I'm so glad the driver is a woman.

She stays in the car, and makes the window go down on Dad's side so she can talk to me through it. My father stays where he is, as if the car *might* just now be his new home and he wouldn't really mind.

She says, "I found him on a sidewalk over on Bacon Street—just *sitting* on the surface of the sidewalk—so I pulled over to see if he was all right, and he seemed confused. I mean, he was sitting on a *sidewalk*."

This is okay, I decide. This is good. I can deal with this. At least my father is *found*. He is alive and sitting in somebody's *car*. This is *really* good. And, of course, I *expect* confusion.

I turn to my father and say, "I'm glad you're all right!"

He gives a look back like to say, "That *is* fortuitous, isn't it?" though no words come out of his mouth.

I turn once again to the driver. She has glasses, closely-cropped salt-and-pepper hair, and is wearing a Ralph Lauren polo shirt—bright pink. "Thank you *so* much for bringing him home. I *really* appreciate it."

On hearing these words, my father and his manners pop up. "Yes. Thank you," he says.

He says it normally and sincerely, but I say my part like, "Thanks for the delivery. We'll take it from here. But *thank you*."

I open my father's door, and he gets out and starts walking toward the house like he's happy he's home—real happy. I'm hoping that that will be it, but, of course, it isn't it—and I didn't *really* think that it would be, though she had been thanked by both of us.

Just as *I* felt she need to be thanked somehow more genuinely and profusely, *she* feels she has to tell her story and does. She tells me how she asked my dad if he was all right, and how he said he wasn't quite sure, which she figured was strange. So then she asked if he knew where he was, and he just answered "No," like "*Should* I?" So then she knew that something wasn't right. She knew right away.

"Anyway. I thought about calling the police, but I figured that would be a big pain for everyone. He looked local, so I could just run him right home if I knew where he lived, and I asked if he had his wallet."

From there, they figured it out that he was just two streets away. And she figured she could drop him off, as long as his family was here. And then she looks at me, like to ask if I *am* his real family—the only real family he's got?

I stick to my spiel using the pills pretext again. I say, "I *really* appreciate your driving him. He does get a little confused here and there. He's on these new pills and…well…he doesn't always take them when he should. But we're working on it."

I'm not sure that's really enough to explain his behavior—his wandering the streets by himself, his not even knowing where he was —and the woman is looking like it's *not* enough, not even close. She's also looking like she thinks I'm awfully young. Like she hopes there is somebody *else* she can speak to…

So then she says, "Is your…mother at home?"

I know what she's thinking. She's thinking there had better indeed *be* a real mom in the house, or at least an adult, and I don't want to show her Aunt Tony 'cause, as we know, she's "really no good at these things." So that's when I get this idea concerning my mother.

"She's at the police station. She was worried to death," I blurt out.

Once I say it, I'm not sure it's a brilliant idea, 'cause now my mom "exists" so to speak. Now she is "at the police station," which is a place a person could check if they wanted. So *then* I say, "He's never really done this before, so we were all worried sick. My mom went to the station for help. But now *you* found him, so I'll call her. She'll be *so* glad to hear. I better call now."

I act like there is real urgency to it, like now I have a mission, like I have to leave so I can call her.

The woman appears to get caught in this urgency, too. She says, "Okay. If you're sure everything is all right, I guess I can go."

"Great. I really can't thank you enough. Thank you."

"What's your name?" the woman asks, as she prepares to leave.

"Maureen."

"I'm Marge. Marge Brannon. But you can call me Marge."

"Well thank you again, Marge."

She nods. And I can tell that she's going to watch till I get in the house and not just drive off—which isn't so bad. I mean, it's really *thoughtful,* if you think about it.

I walk toward our little ranch house, hoping Aunt Tony is not in the window, so Marge doesn't *see* Aunt Tony—I don't want my aunt saying *a word*—but of course Aunt Tony *is* in the window. As I approach the front door, she waves happily to the driver of the car, and I can only imagine a puzzled Marge Brannon waving back.

Chapter 29

That night, needless to say, I'm solicitous of my poor father. I make him something to eat—a sandwich with one-percent milk; no root beer right before bed—too much sugar—lay out his summer pajamas for him, and make sure he takes his two pills. I stand and I watch. I even retrieve the day's comics for him from the *Globe*. He seems foggy, slower, tired, yet relieved to be home. In fact, 'cause of his relief, I'm thinking this might be a turning point for him. For the better. That maybe he'll behave from now on. You know, take his pills, only go out when somebody is with him. I'm thinking this might be a beginning—somehow.

Apparently, though, someone else is deciding the same thing, for I hear noise from Aunt Tony's small room—so much noise, that I'm thinking it will keep my father up, so I go check it out.

She's packing.

She's got her suitcase laid open on her bed, and her smaller, matching, carry-on tote beside it. They're both chartreuse—I don't believe I mentioned that to you before, but they are. *Nobody* sane owns *anything* chartreuse, except my aunt. Plus, the color totally clashes with her red hats.

"What are you doing?" I ask. I can see perfectly well what she is doing, but this is what you're supposed to say in situations like this.

"Packing," is what she says back. This, too, is what everyone says when asked such a dumb question. They tell you the facts.

"Where are you going?" I say. This is better.

"I'm going back to Miami to live with Phil. We've been talking, as you probably know, and he wants me back. And I want to go back." Then, before I can say another word, she adds, "I just can't take it anymore, Mo. Your father wandering off was the last straw. My heart wanted to leap from my chest. And you're not equipped for this, either, whether you know it or not. Your father needs help, Mo, and it's more than what we can provide—me and you."

She looks at me as she announces this news, but just for an instant. Then she goes back to her packing like a guilty party would. I'm totally stupefied. She is utterly and wholly irresponsible. How can she can just up and *leave* us?

She says, "I'm not going to leave you high and dry"—pack, pack —"I've made a bunch of calls while your father was gone. I got in touch with a group called Elder Services. I talked to a woman named Kara Hunt"—pack, pack—"She said there's all kinds of help you can get, most of it cheap, depending on his income. That's how they typically price it—on his income. He just needs a baseline evaluation. They can even come right into your home, depending on what he needs."

She goes on—pack, pack—"Anyway. I wrote all the info down. It's on the kitchen table for you."

Finished, she *keeps* packing, not looking at me anymore.

I'm speechless. I know that sounds trite, but I am. Eventually I say, "You did *what?*"

"Kara's expecting your call, but I gave her your number, too, just in case."

Betrayal, I think! Judas! Brutus! This is between my father and me—not her. She's an intruder. My mother never even really *liked* her.

I stare at her in abject shock.

My father and I are kin, is what I think.

Blood.

She's not even *related* to my father. She's just a leech from outside. Plus, I've toiled so long and so hard to keep it together, and she, with one phone call, destroys all I've done. Who died and made *her* the big boss?

I *keep* staring. She thinks she can just up and *leave?*

"I can see you're angry," she next says, "but you'll thank me for all this someday. Your father needs help, Mo, and it just isn't right that he not get it."

I watch her. She's accelerated her packing like she's catching a train pulling up. She packs all her ridiculous stuff, like her ridiculous workout-wear, and her ridiculous "yachting" wear, and her ridiculous skimpy peach top with the spaghetti-type straps, as if she's *fifteen.* For all I know, there's even a ridiculous French-maid outfit in there somewhere.

"It's the best thing for all," she goes on. "The best thing."

She nods to herself as folds, rolls and desperately squeezes junk in. She's got too much stuff—way *way* too much. It will never fit into her bags. She'll end up cramming it into plastic bags and making fifty trips to her car, *and I won't lift a finger to help!* I won't help with her lumbar-support cushion, I won't help with her George Foreman grill, I won't help with her ludicrous wok…

"I'm leaving tomorrow," she says, "first thing. I'd like to say a better goodbye then, but if you're not up, maybe we should say our goodbye now?"

She's looking at me again. Her betrayal duly confessed, she finally can. She says, "I'll call you," and moves in for a hug.

"Janie can't stand your red hat," I remark. I mean, what else can I say? I have to escape—I don't even know to where to escape to—so I find myself standing in the kitchen, where the *one* brand new thing in the room is the paper with the notes my aunt wrote. I pick the vile white paper up and there it is: The name "Elder Services" underlined; phone numbers printed beside it; services offered in shorthand or at least—in my aunt's flaky version of shorthand which seems to omit pesky vowels from words resulting in "asst lvng" and "hseclng," and the name Kara Hunt underneath.

Complete. *C'est ca.* Well done. And then I think: *Wait. My aunt's the one who dreamt this up scenario, so she's the betrayer who should have to deal with it. She should call Kara Hunt up tomorrow, and discuss with her my father's needs, and schedule a "baseline eval" or whatever it is...I don't need to call Kara Hunt. This isn't my handwriting. My aunt is the one with the plan for my father!*

Besides, is what I think next, *she's the adult. If my father is sent to live in a home, they're not going to place Aunt Tony in foster care, like they will me!* And then I realize this: *This is God's way.* Aunt Tony now threatening to leave is God's way of making push come to shove, so I'll honor my prophecy and become a nun. After all, my spirit guide told me I must "rise to the occasion," and by doing so, I'd accomplish my "mission in life," so, I mean, I *have* to fulfill it. I don't think I have any choice. After all, it's a "prophecy," right? And my aunt isn't the recipient of the prophecy: I am. I can't let *God* down…

So then I settle on this: I'm going to beat my aunt to it. I'm going to leave this old manse before her, go to L.A. where the Center for Spiritual Union is located, talk to the monastics, and do whatever I must to become a postulant and move into the postulant house. I'll have to play down my real age, maybe even have a birth certificate forged, but in L.A., I'm sure you can do that. Mostly, I need to explain to the monastics about my prophecy—how God has sent me to them, how I've been called and how my life's already been mapped—and they'll *have* to acquiesce! It's a prophecy, for Heaven's sake!

Now that I've decided, I need a definite plan that I can implement fast. My aunt is leaving "first thing" in the morning, so I have to leave "*before* first thing." Once Aunt Tony sees I am gone, she can't, she wouldn't *dare* abandon my father. She'll have to make the call to Kara Hunt.

I decide to book my trip online, then pack, then leave a note on the table that I'll follow up later with a call. I have to admit that I've fantasized about this many times in the past—the leaving, not the Aunt Tony part—so I have a *bit* of an idea of what to do. That's to say, I'm not *entirely* lost. Only partly.

I wait until everyone's asleep, then I go online. I know to travel by train to L.A., since I don't like to fly, and buses are the worst, so I Google "Amtrak" and find out the following, which takes about forty-five minutes: I have to take three separate trains to get to L.A. The first one—the one I buy a ticket for, which is only one-hundred-and-eight dollars by the way—leaves from South Station tomorrow at eight-twenty in the morning, and arrives eight hours and ten minutes later, at Washington Union Station, DC. The next leg of my trip leaves from arrives approximately twenty-four hours later at Chicago Union Station, Illinois. The third and final leg arrives approximately *forty-three* hours later, at Los Angeles Union Station, California. That's a shitload of hours. I only book the first leg of the trip so that I can rest in between legs, which means I won't know exactly what days I'll be traveling. I pay with our gold-card Visa, which means Dad will get the bill. That's bad, but I can't stop and think about that now.

What I think about instead is my aunt. With any luck, Aunt Tony will pay all the bills (including my Amtrak trip), by having Dad wobbly-Hancock the checks, the way I used to have him do. Or better yet, she'll get her name on the account, so she won't have to ask for his signature at all...I should really add this suggestion to the note I'm leaving, but I don't have the time right now. Plus, if I start to write one thing, I'll think of another and another, and I'd rather not frighten my aunt with too many things. Just my leaving her alone will probably be frightening enough. I'll call and relay this stuff later, though it does make me pause and rethink things—for a moment.

Besides my aunt paying the bills, I wonder what else she'll have to do without me around? Buy the groceries, and make sure my father is fed. Mow the lawn—at least through October. The lawn mower's right in the garage, and she's seen me do it like hundreds of times, and it pretty much self-explanatory anyway, I would say. It's a gas mower. The kind you push, not ride. The only tricky thing is, you have to yank the cord about three times before it starts up, otherwise zilch—when I call, I'll tell her about that, too. Then there's the trash—it goes out on Wednesdays—but I think Aunt Tony knows all of that. There's the gathering of mail and the wash—I *will* definitely have to call with a list—and of course, there's the housecleaning, which I *know* my aunt doesn't like to do, though she can learn to muddle through, like I had to do. Now that I look at it harder, I can't see them staying together all that long in the house, but then there are the services Aunt Tony mentioned. All of those wonderful services that Elder Group provides that my aunt jotted down for me. Hopefully, my aunt will take advantage of the services and they'll stay. The house is paid off. She could live in it strictly rent-free. There's more than enough of Dad's money for them both, what with his pension and all. I mean, what's Miami, when you really take a look, compared to "The City to Watch?" Oh, and she'll have to get the gutters cleaned, of course, the house painted once in a while, but that's not so hard. That just takes making a call. That applies for anywhere you live.

I print my newly-bought ticket on our old laser printer. Once the transaction's complete, I check the T schedule for trains to take me to Boston. I need something early to A) leave before my aunt is up, and B) guarantee I make my Amtrak train, and the six-forty-nine T will surely do that. Plus, it's the earliest one that they have. So that's done. Accomplished. *Finis*.

As for my not liking to fly, I never have. Everything in me screams no. Being shut in a sealed metal tube where you have no control, and the air is conditioned for you, and even a very small hole in the plane could mean the difference between life and death, 'cause air could shoot out—or suck in, I forget the specifics. Plus, flying defies laws of gravity—it positively *does*—so I'm against it for that simple reason if no other. Plus, it's squishy, and I typically like to have a window seat, but then when you *do* have such a seat, whenever you have to go to the bathroom, you have to bother like *two* other people, and sometimes they have their trays down, so they then have to put their trays up, and if there's a meal on their trays, it makes it even more complicated. And sometimes it's just too cold on a plane, but most of the time it's too hot. And those fans that shoot down on your head do nothing at all, and I'm *young*. Imagine how hard it must be for somebody *old?* There's really nothing about planes I like, so it's good I'm taking a train—why I am even *thinking* about *planes* I don't know.

Okay. Enough thinking. I really should get on the ball.

On to packing.

I do it very, very quietly so as not to unduly disturb anyone. I pack only warm-weather stuff, 'cause I'm going to L.A.! In L.A., Winter stuff's for losers.

Luckily, it's summer in these parts right now, which means my summer stuff's right in the front of my closet—my winter stuff's in back, so this makes it easy. But as I pull different articles out, I realize I'll need new clothes. There's a pretty strict dress code for nuns. Skirts below the knees. Nothing form-fitting or "revealing." No exposed shoulders or tank tops allowed...not that my clothes are all *that* revealing. Janie calls them "Disney clothes," but still, they're not exactly postulant articles either. I'll have to buy mostly new stuff. Go on a nun-to-be shopping spree...

And even though a postulant isn't allowed to wear tank tops, or shorts, or pants, I still pack a couple of each, since there still will be days on the train, and days when I'm waiting for my interview, and days when I'm waiting for the *results* of my interview, and I'll need to have *clothes*. And even when I'm finally a postulant in the postulant house, there still might be certain exception-type days, like when we all load a bus for the beach—you never know—plus, I really don't *have* other clothes.

When I get around to packing my sneakers—New Balance cross-trainers—tears begin to fill my eyes. Janie has always detested these things; they're the most "Disney" thing that I have per her. "Women," she feels, should wear sandals in light-hearted summer, to show off their skin; in autumn or winter, "women" should wear boots. If you *have* to wear sneakers, she thinks, they should at least be a brand that is "in," like good old Chuck Taylor's. Janie's consistently instructed me in this.

I'll miss Janie. But I can't stop and think about that now.

Right before I zip my duffel bag shut, I final survey my clothes. They're nowhere *near* as ridiculous as Aunt Tony's clothes—I don't pack a "French maid outfit" for example—which just goes to show how *I* am the sensible one. How *I* know what I am doing. Not her.

It's two o'clock. I'm sure I didn't pack *everything*. I'm sure I forgot at least *one* crucial thing. It's hard to remember to pack *everything*…oh, well, so I sit around twiddling my thumbs 'cause there's still one thing left for me to do, and that's to write a note. So I twiddle. I can't even contemplate sleep, and it's still too early to leave. I don't want to walk around Waltham in the middle of the night, *especially* with luggage, which makes me remember how I have to call a taxi to take me to the T, since I'll have luggage to tote, so I call the taxi.

All set.

It's still too early to leave, but since I'm not ready to write my good-bye, I think about the other hard stuff—the stuff I was pushing away while rushing around—'cause I have to deal with it sometime.

I start with Janie.

Janie I'll miss a whole ton, though I'll call when I have a block of time, and when it's not still an hour when vampires roam. Janie will appreciate *that*! I'll just explain it to her. Janie will *have* to understand: it's what friends do. Plus, it's not like I never brought it up with her before. Besides, Janie will make new friends…

Then there's Cameron.

Cameron I feel bad about. Very. I'll have to use e-mail with Cameron, not call, 'cause calling would be hard, and I wouldn't have a clue what to say, and my voice just might crack. I don't want Cameron to *hear* my voice crack, 'cause that would just tell him I like him, which I don't want to do 'cause if he harbors feelings for me, too, that would make it even harder hard, so I'll keep things upbeat in my e-mails. I won't say a thing about feelings. I am guessing he'll be somewhat disappointed by the news but he's a guy. He'll get over it.

Aunt Tony, as I've said, I'm going to call, go through a list of logistics with her and hope that she'll stay.

That really just leaves my father, who I'll have to call, too, though I really can't think about that. Hey, they'll still let me visit, right? Just not that often, I'd guess. Actually, I don't really know, since I never did ask, but I'm sure I can get out to visit once in a while. I mean, they *have* to let you sometimes see your *family*, right?

I feel bad about my father, but I am going to give him a call. If I have second thoughts along the way, I decide to tell myself this: Everyone alive has second thoughts. It would be weird if I *didn't* have them. Even the saints, who've experienced *God*, have had second thoughts.

Sure it's a little bit scary leaving home, but it's not like they've given me a choice: my aunt, taking charge the way that she did, my father destroying my life, my mother dying. What did they think I was going to do? Ignore everything and tay here forever?

I go and retrieve a sheet of lined paper from the drawer, then I write this:

Dear Aunt Tony,

I've left to go off and be a nun—to join the spiritual group I told you of.

I had to do this now 'cause, well, you said you were leaving, so I had to. Plus, a prophecy's been told about my life that pretty much says that I'm going to be a nun at the age of sixteen and I'm sixteen now.

Please take care of Dad. I know you will. You're better able to do this than I, 'cause you're an adult. Besides, my life's already mapped-out. I feel it in my bones. Please understand.

Thank you for doing this. You will be blessed for it, I know. I will call as soon as I can to see how things are.

Love,

Your niece,

Mo

I add the "your niece" part just to remind her.

There's still a whole half-page that's blank. That's meant for my dad.

Hmm…

Right…

Where to start?

I sort of want to just pass the news on through my aunt: "Please tell Dad I love him, and I'll talk to him soon"—'cause what can I say? What can I *possibly say* in a letter. But that's the coward's way out. If I'm going to write a letter at all—I've already written Aunt Tony—then I have to write Dad, so I come up with this, which I add to the bottom of Aunt Tony's note:

Dear Dad,

I'm sorry to do this—to leave—but I must. The time is right, and if I'm going to be a nun, I really have no choice. I'll miss you. I love you a lot. Please don't worry about me. Aunt Tony will help take care of you, and I'll call. I promise.

That is the most I can write—more even—so I sign it after my "Love" and I don't read the note back again. I don't even look at it again.

I tell myself this: I'm not leaving Dad all alone—Aunt Tony will be here. I tell myself that I'll call him several times along the way to try to explain. I tell myself I was going to have to leave the old nest *sometime...*

Okay. Wait. I've got one more confession to make, in addition to the one about my thinking through a bit of this before. Another reason I want to be a nun is that my father losing his mind flips me out. Totally. Maybe it shouldn't flip me out, since he is, after all, my *father,* but it does.

There. I said it. I'm being honest with you...It totally flips me out.

And it hurts, too. My mother's dying hurts—I mean, it *really* really hurts. My father losing his mind hurts...

Everyone's leaving me.

Chapter 30

At precisely five-thirty, the taxi arrives. It's a little bit early for the six-forty-nine T into Boston, but I have to be out before my aunt, plus, it's not like I'm going to get any *sleep* waiting here. I had asked the driver to please pass by our house and wait at the neighbor's next door, so he does. I heave my bulky luggage out the door.

I didn't want to travel with *too* much stuff, but one *always* packs way too much stuff, so what I have is a large duffel bag, and a backpack. The backpack is snug on my back, but the duffel bag I carry in my arms like it's a baby, or an overstuffed bag full of groceries, or a rubber-tree plant—too big to lug by the straps, which is too bad.

I try to be quiet. I try to be as quiet as an itty-bitty mouse.

The driver gets out of the taxi, opens the passenger door, then puts both my bags in the trunk. He's got this bright look on his face, like five-thirty in the frigging morning is the very best part of the day, and, truth be told, maybe it is. For him. In any case, it helps to remind me to try and appear wide-awake, as my day is just starting.

He takes me straight to the T, like my train's coming now—it isn't. He doesn't ask *why* I'm going to the T station, or *why* I'm so early for the train, he just gets out, opens the trunk and lifts out my bags for me. I pay him and he drives off. We didn't even talk. Then I'm alone with an hour to kill, and the sun's not quite up.

If I'd been smart, I would have asked the driver to take me to Dunkin Donuts, where I could have gotten coffee, juice, and a fresh sugared blueberry muffin—which I love, especially when heated with butter—but I wasn't that smart.

I think of walking to the donut shop and back. I have enough time, but then there's my luggage to consider. It's too much to schlep the whole way. So then I consider just stashing my luggage in the bushes, and retrieving them when I get back, but I soon chicken out. I mean, if anything bad were to happen to my bags, plus, the sun is finally up and getting brighter all the time. Somebody might see them. Plus, there are homeless people who live in "The City to Watch," and they could be watching. So I basically have this whole hour to kill.

I sit in this Plexiglas enclosure, on a black plastic bench full of holes, which is to say it's *made* with these holes. They cover the surface of the bench. Little symmetrical holes. I wonder if it's made like this to save on materials' expense? I wonder this 'cause I have time to wonder. I also read the following sign that's part of the "See something? Say something" campaign: "When something doesn't quite add up, call this number: 617-222-1212. We want to know. If you see an unusual package, item, person or behavior" *et cetera*. Below the message is a picture of an eerily-empty park bench, with a dark suspicious crate underneath it. Below this is the picture of a woman smartly making a call. Just beyond is a bright constantly changing sign, displaying the very same messages over and over like "See something? Say something," "No smoking, please," "Waltham station" followed by today's date, "Trains operating on or near schedule."

This is interesting: On the station building itself—which is a red clapboard structure—there's a sign that says: "Welcome to Waltham, the City of Choice." I've never heard it called *that*. It's always been "The City to Watch." *What's up with that*, I wonder?

Weird.

Huh.

Moving on…

Eventually, more and more people show up for the train. Most have coffee, laptops, the paper, novels, work…they all seem well prepared for this trip.

The train arrives two minutes late.

I get on. It's the start of a brand-new adventure.

The first thing that happens as I'm standing on the T is I'm thrown. I have to stand when I get on 'cause it's so packed, and the minute the train starts to move—off I go. I'm actually thrown like a couple of steps, so then I hold on tighter. I widen my stance and try to lower my center of gravity some, or at least I try to feel I *have* a center of gravity by sending my energy there. Still, I'm not used to standing up on a moving train, for at each acceleration and swerve, I'm thrown again for a ride. *The driver's a cowboy,* I think, though others seem to be managing fine. But then again, I have my duffle bag wedged between my feet, which makes it hard to stand. I try to hang on and concentrate on remembering that it's only a couple more stops. Well, four to be exact.

As we enter North Station, I think, *I am 10.8 miles from home which means I am also that many miles closer to where I am going.* In any case, everyone disembarks here. This is Boston.

From here, I have to go to South Station, which is where I'll catch my Amtrak train. To do this by T, I'd have to take two different lines—orange to downtown, then red—so instead I take a taxi.

This driver doesn't talk either.

Once at South Station, I check the time. Seven-thirty. My train doesn't leave till eight-twenty, so I still have time.

Everyone's starting to swarm like they all know exactly where to go—I don't. I put down my bags and check the signs. Nothing's totally clear, so I decide to inquire at an information booth. I figure I'll locate my platform, then get something to eat—I'm starved! It's too bad really, for if I had thought of it, I could have brought some snacks from home for my trip. That way, not only do you save money, you also get to eat your favorite snack foods, like Pringles, or apples, or Ring-Dings and stuff. Or come comfort food—I could really use some right now—like a sandwich with turkey and swiss made with your very own hands in your very own favorite way—in my case, slathered with dollops of Hellman's. Made from home is *always* better.

The lady at the information booth points to a sign, which leads to an escalator, which leads me upstairs to more Amtrak signs, and eventually to the right platform. I check out the lit-up departure time board and—there it is! Train number one-seven-one, heading for Washington, DC. On time, it says.

I'm all set.

I go back down the escalator, to get some food. My duffel bag's a pain in the neck, and my back is starting to hurt from my overfull backpack, so it will be good to sit down.

From a Dunkin Donuts, I buy a bagel with cream cheese, a coffee with cream, and a juice. I still believe I'm starving, but when I sit against a wall to eat my food, I really don't feel like eating that much. Maybe I'm *not* starving? Maybe…

I check the time…seven-forty-one…my train will be here in thirty-nine minutes.

Okay. I'll admit I'm antsy, but traveling just somehow does that to you. Something about needing to be on time and needing to know where to go and not being fully in control of all things. I suddenly have a strong feeling I'll be checking the time a lot.

It's seven-forty-two now and I wonder what Dad and Aunt Tony are doing. By now they've surely discovered the note and read it through. I wonder what my father is thinking? I didn't say goodbye to him in person. The least I could have pulled off was a decent goodbye. *This is the stuff of bad karma*, I think—not saying goodbye face to face. How am I supposed to start my life as a nun, when my very first act brings bad karma? One thing you cannot escape is negative karma.

If I was *really* supposed to be a nun, wouldn't God somehow lay it out for me better? Not take my mother from my dad? Or not give my dad early Alzheimer's? Or not make it so my Aunt Tony wants to leave right now, too? It's like God is putting up roadblocks. How could He want me to be a nun and keep putting up so many roadblocks? On the other hand, all of those stories you read—the big epic ones like *Lord of the Rings* and such—the characters all experience major roadblocks. Lots and lots of them. So maybe such setbacks are actually good?

I feel confused and wonder if this is the way my father feels a lot of the time. Will he *ever* understand? Maybe he'll think that I've left for a weekend retreat, and I'll be home again Monday, and Aunt Tony will have to explain it to him. "No," she'll dramatically say. "She's gone for good. She's left to be some kind of nun." And my father will answer: "Oh. Well I wouldn't say *that*." That sounds like what he'd say, doesn't it?

He believes in the lyrics to those songs, the ones that his uncle used to play on the piano when they lived up in Maine, that are *beyond* corny: *It Had to Be You; Night and Day; They Can't Take that Away From Me…*

Not only does he *believe* in them—he *sings* them. I remember how, soon after I'd entered my teens and started to show at family dinners less often, how the few times I did show he'd say, "*There* she is! Strike up the band!"

My mother would always smile, but I'd give *him* a look.

"Maybe we should hire the Rockettes to put on a show!" he would say.

I'd look.

"Maybe we should set off some fireworks!"

He was teasing with all this, of course, and I'd show him the appropriate disdain a good teenager must, though he *was* glad to see me.

I also now recall how we used to goof around with a beach ball when I was a kid, and I used to want to just volley, to get as high a combined score as possible as a joined team, but Dad would mix it up on me. He'd volley for a while, then hit the ball to my left—just out of reach—saying, "Boop!" Or he'd hit it just a bit to my right, calling, "Oops!" He'd do these moves over and over, till I would say, "*Da-ad!*" He'd do anything to get a rise out of me.

Another time—this was in middle school—I had to prepare a report on the fifties, so I decided to question my father, since I knew he came of age in that time-frame. I said to him, "Dad. I need to know some things about your childhood. Back then, at dinner you were told to clean your plate. Is that right? I mean, like eat every morsel on it?"

"Ohhhhhh yeeeees," he replied, making his voice go mock-low, like this was some serious business we'd better get straight.

So then I said, "And let's see…it was Elvis' time. Did you ever get to ride around on *motorcycles*?"

And he said, "Ohhhhhh nooooo"—again with his mock-severe voice.

So *then* I asked, "What about car hops? With kids serving burgers on skates? Did you ever go to *those*?"

"Ohhhhhh yeeeees."

And that was pretty much it, except—and I don't know just how to explain this in full—but it was pretty much fun for us both. His teasing, and me being the typical straight one. He was happy just to have me around, like my *breathing* was enough for him. We were one, overall, happy family.

How can I let him down now? I mean, he likes to play the "Ope!" game with me! I don't care if he *is* slowly losing his mind: It's an important aspect of life!

Then I think, *when my train makes its way down the tracks, I won't be on it. I'm going home.* And one final thing you should know —and this I'm not proud of—I kind of made the prophecy up. I know…that's *really* bad, though I'm sorry about all of that. I mean, I *was* almost hit by a car when I was twelve. And a woman *did* come up to me afterwards, and asked if I was all right, and then looked at me oddly—as if there was an aura around me or something, as if she could see deep into my soul—but she never said the rest. The rest I guess I made up so I could tell Janie and whoever my reason for wanting to leave. So there *could* be truth to it, even though it wasn't true.

I never had *that* close a call. I was never approached by a stranger who foretold my life. I was never like *one-hundred*-percent certain I was indeed going to become a nun.

BIG HEAVEN

Chapter 31

To get back to Waltham, I have to reverse all my steps. That means—take a taxi back to North Station, then take the Purple Line four stops to Waltham, then take another taxi one final time to get me back home.

I begin the long process.

In the first yellow cab, I think this: *It's good I'm going right back. My aunt doesn't even do the dishes every day. My father's not used to that life. Plus, what if she forgets to pay the bills, and the power goes off? Or what if she simply takes off? Or takes up with a disreputable man? She did it before (or almost), with a guy with a family yacht, and look at how that all turned out. What would prevent her from doing it again with a Harley owner? She could end up riding on the back, and they could get in a horrible crash, and my aunt could die, God forbid. Plus, she isn't "real good" in emergencies, as she has made perfectly clear, and there will undoubtedly be more in the future…*

That's what I think in the first yellow cab.

Later, once I'm ensconced on the T, I check out the people on the train, and think this: *I don't know these people. I mean, there are so many different people on the train—like, in the world—and I know none of them, really. They're all strangers to me. And California will be filled with strangers, too. Even the people at the ashram...they'll be strangers...I won't know them.*

Then I start thinking how I used to think this about Dad—how I didn't really know him. Not the way I'd come to know my mother. Not in the way I know Janie, for instance. My father's a male, after all, and they're not that easy to know. But now I see that I *do* know him. I mean, I might not know his deepest darkest fears, or his most intensely-held secrets, or the wildest dreams of his life. I might not know how it feels deep down to be him, but I do know this: He stayed married to my mother for thirty-two years, and never once cheated on her. He worked to support us for most of his life. He did his duty and did it well, and by "well" I mean without reservation. Or no, I mean as if it was a true privilege to serve—this rarified honor he had—at least, that's how he made it all seem. Besides, he's my father.

And this I additionally know: I know the way he looks at me when he wants to play the "Ope!" game with me. I know how his eyes go all hard when he thinks I am giving him "the run-around." I know how much I mean to him.

It's not like being back there is going to be easy—every single minute of the day—but it's the right thing to do. That's what I think on the T.

And finally, ensconced in the black Waltham cab, I also think this: *My dad could wander off at anytime, if he ends up getting upset enough, and the fact of my leaving is upsetting. He could leave without wearing his shoes, which would be bad. He could fall. He could really really hurt himself. I have to get back.*

That's what I think in back seat of the taxi.

Anyway, by the time I make it home, it's after nine. My aunt's Dodge Neon is gone, and the door in the front is wide open, with just the screen door to keep out bugs.

I push my way through. I'm carrying my bags, so it's clear I was just up to *something* before I walked in, even if my father somehow *didn't* read my note—though I bet he did. Besides, isn't it time I stop all these cowardly games?

He's there…as soon as I walk in…standing up.

"Hi, Dad," I barely choke out as I put down my bags.

"Maureen."

I rush right over to him and we hug. He's got one shoe on, one off, so he's lopsided.

"I was afraid you left," he gets out.

"I wouldn't do that," I say, holding on tighter.

"Well gee. I didn't *think* so…but Aunt Tony…"

His eyes are all blue and concerned when I step back to look. They're that watery-blue that they are—not deep blue. Not the kind of blue where the person doesn't need anyone but themselves, 'cause they already have what they need. My father's eyes are washed-out. He really doesn't look very good.

"Aunt Tony…" he utters again, sounding confused.

I suggest we both sit down. I lead him to his chair, the one with the lumbar-support pad built in. As soon as he's seated, I notice the whole one-shoe-off thing again. I also notice a scarf looped around his thick neck, though it's August right now. He looks mixed-up. He says, "Boy, I was worried. I don't know what I would have done if you weren't here. If something had happened to you."

"I don't know either," I say. Then I add, "I was worried about you, too."

I sit on the couch so we're facing each other. I watch the air go out of his body, then quickly back in. He looks a wreck.

"Well I'm glad you're all right. I was actually about to go looking for you." He lifts both his feet at those words, and there is the sock and the shoe. "You're my little girl," is what he says next. "You know you'll always be." He looks at me with those watery blue eyes.

"I know," I say. "I know" as tears spring up in my eyes.

"Well, all right then," is what my father says.

Tears stream down my face. They stream and they stream. I don't know where they come from, but they do. My throat starts to ache, and then my heart. I long for my mother…I close my eyes and see her smiling at me, her arms stretched out for a hug, a chicken roasting somewhere in the background, a table set for three—but she's not here. And yet, my father is. I rush over and hug him again.

He hugs me back, although I'm not sure he knows why we're hugging. When I finally let go, I wipe at my still-falling tears, 'cause I really don't want to upset him too much.

We sit for another full minute.

He looks at me, all up and down, like to check my condition. Then he looks over at my bags, like to sort the entire mess out. Again he refers to the note. How Aunt Tony made him promise to wait here, while she went looking for me. How he was "going looking for me, too," and he lifts his two feet. Then he says, "It's a good thing that you are all right. I don't know what I would have said to your mother if something had happened."

I watch him sink into his chair, possibly thinking about my mother. I wonder if he thinks she's alive, or if he simply means talking to her, like he does, or even like he does in his prayers? It takes me back. I remember his sitting on the edge of his bed talking to her picture that time I happened by, saying, "I know dear…I know…I know," and looking so sad. It feels like a lifetime ago, but it was only three months. I wonder if he sits around talking to her picture a lot? I look at my father and say, "Well, now you can tell her I'm fine." Then I add, "In fact—maybe I'll tell her myself."

The minute I say such a thing, I know I should. And then we just sit, my father and I, like we don't know what *else* we should do.

In the past when it's gotten like this, I made him something to eat, poured him some Barrel Head root beer over ice, brought him the fan to cool down, and then disappeared into my room, but now I want something else. I say, "You know what I was thinking while I was gone? There was this song that got stuck in my head. It's one *you* sing, believe it or not. Something about Coliseum…Louvre Museum…How does that old standby go?"

I know how it goes—*believe me*—but I pretend not to because I want to hear my dad sing it right now. He does. He sings *You're the Top!* by Cole Porter. He looks in my eyes as he sings, as if *I* am his "top." It's the corniest song just about ever made, but you still have to like it pretty much. Corny is way underrated is all I can say.

"Is *that* the one you were thinking of?" he asks. I can tell he knows it is.

"Yes," I say. "Well done!"

"Well done" is something *he* says. And then he says, "Gee. I guess the old man's taste is rubbing off. And here I thought all you liked was Soundyard."

"It's Sound*garden*," I say, smiling at my father.

"Yes, and they're simply *the worst.*"

He says it as if—now that this has been pointed out, I'll change, like the band is a bomb about to go off, so now I'll defuse it, or like they're a meteor about to hit our ship, so now I'll change course…any number of things.

To change the subject, I say, "Want some root beer?"

"With ice?" he puts to me hopefully.

"Of course!"

"Why that would be *lovely*," he says. Then he looks over at my bags, seeming confused. He acts like they are a guest whom we haven't yet asked to sit down, but won't go away. He acts like we need to remedy things.

"Those were heavy," I say with a nod, referring to the overfull pair. "I'm glad that I don't have to carry them now."

Epilogue

I'd like to write an epilogue for you where I tell you that I stayed on with my dad for some years, and that Aunt Tony did, too, and that I graduated from high school and then went to college somewhere close, and dated Cameron, and ended up marrying him and having three lovely children, and that my father lived to a ripe ninety-two, and that Janie was the one who became a nun. Surprise!

Or maybe I became a motivational speaker on spiritual living.

Or I graduated from high school, and then became a nun soon after that: After my dad got married to a woman who used to be a nurse, and who lived in our neighborhood for years, and who fell in love with my father 'cause of his wit and his charm, and renditions of *You're the Top!*, and who took perfect care of my him. Actually, there's no such love interest right now in our midst, but you never know.

Or maybe I could tell you that my aunt got married, and the man she married ran a day program for elders with dementia, and that my dad attended the program, and lived with the newlyweds at night, and did this for years till he died.

Or maybe that Janie and I opened a restaurant, at which my aunt cooked macrobiotic food for a dedicated group of return customers, and my dad sang, and we were all incredibly happy without being nuns…

Lots of cool happenings *could* take place, though I don't know which ones really *will*. All I know is—it's all going to turn out just fine. I'm putting God and guru on the case—so it better!

Oh, and just so you don't worry: Aunt Tony is staying on for awhile—just for "awhile," she says—and we have a very nice woman from Elder Services coming by to help with my dad four times a week, and my dad seems to love the attention. So that's all going well.

And one more thing I should add—and this could be of help to you, as well: While I know that there are going to be hardships in my life—"trials" as the monastics call them—I also, deep down, believe this: Sometimes, something good comes out of a situation when you don't expect it. And sometimes, you have to go through a trial first to have the good thing happen, though you don't know the good thing is coming when you're struggling *through* the trial…that's just the way it all works.

Here's an example: Say you're going to a dance, and that night—*that* very night—there's a snowstorm, and the boy who asked you to go, calls and cancels. Maybe he uses the storm as his excuse, who knows? But *you* go there anyway. Somehow you make it. That is the "trial," by the way: your deciding to go and your actually making it. And, while there, this really cute boy asks you out—a boy ten times cuter than your "date." That is the reward. Well—it *could* happen. It's those kinds of things I'm referring to, anyway. It's that very basic idea. I personally think such things happen in our world all the time; you just have to watch for them. You just have to wait and be ready.

Which I guess is my way of saying that I am quite hopeful. Plus, I'm not forgetting the prize. I'm still going back to God…

We all are.

Eventually.

About the Author

Charlotte Hebert is the author of the novel, *Numbering Stars* (a finalist in both the *Hemingway First Novel Contest* and the *Thomas Wolfe Fiction Prize*), and the nonfiction book, *Meditate and Experience God: Saints, Scriptures, and Science Point the Way*. Her short fiction has appeared in over half-a-dozen literary journals, and her essays have appeared in the *Boston Globe Magazine* and the *Worcester Telegram and Gazette*. She lives with her husband and their son in Northborough, MA.

Visit her at: http://www.bit.do/CharlotteHebertOnAmazon

BIG HEAVEN

If you enjoyed *BIG HEAVEN*, consider these other fine books from Savant Books and Publications:

Essay, Essay, Essay by Yasuo Kobachi
Aloha from Coffee Island by Walter Miyanari
Footprints, Smiles and Little White Lies by Daniel S. Janik
The Illustrated Middle Earth by Daniel S. Janik
Last and Final Harvest by Daniel S. Janik
A Whale's Tale by Daniel S. Janik
Tropic of California by R. Page Kaufman
Tropic of California (the companion music CD) by R. Page Kaufman
The Village Curtain by Tony Tame
Dare to Love in Oz by William Maltese
The Interzone by Tatsuyuki Kobayashi
Today I Am a Man by Larry Rodness
The Bahrain Conspiracy by Bentley Gates
Called Home by Gloria Schumann
Kanaka Blues by Mike Farris
First Breath edited by Z. M. Oliver
Poor Rich by Jean Blasiar
Ammon's Horn by Guerrino Amati
The Jumper Chronicles by W. C. Peever
William Maltese's Flicker by William Maltese
My Unborn Child by Orest Stocco
Last Song of the Whales by Four Arrows
Perilous Panacea by Ronald Klueh
Falling but Fulfilled by Zachary M. Oliver
Mythical Voyage by Robin Ymer
Hello, Norma Jean by Sue Dolleris
Richer by Jean Blasiar
Manifest Intent by Mike Farris
Charlie No Face by David B. Seaburn
Number One Bestseller by Brian Morley
My Two Wives and Three Husbands by S. Stanley Gordon
In Dire Straits by Jim Currie
Wretched Land by Mila Komarnisky
Chan Kim by Ilan Herman
Who's Killing All the Lawyers? by A. G. Hayes
Ammon's Horn by G. Amati
Wavelengths edited by Zachary M. Oliver
Almost Paradise by Laurie Hanan
Communion by Jean Blasiar and Jonathan Marcantoni
The Oil Man by Leon Puissegur
Random Views of Asia from the Mid-Pacific by William E. Sharp
The Isla Vista Crucible by Reilly Ridgell
Blood Money by Scott Mastro
In the Himalayan Nights by Anoop Chandola

On My Behalf by Helen Doan
Traveler's Rest by Jonathan Marcantoni
Keys in the River by Tendai Mwanaka
Chimney Bluffs by David B. Seaburn
The Loons by Sue Dolleris
Light Surfer by David Allan Williams
The Judas List by A. G. Hayes
Path of the Templar - Book 2 of The Jumper Chronicles by W. C. Peever
The Desperate Cycle by Tony Tame
Shutterbug by Buz Sawyer
Blessed are the Peacekeepers by Tom Donnelly/Mike Munger
Purple Haze by George B. Hudson
The Turtle Dances by Daniel S. Janik
The Lazarus Conspiracies by Richard Rose
Imminent Danger by A. G. Hayes
Lullaby Moon by Malia Elliott of Leon & Malia
Volutions edited by Suzanne Langford
In the Eyes of the Son by Hans Brinckmann
The Hanging of Dr. Hanson by Bentley Gates
Written in the Stars - An Anthology edited by Sabrina Favors
Flight of Destiny by Francis H. Powell
Elaine of Corbenic by Tima Z. Newman
Ballerina Birdies by Marina Yamamoto
More More Time by David B. Seaburn
Crazy Like Me by Erin Lee
Cleopatra Unconquered by Helen R. Davis
Valedictory by Daniel Scott
The Chemical Factor by A. G. Hayes
Quantum Death by A. G. Hayes
Running from the Pack edited by Helen R. Davis

Coming Soon:
All Things Await by Seth Clabough
Captain Riddle's Treasure by GV Rama Rao
Libido Tsunami by Cate Burns
The Adventures of Purple Head, Buddha Monkey and Sticky Feet by Erik Bracht
Cereus by Z. Roux
In the Shadows of My Mind by Andrew Massie

http://www.savantbooksandpublications.com